by

# The Lost Civilization

by

K. J. Goss

# The Lost Civilization



ISBN Number: 979-8-9903350-0-4

# The Lost Civilization

For My Beloved
Cynthia and Joan

# Introduction

After another more than successful time in the Yucatan, Eric Dexter could not wait to return to Dove of Spring, his Navajo love.

The trip back to the Navajo country was unfortunately riddled with delays. Eric found himself acting like a typical tourist. Finally realizing he had no control over the weather delays, nor did the airlines, he sat back and relaxed, reflecting on the last season in the jungle.

It was more than a success. They had discovered things unimaginable. The highlight, of course, was the Golden Lady. More research was obviously necessary to work out the connection of Egypt and the Maya, and who knows who or what else.

There was only the five of them to date that had actually witnessed these connections. Though there was also the connection of the Navajo contracts that were still being researched.. How to prove to the rest of doubting world the truth of these discoveries was going to be a never ending task. The odds of the five of them against the world were not a very comforting thought.

The weather finally cleared and I was on my last journey leg. I had arranged earlier by phone to have Lone Buffalo meet me at the airport. I truly wanted to surprise Violet.

# Chapter  1

**D**an was overwhelmingly happy to see me as I walked down the exit ramp to the airline terminal.  He acted as if I were long lost family.  After his bear crushing hug he inquired about everything I had done and discovered in the Yucatan.

"**T**here is much to much to tell in just a few minutes.  You will have to wait and read my journal," I suggested.

**H**e knew I was right but admittedly was anxious to know about my new discoveries.

**W**e tossed my bags in the truck bed and were on our way home.

*"Funny,"* I thought to myself, referring to the reservation as home knowing my house was in Vermont.

"**W**ell ! Aren't you even curious ?" He asked.

"**C**urious about what ?"  I smiled in answer knowing he was referring to Violet.

"**W**hy, Dove of Spring of course," he answered almost shouting.

"**O**h  her," I answered indifferently.

"**W**hat do you mean, Oh her," he said in a slightly raised voice.

**I** answered in the same not concerned monotone.

"**I** assume she's OK.  I really don't know.  I haven't heard otherwise."

**L**one Buffalo pulled over to the side of the road and stopped the truck.

"**I** thought she meant something to you," he almost yelled.

**T**hen he saw the smile on my face.

"You're mean. Do you know that," He replied slowly growing a smile to match my own.

"I've been called worse things."

"I'll bet you have," he replied. "And rightfully so," he laughed.

Turning serious I finally answered truthfully.

"I missed her terribly but I'm not sorry I went to the Yucatan. Our discoveries were worth it."

"She missed you also but tried to hide it. I think Whispering Wind and myself were the only ones who knew better."

"Thanks Pal for the insight. You really don't know how much I missed` her. It became difficult at times to concentrate on what I was doing."

"I'm almost happy to hear that because I knew she also had a hard time but kept her feelings to herself. You two were meant for each other."

"I hope so," Eric answered feeling himself blush. He changed the subject and asked about the teens and their pyramid observations.

Dan picked up on this and did not pursue the Violet subject any longer.


It was great seeing the desert again with all its open beauty. The heat was of a different sort than the jungle. By contrast the terrain was totally different yet I loved them both. I really could not pick a favorite.


"I'm going to drop us by my office, then you can decide what you are going to do," Dan suggested, "It sure is nice to have you back."

As the truck neared Dan's office, Dove of Spring was just leaving the school building and spotted Eric. She dropped the books and papers she was carrying and ran to the truck. Before Eric was completely out of the door she crushed him in a loving hug almost sending them both to the ground. Lone Buffalo smiled almost laughing as he walked away.

*"This was their moment alone,"* he thought.

After an extended moment of hugs and kisses the pair finally caught their breaths.

"I suppose we're acting like children," Violet said.

"**W**ho cares," replied Eric warmly as he enfolded her close in his arms.  They were content.

"**I** know I said I would let you go because I love you.  But no more."

**E**ric gazed at her questioning.  Violet raised her head looking at him directly.

"**O**h you can still pursue your dreams and research of discovery, but from here on out I will be with you.  These last few months I went through hell without you.  Please don't leave me again.  Please."

**S**he sounded like a little girl begging for ice cream.

"**Y**ou need not worry my love.  From here on we will never be apart," Eric heard himself say.  He even surprised himself saying these words, yet deep inside he knew he meant them.

**T**hey stayed silent holding each other for the longest time not caring about the world around them.  At last regaining their composure they moved to retrieve the books and papers Dove of Spring dropped.  Lone Buffalo was just approaching and was heard to say,

"**W**elcome back to the real world you two.  You do know there are other people living here, not that either of you care."

**H**e said this of course with a big smile.

***Welcome home my son,*** were Whispering Winds words, which only Eric and Violet heard.

"**Thank you,**" Eric answered.  Violet added, "**We will see you soon.**"

**A**gain the earlier words of Whispering Wind haunted Eric's mind.

*"**S**he will be here for you but you always knew that.  She will be of great assistance to you in the future.  Do not let that escape you."*

**A**n air of contentment overcame Eric.  Suddenly all was right with the world.  At least in his world.  He took hold of Violet's hand and squeezed it lovingly.  She returned the pressure, both accepting their future.  They again turned their attention to Lone Buffalo.

"What are your plans now ?" He directed his question to Eric.

"I honestly can't answer that yet. This beautiful vision has got my mind totally up side down."

Dove of Spring was embarrassed but lovingly smiled, not letting go of Eric's hand.

"I don't mean right this moment, I mean after the wedding, which, of course, I'm invited to."

"Whoa, slow down Dan. Don't you think you're rushing things a bit ?" returned Eric.

"No" answered Violet with a broad smile and a sparkle in her dark eyes.

Eric looked at her not knowing what to say but did smile.

"Tell you what," continued Dan. "When you guys make up your minds let me know. I'll be in my office trying to work." He laughed as he walked away. "See you later."

Eric looked at Violet, smiled and asked.

"Are you serious about getting married ?"

She kissed his cheek and quietly replied,

"Of course my love. I want nothing more." There was a pause then she added, "Now let's go see Whispering Wind."

He allowed her to pull him in that direction. Silence reigned for a few minutes.

"I want to hear all about my rival, the Golden Lady."

Before Violet spoke again, a now more relaxed Eric smiled in answer.

"I want to share everything with you, especially the Golden Lady, but I have a lot of film to process first."

"What about the danger you were in. To tell you the truth I was very upset for a very long time."

"Oh that. I have it all recorded in my journal. It was no big deal. They just wanted to make me a human sacrifice but I told them they would need your permission first. So they let me go."

Dove of Spring looked at Eric laughing as she slapped his arm. I'm being very serious you clown."

"Isn't that spousal abuse ?" returned Eric laughing.

"No" she answered firmly, because we are not married."

"Oh so that makes it okay for you to beat me ?"

"Yes" she laughed.

"To be serious for a moment, hearing your voice or at least your thoughts meant the world to me.  It not only gave me the strength to carry on but it also made me realize how much I loved you and missed you.  I'm sorry I did not follow up on showing you the telepathic connection.  I assume you were shown by Whispering Wind."

Violet smiled in answer.

"I will be forever grateful to him.  Hearing your thoughts and love pulled me through a number of tough spots."

Eric saw the worry in her expression and tried to comfort her.

"There was no immediate life threatening situations but your words, as few as there were, pulled me through.  Truth be told I could not wait to return to you, yet I knew I had to finish my work."

Dove of Spring again glowed with pride and love as she kissed his cheek.

Before they realized they were at Whispering Wind's hogan.  Of course he had sensed their arrival and bid them enter before they could announce themselves.  Dove of Spring addressed him in their native tongue while Whispering Wind greeted Eric by telepathic messaging. Then in broken but understandable English he voiced;

*"Yes, I will marry you. Is that not what you came for?"*

Eric and Violet answered together.  She said yes and he said no.  They looked at each other and laughed.

"Here we go again." stated Violet.

Eric then clarified his no answer with "Yes marry us but no I did not mean this very instant."

This satisfied Violet and she glowed while reaching for his hand.  Whispering Wind smiled and was happy for them.

*"I know your trip to the land of our brother the Maya was successful, but perhaps you can fill us in with more*

*detail. I spoke with your King who teased me about the Golden Lady."*

"**H***ere we go with the riddles again*," thought Eric.

**S**he is exactly who I want to share with you and, of course, all the elders."

"**D**on't forget Dan," added Violet.

"**N**o never. I will share all with him. He has been most helpful in the past as I know you will be in the future."

**B**eaming the smallest grin Whispering Wind addressed Eric privately.

*"A very wise decision, my son. You will always be able to count on her as I have voiced in the past."*

*"Now getting back to your visit here Eric, I am fully licenced by the state to perform your wedding, unless you object we can do it right away or in a few days so that all our people can take part in our tradition."*

"**I** think I would also prefer your traditional ceremony and the sooner the better."

**T**hen smiling at Violet continued with:

**W**e have a lot of work ahead of us."

**S**he was now truly glowing with love and pride. Eric could not believe his own eyes as he viewed Violet's grandeur. He knew this was the right decision for him.

**S**uddenly this loving glance at Violet's beauty rang a bell in his sub-conscious. Why, he could not tell, he just knew there was a hidden attraction there.

**P**ulling himself out of his dream world he addressed the elder.

"**G**ive me a few days to get my film processed and my notes in order then I can make a proper presentation for all. I know you all will be impressed as we were upon the discovery."

**W**hispering Wind smiled his acceptance of Eric's words.

*"**G**o then my son.  Do what you must but do not neglect the beauty beside you."*

**D**ove of Spring felt herself go crimson as she answered; "**I** will not let him.  We are now one and always will be."

**T**hey took their leave of Whispering Wind.  Once outside the pair remained silent on their return walk to the school building.

**E**ric did not want to part but knew he must.

"**N**ow my love you attend to the nuptials of your choice while I get lost in the dark room."

**T**hey kissed unashamedly and parted reluctantly.

**A**fter a routine, almost boring day Eric was pleased that the film processing was complete.  He looked forward to time with Violet.

# Chapter  2

The next few days passed quickly because of a heavy work load.  Eric now felt he was ready to meet with the elders.  All was set in the council room.  Eric, out of respect, wore his eagle feather much to the delight of Dove of Spring.  The elders were also pleased he showed respect for his newly acquired family.

The presentation lasted for close to two hours.  Eric went into as much detail as his memory allowed.  He also made his personal journal available for all to read.  The elders agreed with their Maya counterparts in that this would be a difficult thing to sell to the reigning scientific paradigms.

Slowly the council room was vacated leaving only four people.  Eric, Violet, Dan and of course Whispering Wind.

*"Sit for a time,"* instructed Whispering Wind.  *"I have something to share with you."*

He continued in his native tongue.  (Dan and Violet took turns with the interpretation of his words.)

*"After many years I feel that you, Eric, are the one to continue my work."*

The three others, now captivated by his words, dedicated their full attention to the wise one.

*"As you well know, we too have had contact with the distant Egyptian Culture, but again no one wants to believe our words.  I now have something to share with you*

*that will, if ever believed, change history and the way modern man believes and thinks."*

**E**ric looked at his two companions only to see the same inquisitiveness that overtook him.

*"My friends, as old as our history is, there is yet a civilization older than ours. Your king Eric, as I'm sure you have already surmised, is from that ancient civilization."*

**E**ric answered; "The king also instructed that there were others like him from that ancient past whose job it was to enlighten other cultures, not to control them but to benefit them. And as you already know their teachings were falling on deaf ears, hence the world we have today."

**D**ove of Spring changed Eric's words to Navajo for Whispering Wind. He silently nodded his knowledge and acceptance of Eric's words. He then continued;

*"**I** am in possession of some information regarding that Ancient civilization which I am now going to pass on to you Eric. As your king has already chosen you, I too am choosing you. You are true to your heart and if anyone can find any remains of this historical epic it is you. You already have with you two others who are also worthy. You have a knack for finding lost history. I have faith in you to also find our lost past. Not just the Navajo past but of this whole continent if not the whole world. In the words of your king, Eric, you truly are a chosen one. My full trust is in you, knowing that you will succeed."*

**H**ere he paused momentarily then slowly continued.:

*"**I** must go and rest now. I will have words with you on another day."*

**W**ithout hesitation Whispering Wind arose and left the

council room.

The three remained speechless staring at nothing. The silence was at last broken by Dove of Spring.

"I knew you were special my love. I just never knew how special you were."

Her broad smile was also shared by Lone Buffalo. Her words appeared not to have been heard by Eric. He just sat there gazing out the window watching Whispering Wind with his fast gate heading for his hogan. Violet and Dan looked at each other and silently agreed to let Eric have his time. They quietly arose and left the building to wait outside. They both understood the heaviness of Whispering Wind's words. They were a tremendous charge for anyone. Violet felt for her new found love but knew she would stick with him no matter what his decision.

A good fifteen minutes had passed when Eric finally joined his two friends.

"Okay, what say we think about a place for dinner. I'm pretty hungry."

Dan and Violet just looked at each other dumbfounded. Dan spoke first.

"Well"

"Well what," Eric stated back.

"Are we going searching or not ?" Violet put forth.

"Searching for what?" Eric questioned in return.

Violet threw up her hands saying; "The wedding is off," She turned and walked away.

Stunned in disbelief Eric immediately went after her.

"Wait, where are you going ?"

When he caught up to her she faced him wearing a broad grin. "Two can play that game you know."

"I give up. You two act like you have been married for thirty years." said a frustrated Dan.

The lovers returned to where Dan was.

"I accept Whispering Winds challenge, but it includes both of you." stated Eric.

"Don't forget, I still have classes to teach." Dan reminded.

"I am well aware of that and I'm sure we can work something out to both our advantages."

"**I** am yours one hundred percent," added Violet.

**W**ith a serious face Eric stated;

"**N**ow what's with the wedding plans.  I want to get this over with."

**W**ith that Violet swatted him again.

"**Y**ou're a witness Dan to spousal abuse."

**D**an turned and walked away shouting back, "Let me know about dinner plans.  I'll be in my office.

**A**lone now Dove of Spring asked Eric.  "Do you really want to cancel our wedding ?"

"**N**ot on your life.  I'll never let you go."

**O**n tip toes she kissed his cheek.  They started walking, not knowing to where.


"**I** will meet with Whispering Wind tomorrow and get as much information as I can.  I really have no idea of what or where he is referring to.  I hope you don't mind but I must do this alone."

"**I** understand completely.  There is no need to worry about me. I will always be here. I will make the wedding for day after tomorrow. A lot of the old traditions were given up a long time ago but still all will attend.  Then we will be escorted to my house.  I don't know if you were aware but the Navajo is not exactly a matriarchy but a lot leans to the woman's side of the family, thus my house.  Not to worry though in actual practice it is pretty much like any normal wedding.  We may want to keep it small and quiet but that is not possible here on the reservation.  Please have patience with us."

"**N**o need to fret my love.  This is your show.  Mine is finding lost history."

**T**hey each squeezed the others hand firmly as in total acceptance.

# Chapter 3

Eric and Violet reluctantly agreed to this necessary time apart, Violet to pursue the wedding preparations while Eric needed to finish the film categorizing and notes to send to his Maya friends at the Arizona college. Also, of course, he set aside time to meet with Whispering Wind.

The photos and notes were soon in order and after a quick lunch Eric found himself on his way to the hogan of Whispering Wind. He was looking forward to this particular visit, yet at the same time had a feeling of uneasiness about what he was soon to learn. The unknown always triggered this uneasiness along with an excitement that he looked forward to.

*"Come in my friend. You are most welcome."*

Eric knew this communication would be strictly by telepathy, a function he was growing quite fond of because of its total privacy. Those who used this technique could choose who and when was to be part of the communication.

Even though Eric had been in this hogan a few  times before, he still marveled at the history it contained. *"A lost history."* he thought.

*"Sit my young friend and share my lemon drink. I wish you to listen carefully and patiently to what I am about to reveal. Some would find my words hard to believe but I know your true heart. I know you will accept my sharing as you did your Mayan king. Hold your questions until my tale is finished. You will have many of the answers at that time."*

Whispering Wind sat and made himself comfortable and

looking deep into my eyes started his story.

*"**O**ral history has been passed down for many hundreds if not thousands of years. Too many to really count. We were once a mighty nation and a proud people, as were others in this land. This was long before the European conquest. The best I can decipher is long before even European advanced civilization, there existed a technology that was far advanced from today's so called modern world. Even with that advanced knowledge, we still lived in harmony with the land and its other creatures. I know you are aware of some of those powers that were harnessed by the ancients. Your Mayan king enlightened you to their wonders. They were meant to help all mankind without exception."*

Eric wanted to ask questions but Whispering Wind begged his indulgence a bit longer. He realized all would be answered in due course. The senior elder continued.

*"**T**hese ancestors lived in untold of peace with all nations on all continents. Disagreements, the few that there were, were handled by those of clear minds with fairness for all. War was all but forgotten. It was just a word from the past."*

Here Whispering Wind paused to refresh himself with his lemon water. Yet again Eric wanted to speak but controlled his urge.

*"**M**utual respect and sharing ruled all without disagreement or prejudice. The world was as it was meant to be and as it should be."*

Here he paused again, his eyes gauging my acceptance or not of his tale. Seemingly satisfied he turned his gaze to the fire embers as if lost in the world past. I respected his silence. Studying his facial expression it appeared to be lost in the world of the ancients. After a very long three minutes he continued speaking as if he had never ceased.

*"Then it happened. As advanced as our culture supposedly was we were totally unprepared for the fury of cosmic events."*

Eric's attention was now piqued like never before.

*"An extremely large celestial body penetrated our galaxy. It breached earths orbit. Its path unmistakably headed for collision with our home planet. We had no control whatsoever over the events that followed."*

Eric could feel himself growing tense, as if he himself were witnessing this catastrophic event. Whispering Wind noticed this and inwardly smiled knowing what Eric was picturing and feeling.

*"The whole world was affected but the northern hemisphere in particular. North America, our homeland, was its main impact site. The devastation that followed was total and complete. No man could have predicted it. Man, animal and the very environment were completely wiped out, absolutely not a trace left of man or beast. The massive impact naturally caused uncontainable fire damage almost world wide, which in turn led to a smoke curtain that blanketed most of the planet. The repercussions of this again caused a severe temperature drop; hence an ice age particularly in the northern half of the globe. This lasted for hundreds of years before life as we now know it slowly rebuilt itself."*

Whispering Wind sheepishly smiled with a correction of his own story.

*"Forgive me. Your own king and many others like him whom they called The Chosen Ones, were sent out on a mission of teaching, which as you know was not received very*

*well.  By the way, which I'm sure you have already surmised, our Ancient Ones were those advanced peoples, but all was lost in that cosmic conflagration. Your king, I believe, is the last of his kind.  He was lucky enough to have met and taught the Maya.  As you yourself now know the Maya were far ahead of others of their time, in science, mathematics, astronomy and building and education, which includes writing.  They were true receptors of the Chosen Ones attempt to transfer that knowledge.  They did indeed learn and accept.  Then to make matters worse, the invading Europeans, looking for riches, destroyed unimaginable amounts of history out of pure ignorance, history that to date has been unrecoverable. Books and texts containing history and that advanced knowledge are irretrievable.  Their ignorance has held back our growth as a people who are only now making scientific advances, yet not necessarily the correct ones.*

Eric could detect the sadness and sorrow emanating from Whispering Wind.  He wanted to comfort him, but rightfully kept his emotions to himself.  The silent pause was only interrupted by the almost soundless sips of the elder's drinking of his lemon water.  The short pause was finally ended with a whole new Whispering Wind.

*"Now my young friend, this is where you come in.  I know you wish not to hear this, but you, as your king has told you many times, are a modern extension of the "Chosen Ones"  Your abilities to find lost history is unmatched.  And now you are going to put that talent to work again.  You cannot refuse, and as you already know, you wish not to."*

Eric knew his words to be true.

*"In my readings and studies of the oral history of my people there still survives a trace of this ancient civilization.  I am tasking you to find it.  I will provide all the clues at my disposal.  I know this will be no easy task but my*

*faith resides in you.  You now also have Dove of Spring at your side as I predicted.  I am also certain your Mayan friends will more than willingly assist you."*

**W**hispering Wind was silent for a moment.

*"Now you may ask your questions,"* He finished with a smile.

**M**y mind was racing with questions, so much so that I couldn't speak.  Happily embarrassed I finally managed a few words.
**"W**here is this starting point ?"

*"**I** see your king was correct in his assessment of you,  right to the point.  Actually it is not far from here, but I'm afraid it will be a great distance underground.  The pressure of the ice for over a thousand years has more than done its job."*

**F**inally collecting his wits about him, Eric's mind was fully engaged already making plans.  He was actually more excited than he felt in the Yucatan.
**W**hispering Wind ended their visit much to the disappointment of Eric.

*"**Y**ou must concentrate on your upcoming ceremony with Dove of Spring.  When all is settled we will talk again and all will be revealed."*

**E**ric was naturally disappointed but knew this respected elder was right.  One more day after thousands of years will not change a thing.

# Chapter 4

<br>

Eric liked this idea of always having someone to return to. Once back with Violet he was naturally curious about the wedding plans.

"Why ? Are you getting nervous ?" she teased.

"No. I just have not been here to take part in the planning."

"All is going well so far. I believe I mentioned earlier a lot of the old traditions have been dropped, but a few are still maintained, which I would like to maintain. It is not too common that one marries out side of the nation. So I will briefly outline the ceremony for you so that there are no surprises."

Eric liked the idea of no surprises. He has had more then his share over the last few years.

"First, the ceremony will take place at my hogan. Well in this case my house. The wedding will take place at sundown."

"Good." interrupted Eric. "I hate drinking parties during the day."

Again he received a slap on the arm.

"Clown," she smiled. "I am not to be seen by the sun or sunlight; therefore my head will be covered with a blanket."

Eric smiled again.

She smiled again. "Please bear with me," she grinned in return.

Eric said not a word but threw both hands up as if surrendering.

"You my Love will arrive by horseback. Just before the actual sunset. Lone Buffalo is arranging that for us."

"I like that idea," Eric voiced sincerely.

Violet was pleased by his remark.

"The saddle will be removed and taken into the house."

"Keep going, I think I am truly going to enjoy this."

Violet was more pleased by the minute.

"A wedding basket to hold corn meal and blessings will be placed with the opening facing East. This is the sacred direction from where the sun rises and from where no harm or evil can come."

Violet paused here asking sincerely, "Are you still with me. I hope you are."

"All the way and forever," Eric replied looking straight into her eyes.

She leaned over and kissed his cheek. Smiling and happy Violet continued.

Whispering Wind will then sing a blessing after which corn meal is placed in the basket and blessed. A water gourd will be given to us to wash each others hands before eating. This is for cleansing and purity. We will take turns eating a pinch of corn meal, moving to all four directions of the world.. Whispering Wind will speak of our mutual new relationship and duties to each other and again give a blessing."

She softly laughed here saying.

"Then you're stuck with me."

"Forever I hope," Eric answered.

"After the official ceremony we join hand in hand and return to my hogan."

Dove of Spring shyly smiled; "The next day we party. Remember as I said, the entire reservation will be in attendance, so you can't back out. Now, I still have preparations to take care of, as do you I'm sure. We will see each other tomorrow night."

She kissed him lovingly and walked away.

Eric just stood there. He never tired of her majestic beauty. Again a tingle in his brain hinting at something familiar about her.

"What are you standing there for, we have work to do, besides the bus doesn't run here any more."

Somewhat startled Eric turned to see Dan grinning.

The rest of the day went quickly as did the next. By late afternoon Eric was prepared.

The ceremony was even more intriguing. This, Violet had

spoken of and the new groom was extremely impressed.

"I feel truly at peace now.  I guess this is what I have been unknowingly searching for my whole life," Eric softly said to himself.

# Chapter 5

Five days had passed, and the lives of the newly married couple finally slowed down a bit.  Eric had not yet met with Whispering Wind for further information on the past civilization.  As much as his life was occupied with the recent nuptials he still allowed time for reflections of the words of the honored elder. His fascination with his words constantly filled his mind.

*"What made me so lucky to have both the King and Whispering Wind influence my life is a complete mystery to me,"* thought Eric.  *"I'm not going to fight though. I never believed in all that destiny stuff, but after the last few years perhaps there is something to it.  I am actually looking forward to the unknown. I feel even more fulfilled now that I have Dove of Spring at my side."*

Now for the final moment.  I bid my good bye to Violet and made  my way to Whispering Wind. As expected, he bid me enter before I was near the hogan.

*"I am aware of your anxiety my young friend, but do not let it cloud your mind.  As you have experienced in the past, patience allows you a multitude of answers."*

Chagrined at my own foolishness, I sat down where instructed and awaited the words of wisdom and discovery of my learned colleague.  Whispering Wind continued his story of the past as if a week had not past.

*"Our land was of many nations as was Europe of the time save for the fact we were not as unlearned as the Europeans.  Our advanced lifestyle was far beyond their realm*

*of understanding.  Hence the "Chosen Ones" reached out to teach which, as you have learned from your King, fell on deaf ears.  That, my young friend, was the result of misplaced self pride and greed, the downfall of many a society.*

*Enough of my boring stories.  You are here for the future of the past."*

**M**y sudden renewed interest must have shown.  The almost imperceptible smile on Whispering Winds face indicated that was so.

*"In the North East corner of our reservation lies a spot of extreme interest.  It is at what all refer to as the four corners in Utah territory, but that  matters not.  It is still Navajo land.  I will not journey there with you but from my sessions with your King I believe you will locate the place of our past history.  Do not expect to find identifiable structures. Remember we are speaking of thousands of years past.  We are but infants to their world."*

**F**rom an old earthen jug Whispering Wind retrieved a scroll. This was not a contract scroll though.  It was an intricately drawn map that left nothing to the imagination.  Right away my thoughts went to Lone Buffalo and his sonar sled.  What worked once before was worth trying again.

**I** detected from Whispering Winds smile he was reading my eager thoughts.

*"**R**emember my son, there is no time line on this adventure. Do not foolishly rush into what could be dangerous. You have a whole new life ahead of you with Dove of Spring. Do not become overwhelmed with foolish mistakes.  The advanced knowledge of eons ago awaits you.  Do not allow it to rule you as I know you will not."*

**H**e passed the scroll to me which I received as the treasure it was. "How ?" I asked , "Where and did you get this map ?"

*"That is not for you to distress over right now.
All will be revealed in its own time."*

He placed his hands on my heart and repeated some Navajo words several times. Whispering Wind dismissed me with the words:

*"Stay true to your heart, oh Chosen One."*

I felt humbled and knew I was dismissed. I silently took my leave returning to Violet.

I was welcomed home by my new bride with a kiss and a warm hug and questioning eyes. I smiled showing the map clutched in my hand. Instantly Violet pursued with;

"When do we leave ?" followed by a smile. "Remember, from now on we do this together no matter where it takes us."

Eric smiled and renewed his promise.

"Before we take off blindly I have to talk with Lone Buffalo."

Violet was anxious but knew Eric was correct. Get everything in order first.

"Let's plan on first thing tomorrow. It's probably a two plus hour drive so we can leave early.

"Good by then I will have everything ready." Violet answered.

Eric looked confused.

"Food and clothes silly and any other odds and ends you can think of."

"In the meantime I will go to see Dan. We may need his truck and or backhoe sooner or later."

"You go ahead "Oh Chosen One" and do what you must."

As soon as Violet said this she noticed an upsetting look on Eric's face. She instantly apologized.

I'm sorry my love. I know how that bothers you. I promise not to tease you any more. Just remember, you are my chosen one."

Eric smiled, "That, I can and will accept."

The rest of the day was routine for both yet they were

excited about their tomorrow.

Up and out early, Eric and Violet were like two school children heading for a class outing.  After just under two hours they were at the  map's destination point, basically empty desert area highlighted by a few sandstone monuments that broke the deserts monotony.  There were, however, a few not in the greatest conditions, small shacks.  One was a bit larger than the other three.

"I know this place," Violet said excitedly.  "I was here a few times as a child.  My father always spoke to an older person in that building. I believe she was called "Keeper of the Past" pointing to the larger of the four.

"That's the very structure Whispering Wind indicated on his map."

Now both showed their curiosity.

Slowly they  exited  Violet's car and  stood  for a while taking  in the natural beauty of the desert.  After double checking the map again they strode to the indicated building hesitating a bit.  Finally Eric knocked softly.

"Come in, " was the reply in Navajo.

They entered letting their eyes grow accustomed to the low light.  Soon they focused on an elderly lady in a rocking chair.  The inside surrounds were decorated with an amazing eclectic mix of things from the most horrid modern art to unidentifiable pieces of who knows what age.  The elder spoke with a surprisingly young voice but in the Navajo words.

"What can I do for such as you ?   I see you are newly joined together. May you have a long life."

Violet  translated  for  Eric  who  was  surprised  by  the comment.  He smiled and nodded his head.  Violet mentioned having been here long ago.  The woman said she remembered that time and that she was here with her father.  She described both of them as well.  Violet was surprised by the woman's  memory.  She had every detail correct.

"I know why you are here.  Whispering Wind said you would show soon.  I will speak with only your man now.  You may look around."

Disappointed and hurt somewhat, she translated to Eric and

moved away.  Eric, a bit uncomfortable, looked at his hostess with caution. Words entered his head, as with the King and Whispering Wind.

"I have been expecting you for many moons, more than I care to count.  You are he ? Are you not ?"

Eric stood there in shock not saying a thing, not even knowing how to approach such a question.  Who is this he, he wondered.

"I sense you are the he who was promised to come to me."

He firmly answered, "Who is this he you speak of? I'm afraid you have me at a disadvantage."

The old lady smiled now.

"Your humility is admirable.  You  have already answered my question."

Eric was becoming annoyed now.  Why must people play games with words.  This is as bad as the King's riddles.  Ahhh the King ! I wonder if he is involved with this.

"No need to wonder.  Your King and I have been acquainted for some time. I see now that you are not receptive as of yet. Perhaps another time."

She stopped speaking to me and just smiled.  She called Dove of Spring and said we may leave now.

" You may return when you have been enlightened more."

Eric did not say a word.  He took Violet's hand and urged her along as he exited the dwelling.


"What's the matter Eric ?  What has got you so upset ?"

Eric did not answer right away.  He entered the car on the passenger side.

"I'm afraid you will have to drive for now,"  He stated. Then remembering who he was talking to added a polite "please"

"Of course Eric. Try to relax and don't talk now but please explain when we get home.  Remember, I'm on your side."

Eric smiled and reached out and squeezed her hand.

"Thank you,"  He was silent again.


They arrived home late afternoon not having spoken a word for the whole drive.

Eric headed straight for the rocking chair on the back patio. Violet headed for the kitchen for a mug of coffee for him, black and syrupy just as Eric liked it. Minutes later she stood next to him coffee mug in outstretched hand.

"Hey, remember me, I'm the one who loves you," she whispered with her super smile and glowing dark eyes.

Eric looked up at her smiling. "Thank goodness for that," he answered as he took the mug and set it down on the nearby table. He then grabbed her and pulled her down to his lap. She smiled and giggled as he held her tight in his arms. "I need you." was all he said. After a few minutes of silence Eric reviewed his feelings with her.

"Frankly I'm tired of everyone saying I'm something or someone special. I'm just plain old Eric Dexter, photographer in love with a super special lady."

Violet, of course, knew how special he was. For the last few years he proved it with his new discoveries of ancient history. She was also aware of how much his Maya friends loved and respected him. She had instinctively known of his humility and that he did not like being paraded around like special royalty. She then decided it was her job to calm him down and allow him to accept who he is and to show him how proud she is of him and his history changing accomplishments.

"Please Eric, I have a general idea of what's bothering you but I would rather you explain all your feelings to me. We are one now and I believe together we can get through anything."

Eric was silent, staring at nothing. Slowly a half smile showed as he looked deep into her eyes.

"You are absolutely right my love. And I apologize. From now on there will be no secrets, except  of course, of my other three girl friends.."

Violet swatted his arm. "Now that's spousal abuse." she said with an equal smile.

Eric became serious again. "Okay, I'll give you the whole story of my feelings."

He went on to relate everything from the very beginning with his Yucatan adventures, more detail than was in his original journals. He ended his story with today's meeting with the Elder Navajo woman.

Dove of Spring empathized with him and silently vowed to lighten his burden for both their sakes.

"It was enough with the King pursuing the idea. I unwittingly went along with it telling myself he was from a different time and place. Then Whispering Wind, in an innocent way I know, alluded to the same specialness of my being. I did not push back too much out of respect for who he was."

He paused here and sipped his black liquid.

"Then today, a total stranger addressed me along the same lines as if I were not Eric Dexter. I am not special as these few from past civilizations want me to be. I would like to be treated as the plain person I am. Is that too much to ask ?"

They were both quiet now, each in their own thoughts. Some time passed in total silence. Violet took Eric's hand in hers asking.

"Do you trust me ?"

Eric instinctively knew she was serious and answered.

"Implicitly."

"Good then tomorrow we go back to the elder and I will speak to her first. Trust me completely on this and then you will have the necessary information you need. Then My Love, together we can search for this lost civilization, and I mean together. No more having you go off by yourself to be sacrificed in the jungle."

She smiled her love and Eric joined in that smile.

# Chapter  6

-27-

Early morning found Dove of Spring and Hunter of Stories on their two hour drive to the location of Whispering Wind's map again. Arriving at the now far from nowhere location they remained in the car, again taking in the scene of natural beauty interrupted only by the four structures that did not appear to belong.

Smiling Violet voiced, "All right Love, let's do this."

As they neared the house the same elderly voice bid them enter.

"I knew you would return," Eric received in his mind.

He half smiled and looked at Violet who immediately answered her elder in the native language.  Out of respect she addressed the woman as "Shima", her native word for mother.  The older woman had Violet by physical age but Violet was truly a tribal elder and gently asserted her status. The two conversed in the Navajo, which Eric did not understand.

(He mentally told himself he should learn at least some of the basics, then remembered he had the rest of his life for that now that he was married to Dove of Spring.)

Violet did most of the talking.  The old lady was humbled but did not take offense.  Dove of Spring was truly caring in her words. When she finished she turned to Eric and quietly whispered "I will wait outside."

The elder viewed me with somewhat smiling eyes. Then my mind picked up her words.

"Now my young friend, I am aware of your discovery history.  What I am about to reveal to you will fit in nicely with your previous discoveries.  Listen carefully. All I am about to say is clear only to those deemed receivers."


Eric was still a bit annoyed with everyone's indistinct wording, but for Violet's sake he held his tongue.

"Eons ago, those who came before us were far more advanced than today's world, no matter what some of our leaders tell us of today.  The history books of today tell us we were settled long after Europeans and Middle Eastern country's.  But that is not so.  Our ancestors have been here for many thousands of years.  Advancement in civilization went from west to east, not the other way around; hence the Egyptian encounters that you are now familiar with.  The Maya and others of Central and South America were an extension of our ancestors.  There are many places throughout this world that still exist, such as structures, as testimony to this advanced people and technology."

Eric had read about such places and was as mystified as the experts as to the construction of these stone structures, yet this old lady appears to have an unknown knowledge of such things.

I saw a glint of understanding in this woman's eyes as if she had read and understood my thoughts.

"Beneath where we are now sitting is that lost technology, an unknown city, nay a massive community dedicated to advanced technology and equality without prejudice.  Unheard of Cosmic forces put an end to that world, an end to that world and all that was good for the planet."

My elderly instructor paused here as if gauging my reception of her words.  I remained silent but urged further with my eyes.  With an affirmative nod of her head and soft smile she resumed her narration.

"Not far from where we are sitting now is a portal or entranceway to that lost world.."

This, of course, sent my mind soaring with a thousand questions.  Recognizing this, the elderly Shami held up her hand as an indication not to interrupt.  I bowed to her wishes.

"This portal is not a visible thing.  It has been buried, as the city was, for many thousands of years.  When and if you find this entrance, Whispering Wind will then share with you further documents to the treasured secrets of civilization we have not reached yet."

She lingered here a moment as if in deep thought.  Looking directly into my eyes, the Shami asked:

"Are you  this "Chosen One" to find the world's future, or do we just close the book forever ?"

She really threw me for a loop with her question.  My mind was suddenly filled with nothing.  I was a complete blank for an unknown time.  The memories of the last few years slowly filtered through my brain.: Frank Thurber, the King, my four Mayan friends, Whispering Wind, Dove of Spring, Lone Buffalo.  A warm flush of self confidence filled my being as I turned back to my questioner.  In spite of my own sometimes doubts I firmly and confidently answered ;

"Yes !, I am the one who can do this.  I know I can and I know I want to."

This special elderly Navajo lady smiled and bowed her head to me.  She arose and slowly walked, carefully judging her steps to an old intricately designed earthen jar and retrieved a scroll.

"Study this my son and return it to me.  This is the last communication with lost history.  When and if you find the lost entrance this document will self destruct."

Her words confused me but I was not about to question them.

""You may take this to study but it is not to leave this compound.  You and your loved one have one hour.  It must then be returned to me."

She said no more but handed me the scroll, turned and walked through a door on the other side of the room.  A door I had not previously seen.  I myself exited and went directly to Violet, standing by the car.

I explained all that took place and that I had accepted the challenge to search.  Together we unrolled the scroll and lay it on the hood of the car.  We both stared at it in disbelief.  Nothing was recognizable and we only had forty five minutes left.  In my mind I pictured some of the squiggles as elevated ground.  At the same time Violet mentioned that some of the wording looked like the Navajo language of old.  She suggested Whispering Wind would probably do better with the wording.

"We don't have time for that," I replied.

We were both quiet for a time trying to memorize the

scroll.

"Don't you have your camera with you ?"

"Of course, dummy me; why didn't I think of that, especially after the hundreds I copied in the Yucatan."

"See, I am a help to you already," she teased smiling.

I retrieved the camera from the car and photographed the scroll in sections as close as I could.

"I wonder if now my film will self destruct after an hour."

With the camera put away we used the remaining time to physically study whatever we could, trying to commit as much as we could to memory.

With five minutes to go we returned the map to the Old one.  I thanked her as best I could while Violet was more sincere in her native language.

"May the Great Spirit follow you on your chosen journey." were her final words to me as we drove away.

We were naturally eager to get back to Whispering Wind for his input on the mysterious scroll.


The usual routine, still a good thirty feet from his hogan, he bode us enter.


*"I am glad you accepted the challenge Hunter of Stories.  With Dove of Spring at your side you will not fail. Listen to her council when given and do not hesitate to ask.  I sense you are both here to share something with me."*


He indicated we sit.  Violet handed him the scroll and translated his words.


*"Ah, yes.  I have seen this only once before.  I was but a boy that had not earned my eagle feather yet.  It was my grandfather who was the keeper then.  I'm afraid I will not be of much assistance to you on this."*


He noticed the disappointment on both our faces.

*"You should not be disappointed my son.  It has never hindered you in the past.  However I can assist with one word."*

**H**e pointed to a symbol that meant nothing to either of us.

*"This is from the language of the ancients.  It has been deciphered as meaning crest. That may be of help to you."*

"**M**y topo maps !" I blustered out rather loudly to the smiles of my two companions.  "I'm sorry." I instantly apologized to two smiling faces.

*"You have just proven my faith in you my Son. Now go do what you must."*

**W**e knew we were dismissed but left on a  happy note, hand in hand on our return walk.

"**W**here have you two been all day.  I have asked and searched all day."

**T**he voice of course was Dan.

"**I** have a telegram for both of you."

**V**iolet extended her hand first, then seeing it was from Arizona she passed it to Eric.

**I** looked at where it was from and gazed at Dan questions in my eyes.

"**I** took the liberty of contacting Diego about your nuptials I thought they might want to know and perhaps attend."

"**T**hanks Dan. That completely slipped my mind which was obviously on other things,"  I looked directly at Violet as I said this.

"**W**ell, go ahead and read it.  I'm just as curious as you are," Violet asked with a big smile.

**E**ric opened it and smiled.

"**W**ell go on." urged Violet.

Eric started reading and a smile came across his face again.

"Out loud silly," ordered Violet.

"Okay, if you insist."

He smiled again as he read.  "Eric, you have now officially been thrown out of the "Stupid Bachelors Scientific Club"

Both Dan and Violet let out a soft chuckle.

"She must be one hell of a woman for you to give up all these lonely nights of talking to the trees.  We all suspected something like this while we watched you day dream instead of discovering new things for us."

Dove of Spring was slightly blushing now.

"We will break the news to the Golden Lady slowly but we are sure she will take this as a personal affront.  Joking aside we all wish you the best but we do hope it won't keep you from further outings with us.  There is still a lot of work to be done in the lost city.  Sincere best wishes to you and Violet.  We all hope to meet her some day.  We already know how special she is to have captured you..

Signed:

The best always; Diego, Mateo, Carlos, Mario.

P.S.  Sorry we could not attend but our schedules just did not allow."

Both Dan and Violet were all smiles with Violet still blushing a bit.

"I would like to meet them." she said sincerely.  "They sound like great people.

"They are and you will, I promise.  You will just love it in the Yucatan."


"Okay back to reality.  Where have you been all day ?" Dan inquired.

Both Eric and Violet filled him in on everything to date.

"Now here's where you come in," said Eric seriously.  "We are going to need your sonar sled again and some of your muscle."

"Not a problem, I will set my schedule according to your needs."

"No wonder Eric thinks so highly of you," Violet offered matching Dan's smile.

"I'll meet you here tomorrow, say eight AM," Dan said

and left.

"Now home and some topo map work," Eric suggested.

"Don't forget the film," Violet reminded.

"Oh right, I'll do that right now. I'll see you at home in about an hour or so."

He kissed her and headed for the school building.


A little over an hour and Eric knocked on the door of Dove of Spring.  Within seconds she opened the door.  Looking surprised to see Eric she smiled, kissed him and politely reminded him that he lived here now and did not have to knock.  She jokingly added.

"Keep this up and I'll take away your key."

Feeling awkward and turning crimson, he stepped into the house where Violet threw her arms around him.

"You are so adorable, I guess that's why you're so easy to love."

Recovering in her arms he asked;

"Care to help me look for a lost civilization."

"Now and always, I'll get you some coffee while you set up."


Violet returned with the coffee to find Eric in the midst of many air photos, stereo photo glasses and various topo maps along with some quick prints of the map they viewed that morning.

"I'm impressed," stated Violet. "You mentioned your use of aerial photos in your journals but I never imagined it was this involved. We had a very brief example of their use when I got my engineering degree but never actually used this technique."

"Well you're in luck, my love.  Prepare to watch and learn."

Violet put on a broad smile as she said;

"And from what I know of your discoveries I'll be learning from the best."

Eric felt a bit self conscious by her remark yet felt proud that she felt that way.

"Okay then, see what you can do to match a few of these photos to the topo of the area in question. I'll see if I can equate anything from this ancient scroll to the same area."

They silently worked for ten or fifteen minutes till Violet broke the silence.

"This is actually fun.  I never realized aerial photography was this useful or important.  Now I'm even more impressed with you."

"Welcome to my world," Eric smiled.  "My Mayan friends always teased me about sleeping while pretending to look through the stereo glasses, but they did like the results I came up with."

Violet leaned over and kissed Eric's forehead.

"What was that for ?" he asked confused.

"Just because,"  she smiled and then added, "Back to work."


"I think I have something." exclaimed an excited Violet. "It took a while but I think this couple of photos fit with the map."

Eric took a quick look and confirmed her find.

"That's not fair.  You only glanced at them and yet okayed them."

Eric laughed. "The difference being, this is your first shot. I've been doing this forever.  Wait till I tell my pals of the Yucatan.  They still haven't figured it out."

"You tell them and they will hate me and never talk to me." pouted Violet.

"Who could ever hate you," smiled Eric.  Now to be serious again I think I found something on this antique map.  All we have to do is to try and match it to the air photos and topo."

"I think I'll let you do that." she smiled.  "I'll go see about dinner."

"Quitting on me already ?  I'm so disappointed."

Violet looked at Eric directly, grabbed the old map and turned to the photos. "You go fix supper."  She turned back to the table and went to work.

It wasn't too long when she called to me.  "Please confirm this.  I do believe I have a  match up of all three sources."  She said with a twinkle in her eyes.

I looked at what she considered a match and with a big smile said; "You have the job permanently my dear.  I don't pay much but the job is forever permanent."

I like the word permanent," she said with a kiss.

Now that we had the general location pinned down, I reached for the stereo glasses.

"Now comes the hard part. This will even be more difficult than the jungle."  I was questioned by Violet's eyes.  "The jungle has definite shapes and forms.  Here we only have low meandering slopes constantly wind blown.  A definitive hillock does not last long with the ever changing winds.  The best we can hope to do is locate a general area, then let the sonar sled confirm or deny our guessing.

"Dove of Spring smiled saying;

"I truly am looking forward to this.  I find this whole idea challenging and exciting."

Eric was more than pleased to hear this knowing what possible troubles may lay ahead.

# Chapter  7


The new couple arrived at the school building at five minutes to eight only to find Lone Buffalo, truck and sonar sled ready and waiting.

"If you two were not partying all night you would get to work on time.  I've been waiting here for hours."

Eric replied with, "You also lie a lot."

Smiles went all around.

Off  the trio went in two vehicles.  Reaching the pre-planned location, they unloaded the sled, set up and proceeded scanning. Eric and Dan diligently pushed and pulled for almost two hours with absolutely no results.  Disappointing as this was they were not deterred. Violet even took turns with the pushing and pulling to give the men a break. The scroll printout showed not the slightest anomaly underground.  They did know they were looking for the proverbial needle in a super large haystack, yet the disappointment was showing.  Reflecting back to the Pyramid seemed like an easy chore.  While resting Dan jokingly remarked,

"What we need here is Mr. Blue."

Eric's face lit up with a broad grin.

"That's it !"  He almost shouted.  "Why didn't I think of that.  I hope he's still around."

"That he is my friend.  I even told the teens of his value and speciality.  They in turn do treat him with respect.  As far as I know he's still living in or near the Pyramid."

Eric, with new enthusiasm, turned to Violet.

"Come on Love, we have to go find Mr. Blue, but first I have a stop to make."

He quietly turned to Dan

"Same time tomorrow, Pal." as he ran for the car, Violet in tow.

"Now I know you are absolutely crazy," she laughed.

The stop , of course was the small Pet Shop Eric had been to before.  He was able to get what he wanted just as the last time, crickets, grass hoppers and June begs.

"Nothing like a little bribery I see," Violet smiled.

"Mr. Blue deserves it," Eric answered earnestly.  "Now to the pyramid."

"You sure do like a busy day," she laughed.  "But that's okay, this time I'm with you."  She reached and squeezed his hand.


The Pyramid now in sight, I was pleased to see the teens kept their promise. It was now truly a sight worth seeing.  They had cleared the surrounding landscape which only added to its majestic appearance in the middle of the desert.  Stopping the car a good distance away, the pair walked hand in hand to the structure.  Stopping a good twenty feet from the entrance to admire the view, they were met by Eric's longtime friend who actually acted excited to see him.  Eric immediately dropped to his knees and emptied the box of treats.

"Here you go my friend, but I must admit I have an ulterior motive.  I need your help again.  A place quite a distance from here.  Would you help me once more ?"

Mr. Blue had already struck and stunned all the new treats.  He paused no more than six feet from the couple twitching his legs together.

"Thanks, Pal, I knew I could count on you."

Mr. Blue then went about stock piling his future meals in the Pyramid.

Dove of Spring was again mesmerized by what took place before her eyes. *Eric was certainly special,* She thought.

"Now my friend do you trust me enough to go with me.  It is a long distance from here.  I promise to bring you home again."

Without hesitation Mr. Blue walked to the car and waited.  Using the empty bug box as a scoop Eric set him into the trunk of the car.  Violet, still spellbound, entered the car along with Eric, and they returned to the Old Map location where Mr. Blue was released.  Violet waited silently as Eric outlined to Mr. Blue his request.  They left Mr. Blue alone and returned home.

"I almost don't want to believe what I just witnessed today.  You are amazing."  She looked at Eric and saw his embarrassment and quickly changed the subject.

"**I** think I love you." she stated with a smile.

"**Y**ou have to now, we're already married."


~ ~ ~ ~ ~ ~


**E**arly the next day found all three anxious to get started. Dan checked and rechecked the sonar sled. Violet examined the paper scrolls for performance, while Eric attended to the presence of Mr. Blue. All was ready with Mr. Blue placed on the chosen location. Eric's helpful tarantula circled the spot as if gauging for accuracy. After a few wide circles Mr. Blue took off as if heading for the home of the elder one. Eric recovered quickly and returned his furry friend to the chosen location. Mr. Blue repeated his performance as previously acted. This time Eric spoke in a soft voice trying to get Mr. Blue to return on his own. Once again Eric returned his blue beauty to the sonar sled position. Without hesitation Mr. Blue took off hastily heading for the old broken down structure.

**F**rustrated and disappointed, Eric let him go and looked apologetically at Dan and Violet.

"**I** thought it was a good idea considering what he had done for me before."

**E**ric sat down on the sled feeling rejected and again embarrassed.

"**L**ook, he's stopping." commented Violet.

**T**he large blue creature had stopped and looked back at the three, but turned and once more made for the old building.

"**L**et's try one more time," Eric spoke as he stood and walked after Mr. Blue.

**D**an and Violet soon followed. Mr. Blue glanced back one more time before entering the building through a large rotted hole at the side.

**E**ric now rushed to the old lady's home in fear of Mr. Blue's life. He anxiously knocked on the door.

"Come in young man."

**A**s he entered he saw the old lady standing near his furry companion with her ever present questioning smile.

"I see you also have a connection with nature's creatures. You are truly the Chosen One."

**A**s much as Eric disliked being called by this name he let it pass because of his concern for Mr. Blue.  As if reading his mind the elder one calmed his nerves when she confirmed as having the same gift of connection with all creatures of the Great Spirit.

"You have proven yourself true to your cause my young friend.  The portal you seek may be here.  It is something I have suggested for countless years, but dared not pursue.  Whispering Wind was wise to choose you."

**B**y now Dan and Violet had joined Eric inside the house and caught the tail end of the old lady's words.

"**B**ut this is your home, I can't start breaking it apart." Eric voiced apologetically.

"I spend some time here, but this is not my home.  My hogan is not far from here to which I will now return.  May the Great Spirit bless your search."

**W**ithout another word she took her leave as if she disappeared.

**E**ric, Violet and Dan remained staring at Mr. Blue.  In an apologetic tone Eric addressed his blue helper.

"**I**'m sorry to have doubted you my friend.  I should have realized you would not let me down."

**V**iolet and Dan were smiling now along with tears in Violet's eyes, tears of pride for her man.

~ ~ ~

**T**here was a large knothole identifying a loose board yet not large enough for Mr. Blue.  A quick  nod to Dan and we both set to work tearing up the board.  Mr. Blue instantly scurried into the opening and disappeared.  We further tore up more of the floor.  What we were now staring at was poorly constructed base flooring set up on aged hardened dirt but no Mr. Blue.  It suddenly dawned on me that this could be a good sign, such as he was instinctively following his sense of discovery.

**D**an broke into my thinking with;

"**W**hat now big guy ?  I can't get my backhoe in here."

"**I** guess we start digging by hand then," offered a positive

Violet.

      With a broad smile Dan answered with, "You two were made for each other. You're both nuts. No disrespect meant," he added. "Okay, you guys win. I just happen to have three small shovels in my truck."

      Violet moved to Dan, kissed his cheek, took hold of his hand stating, "What are we standing here for. Let's go get them ."

      "How did I ever get involved with you two," he smiled as he was pulled along.

      After returning with the shovels I joined the pair and we all proceeded to dig.

      "Careful," I warned. "We don't want to hurt my blue companion, where ever he is."

      Heed my warnings they did. In fact Dan decided to remove additional flooring, which he did with the utmost care, so that we could put it back when necessary. The hard packed dirt seemed to go on forever with no sign of Mr. Blue. No sooner had that thought crossed my mind when he suddenly reappeared. He stopped, looked at me twitching his leg and headed off again under the still remaining floor boards. Attempting to listen in the direction he went, I followed quietly. A set of shelves stacked with very old canned goods now stood in the way.

      "Now what," I wondered.

      Within seconds of that thought Mr. Blue came from behind the shelf.

      "Well, hello there friend. Do you have any discoveries for me ?""

      Both Violet and Dan were looking at me strangely. I don't know why. They both knew of my connection with this beautiful tarantula.

      My furry friend turned and disappeared behind the shelf once more.

      "Dan, give me a hand," I asked. He answered with that sly smile that only he and Diego possessed.

      We struggled for a bit hardly moving the old heavy shelf. Without being asked Violet joined in and with extra effort the three of us we finally dislodged the old structure.

      With an "I told you so," smile Violet voiced;

      "Where would you men be without us women ?"

      With true meaning I replied;

"I will always want and need you."

This made her blush as she moved away.


Behind the now moved shelf was more rotted flooring, obviously from moisture over the years. Dan and I easily removed some of the rotted wood. There was Mr. Blue digging at one spot. My face lit up, Mr. Blue and I had connected again.

"More crickets and grasshoppers for you, Pal."

Violet had already retrieved the shovels,  and we commenced digging.  Mr. Blue returned to his original entry point and calmly waited.


All three of us dug steadily for almost an hour.  After resting for ten minutes or so we agreed on only two digging, and rotating in the third person every half hour or so..  It did not look like we were making any progress until we reminded ourselves that this lost civilization, if there was one, was buried some twelve or thirteen thousand years ago.  A lot can and has happened over that span of time.

Time passed slowly until they realized a problem was developing.  Dan and Eric came to this conclusion basically at the same time.  They stood there looking at each other, half smiles on their faces.

"It appears we have been here before," Eric stated.

Dove of Spring looked a bit puzzled, but not for long. Smiling, she now knew what Eric and Dan were referring to and thus stated the obvious.

"Okay, guys.  What do we do with all this dirt and who knows how much more ?"

The three sat down and laughed.


After their enjoyment of the moment they got serious again.

"Do we ask the teens again?" quizzed Eric.

"Not a bad idea, but," replied Dan.  "This is the wrong time of year.  I believe  their studies should take  precedence over our folly."

Eric agreed and apologized for the thought.  "I agree, schooling is more important than our dreams."

I could bring the bucket loader but we would have to remove part of the wall of the house," suggested Dan.

"That's a little much, don't you think.  It's not like it's our own dwelling," answered Eric.

"**G**entlemen." stated Violet. "That may not be outwardly true."

**T**he two immediately looked at her with curiosity.

"**I**f you remember prior to your talk with the elder one Eric I had a very direct conversation with her. It was an honest and above board chat about what you were researching. She willingly disclosed to me her feelings and her part in the overall picture of this seeking adventure. She along with Whispering Wind are probably the only two who know of or at least suspect the existence of a lost civilization."

**V**iolet looked directly at me as she said these words.

"**S**he knows of your connection with the king and of your special relationship with Whispering Wind regarding this lost knowledge of antiquity. She believes in you and your ability in this unique search. She informed me directly, without hesitation, that you were free to do whatever was necessary with the building to accomplish your goal. She accepts without judgement any of your decisions  regarding that assigned goal."

**D**ove of Spring paused here momentarily. Then with a look of love in her eyes continued;

"**A**s do I. This is not for your ego, my love, but for the benefit of all mankind, the past, present and the future."

**V**iolet felt herself growing scarlet. Eric also felt a little awkward. In his mind he was not this special.

**D**an assessing the dilemma voiced his, as always, practical solution.

"**W**ell I guess that's our answer pal. Tomorrow the backhoe."

**E**ric just nodded his approval and smiled quietly. Violet went to Eric and gently put her arms around him whispering, "It's okay love, I'm here with you."

**T**hen addressing all:

"**N**ow that we have had a little break how about some lemonade ?"

**S**miles were contagious as they walked to the car. Relaxing with the cooling drink, the quiet was suddenly disturbed by a slow rolling roar. The trio watched as the rear half of the building they were working in methodically collapsed, sending up a cloud of dust and dirt. Momentarily frozen in place they stared in disbelief. As the dust settled Eric was the first to move quickly to the rubble.  As he drew closer he was shocked at what he was viewing.  It appeared as if it was a planned take down, the key being the earth below now exhibited a cave like opening immediately adjacent to where they had been digging.   Dan and Violet, now standing with Eric, witnessed Mr. Blue at the entrance to this exposed cavern.  He repeatedly moved in and out of this new opening as if saying "this is it".

"I really owe you big time for this one my friend,"  Eric said as the three watched Mr. Blue walk away toward the car.

"So much for the backhoe." Dan smiled.

"What now Eric," Violet asked holding onto Eric's hand.

He looked at his watch and replied casually;

"Have, I guess, a good hot shower and a relaxing meal and a night of much needed rest."

Dan, a bit surprised questioned,

"Aren't you even a bit curious ?"

Eric smiled, "After some twelve thousand years I don't think one more day will make a difference.  Lets tarp over this mess and put up a keep away sign."

# Chapter  8

After a breakfast fit for a king, Eric and Violet were preparing for the day or longer in this newly found cavern.  Four canteens of water, bandanas for masks, no machetes but good sized knives, military entrenching tools, compass, and of course camera and plenty of film.  Violet packed six small MRE's and some energy bars, enough for three.  Last but not least some hard wearing but comfy clothes.

A similar list was given to Dan who was to meet them at the site.

"It appears you have done this before." clowned Dove of Spring, though well she knew having read his past journals.  "Civilization is nice, although I am so thrilled to finally be part of your chosen way of life."

They hugged without shame

Once on location Eric was having second thoughts.  Not about the lost civilization but about finding anything.  This was nothing like a city in the jungle taken over by natures growth.  This was supposedly a piece of ancient history that was catastrophically buried under hundreds of feet or even miles of earth and stone for thousands of years.  We could dig for years and possibly only find a small artifact that would have no definitive meaning to us.

After mulling this over in his mind he decided to share his thoughts openly with Violet and Dan.

Having done so with the utmost concern all was silent for a while.

"You sure know how to kill the spirit of adventure," quipped Dan.

His statement at least broke the seriousness of the moment.

"So what are you suggesting we do ?" asked Violet softly.

Eric appreciated her tender approach but answered with mixed emotions.

"I wish I knew.  My own thoughts even threw me for a loop.  Please my friends, I am open for ideas."

Dan, now joining in the seriousness asked how I had handled such problems in the Yucatan.

"I had four others to help bounce ideas around, which is why I'm asking the two of you."

"And you had the king, riddles and all," said Violet.

At least this raised a smile from Eric.  His eyes told her of his love as he voiced;

"Thanks for the reminder."

Eric drifted away from Dan and Violet deep in confused thought.  Dan was about to say something to Eric but Violet's touch stopped him.

"This is his moment alone.  Let him be."

Dan thought this strange but Violet knew this was the right thing.  She could almost read Eric's mind but purposely ignored her own thoughts at this particular time.  This was his and his alone to work out, as much as she wanted to be part of him.

### *"I sense that you are troubled, my friend."*

The king's voice did not really startle me.  I sort of expected it.  As much as his riddles annoyed me, at this point I could use his council.

*"As always Eric, you know when to question that which is before you.  And now you are troubled by my ancient civilization.  Rightfully so, my friend.  Your Whispering Wind is going by oral tradition passed down through the ages.  He is too young to have been part of this living thing that was my time.*

*The cavern you were about to study will net you nothing.  What was once there has been obliterated by cosmic fallout.  Yes it was once a partial example of my time but never the true roots of our superior intelligence."*

"**B**ut Whispering Wind appeared so certain because of the Oral Traditions," Eric interrupted.

*"As would any knowledgeable person. Don't fault this elder my friend. He did not possess the knowledge of the inner workings of my day. I have just conversed with your Whispering Wind and he now knows the truth."*

"**B**ut what about this woman's house or business. We have all but destroyed it to get to this point. And Mr. Blue, he has never been wrong before."

**E**ric was now upset and disturbed, actually distraught for others because of this folly.

*"I see you are out of sorts right now. I shall take my leave till you sort out your overwrought feelings."*

**E**ric knew from past experience that it would be useless to get the king to return. He took a few deep breaths and turned back to his companions. With a forced half smile he returned to them.

"**T**hat's it for today I guess,"said Dan.

**E**ric put his hand on Dan's shoulder saying:

"**T**hanks for understanding."

**E**ric's eyes then shifted to Dove of Spring. She nodded her head indicating her understanding without saying a word. They returned quietly to the car. Dan was already driving away. Eric assisted Mr. Blue into the car then drove straight to the pyramid.

**M**r. Blue went straight to the entrance and disappeared. Eric laughed at his rush to return home as he sat down in the sand facing theat entrance. Violet quietly joined him.

"**I** don't have much to offer but we do have plenty of water or how about a tasty energy bar ?" she quipped.

**S**omewhat relaxed now, Eric told her the story of surviving on energy bars the day he communed with the jaguar.  They then remained in silence for almost an hour, Violet content with just holding Eric's hand.

**T**o break the ice of silence Violet spoke softly.

"**H**ow about we eat out tonight ?  There is always that little steak house not far from here."

"**N**o, my love, I just want to be alone with you.   I need someone to talk to; thus fortunately for me, you are the one."

**W**ith a beaming smile Violet responded.

"**T**hat's what I married you for, to share your life, the good and the bad.  We are one now my love and together we can surmount any challenge."

"**H**ow can one man be so lucky." was Eric's quiet response.


"**I** know you were in touch with the king which seemed to put you in this off mood. Can I help ?  Please let me help."

**E**ric was already feeling better.


**H**e wanted to share his discoveries with her and felt this was as good a time as any.  He had shared many adventures with his Mayan friends and of course locally with Dan.  This sharing would be different he knew because he yearned for her participation.  He knew the danger of such adventures because he had already lived them.   Down deep inside he understood and accepted her desires to take part in these unknown ventures. He knew she had the strength of character and determination to equal any of his previous undertakings, yet he still felt a deep desire to protect her from any danger.   Her strong determination to be part of his life convinced him that she could and would be of great assistance.

**C**learing his mind he turned to her saying:

"**Y**es, I want your help.  Better yet, I need your help."

**T**he love in her eyes was unmistakable.

"**I** know I have read your journals but I'm sure there is more to you than what you put down as notes in a book."

"**Y**ou are absolutely correct, and now I want to fill in the blanks."

**T**he smile she showed was sincere.

"**B**ut first," Eric continued, "I think I could use that energy bar about now."

Violet instantly went to the car returning with water and the requested treat.

Once settled again Eric felt and acted  like a whole new man much to the delight of Dove of Spring.

He spent the next twenty minutes detailing his three trips to the Yucatan, his experiences with the king, and his time with his four Mayan comrades.

Violet took in every word like a sponge.  She was finally getting to see inside Eric Dexter: his drive, his dedication to the truth, the real man beneath.  He was so much more than just a photographer.

Finished with his adventures and smiling, Eric looked at Violet saying;

"Now that I have bored you to death, what do we do with the rest of the day ?"

Returning his smile she replied.

"Boring you are not.  I am now convinced more than ever that from now on I will be always at your side, even at the sacrificial alter."

Eric stared at her with wonder yet was filled with a happiness he never knew before.

Jokingly, she quickly added, "You will never leave me again except when I send you to the store for groceries."

"I'll drink to that," he quipped in return as he lifted his canteen to sip.

Dove of Spring reached and squeezed his hand.

"Okay, let's get serious again.  What was your trouble with the king this morning ?  I sensed a drastic change in you from early this morning."

Eric smiled, though remained pensive.

"You truly are a wonder.  I now wish I had you on my treks in the Yucatan."

Violet's eyes twinkled at his words.

"Yes, back to this morning.  Whispering Wind was not necessarily wrong in his wanting to search for the lost Era, but was missing complete information.  Both he and the old woman were basing their feelings on oral history that had been handed down through the ages which, by the way, was correct."

Violet was now looking perplexed.

"The history was correct, just not complete. Just prior to or during the early phase of the cosmic impact, the ancients tried preparations for surviving. This is where apparently the oral history went astray. Many of the ancients, including the seven "Chosen Ones," wanted to preserve their advanced society and way of life. I will go into those details later. They set about finding a place or places for that survival, one of which was here on this reservation. Others were spread throughout these United States.. Your Native American heritage is or was directly connected to this civilization as were the Mayans and those who came before them. You were to be the recipient of that advanced culture. The few surviving connections were destroyed in this country by the invading Europeans who had a wrong sense of entitlement. Right up to our modern times we are still wiping out our past in order to build a future and not necessarily a future of knowledge for the betterment of all.

Now, in Central and South America there still survives physical proof of these Ancient peoples. The downside of the jungle, as we view it now, was actually the key to its preservation. Survival in the jungle was the biggest deterrent to complete takeover by the Europeans hence the king's presence, if only in spirit."

Dove of Spring was completely taken in by Eric's tale. "Hunter of Stories" was an accurate name for him. She considered this a break in his story telling and inquired seriously.

"What has this fascinating yarn to do with this morning's debacle."

Eric smiled now which puzzled Violet.

"Ahhh, to use the king's words to me many times, to paraphrase "Ever the curious and right to the point."

Dove of Spring was pleased with the comparison. Eric continued.

"As was obvious I was upset when we didn't find an entranceway. Believe me, I am used to let downs but an answer eventually shows itself. When all I saw this morning was solid earth and then thought about the thousands of years of burial, I realized this was an impossibility."

"But your Mr. Blue went right to that spot," Violet suggested.

Grinning, Eric answered immediately.

"And he was right in doing so. I do believe there was an

actual location, but it has been buried for countless ages.  There would be nothing left."

They were both silent now.  Eventually Eric spoke in an upbeat voice.

"Don't look so down in the dumps.  There is always an answer to a problem.  I will make arrangements for an enlightenment session with Whispering Wind and the king."

He purposely paused here, then with a huge smile added.

"And you will be there also."

"Do you really mean that.  I don't want to be a handicap to you."

"You can only be an asset my love."

She crushed him in a bear hug.


That evening at home, Eric spent time reviewing facts about the king for Violet.  There was no actual verbal conversation.  They communicated with their minds at his request, sort of a preparation for meeting the king.

You and Whispering Wind can converse via your native tongue which, at this moment has me at a disadvantage.  I know you will help me learn your language, but for now we will have to rely on mind transference which, as you already know, has no boundaries of time or distance.

Dove of Spring remained fascinated by this method.

"Our meeting with the king and Whispering Wind will be strictly by telepathy."

She looked forward to the meeting and in particular the king.  The evening drew to a close with Violet excited beyond anything she could remember.

Eric using actual vocal transmission said good night to his new mate and was happy to use his real voice. Nowhere was there two more content people.

# Chapter  9



 

*"Come in my children,"* said Whispering Wind knowing Eric and Violet were approaching.  Neither vocalized their greetings but it was received by the senior elder with a smile of acceptance.

**D**ove of Spring, however, was a bit apprehensive.  She, to date, had limited experience in this use of mind messaging, coupled with the fact she was about to meet the king.

**A**s  was the routine, the arrivals were directed to sit and were served a lemon drink.

*"Before we start our session with the king I must apologize to you Eric, for misleading you on a futile search"*

Whispering Wind said this with obvious humility and contrition.

"There is no need for that.  All are lessons of learning ,Sir, and for further lessons when indeed learned."

Violet was again amazed at the depth and caring that Eric possessed.

"All will be answered with today's session with Atl.  There is no blame to be put anywhere.  Please accept my apology if I misled you to blame yourself.  That was never my intent."

**"Spoken as I would expect from you Eric. You never cease to amaze me,"** were the sudden interruptive words of Atl.

Violet sat there with a somewhat startled look yet a hint of pride at hearing the praise for Eric.  She was surprised even more with what she heard next.

*"You, Dove of Spring represent your name beautifully. Eric has chosen well. You will be a great asset to his never ending curiosity because your heart is also true. Please care for him as I know he will care for you."*

Violet's surprise turned to awkward embarrassment mixed with almost tearful pride.

*"Now for the matter at hand,"* the king voiced authoritatively.

*"You, Whispering Wind have always known about the lost civilization, my civilization, as does the woman known to you as "Keeper of the Past," but has been beyond your grasp understandably. You then met young Eric as did I. That fortunate meeting appeared to have opened doors for you, rhetorically speaking. We have both taken advantage of his talent, I more so than you. It seems now finding the location of the lost civilization has come to the forefront. I myself wonder if this is a good thing or a bad thing. The advancement of our technology could be of great benefit to all mankind. But, and heed my words, it could be the destruction of all mankind. The unacceptable condition of today's mind- set is certainly not conducive to peaceful acceptance. As you know we chosen ones were sent on a mission of enlightenment to all nations, but the inherent greed for wealth and power turned away many of our efforts planet wide. The indigenous peoples, such as yourselves, here and in the lands south of you, were the only beings who already lived in a sharing world. It hurt me to see the invasion from the east come and destroy everything that was good here in this northern*

*place. The southern place to their credit embraced some of our teachings, which gave them an advantage over the conquerors. The known studies and advancements in mathematics and astronomy, language arts, and art itself, not to mention advancement in the technology of matter and the manipulation of magnetic's and the atom itself. Eric here has been witness to some of these manipulations of the electronic universe."*

At this point the eyes of Whispering Wind and Dove of Spring turned to Eric.

*"He being true to himself and thus to mankind has kept them secret, hidden in his heart because of their potential danger to mankind.*

*Now, to the location of our lost civilization. You were right, Whispering Wind. The major part of our community was here on this now reservation. As you all know now it is totally lost and buried under thousands of years of rock, sand, and cosmic debris, totally unrecoverable."*

Atl paused here. A chill ran through Eric's body knowing he was being singled out.

*"A small cache of articles of that civilization are yet preserved here. It is up to you Eric to find them or not. Once found you will know what to do."*

"And where do I find this hideaway ?" Eric asked knowing it was almost a futile question.

*"Review your past successes and perhaps further your reading."*

The king abruptly ended that hint.

*"The balanced and more complete proof of the existence of my time is back where you released me. I'm sure you and your new life partner, along with your Mayan brothers, can locate my history. What you do with it I leave to your discretion. You are aware of all the options. Dove of Spring guide him well to making the right decision and all will be rewarded."*

The hollow sound Eric was so used to surprised the others. The king was gone though Whispering Wind did try to reestablish contact.

"I'm sorry my friend but Atl has finished. When he feels the need he will establish contact again, either as a group or individually.

*"I understood everything but did not realize how he values you,"* stated Whispering Wind. *"You are obviously important to him and his wanting to share his hope for the future, not just ours but mankind's. I must rest now my children to absorb all that has transpired today. Go now and do what you must "Hunter of Stories".*

Eric actually liked when his given Navajo name was used. He along with Violet took their leave of the wise elder. They walked slowly and silently back to the school and Dan's office.

Dove of Spring was deep in disturbed thought the whole way back though she did periodically lightly squeeze Eric's hand. He also was quite pensive in the silence.

Dan had not yet returned to his office so the silent couple agreed to wait in the council room where they were assured privacy. By now they were ready to talk. Violet spoke first with a huge smile of pride.

"I learn more of you every day. There is obviously more to you than just taking pictures. The first time I met you I thought you were just some arrogant souvenir hunter out for a quick buck. My humble apologies."

Eric jokingly interrupted;

"And you married me anyway.  Are you looking for a quick buck also."

Without hesitation she swatted his arm again, but did it with a loving smile.

"I'm beginning to like these beatings.  They keep my muscles in tone."

"Are you ever serious ?" she asked.

"I can be," he answered seriously.  "When people don't make me out to be something I'm not."

"Point taken, but you are still more than special to me."

"That I can and will accept."

"Now ," Violet took the lead, "To be serious once again. I see what you mean about riddles. Does your Atl do that with everybody ?"

"I assume so, but I don't really know how many others he converses with, other than myself and my four colleagues in the Yucatan. So you also picked up on his book reading reference."

"Yes, to me it sounded like the riddles you spoke so much of.  But what does it mean ?"

"That's where you come in," Eric replied with a smile.

"Me ?"

"Yes, now there can be two of us confused."

She laughed.

"Seriously though, the only book I can recall with the pyramid was the large ancient book that was wrapped in the rare silks."

"You mean the one I did not believe in," she smiled.

"Dan and I had not come across anything else that I would call a book.  A few small scrolls but not a  book.  And that particular book I did not and could not read."

"Then  perhaps when the king said further reading he meant looking further than the book."

Eric perked up like he had just been stuck with a pin.  He leaned forward and kissed Violet.

"You are wonderful."

Just then they heard an all too familiar voice.

"Don't you two have a house for that sort of thing ?"

Of course it was Dan in his ever joking mood.

Eric and Violet proceeded to give Dan the details of their shorter than expected meeting with the king. Eric finished with;

"And this marvelous woman, I believe, just solved the king's riddle."

"I hope I don't have to meet your king because I'm terrible at riddles, " smiled Dan.

Eric pushed on, "Seriously though you and I have to go back to the pyramid to where we discovered the book."

Violet rather loudly cleared her throat. Eric looked at her smiling face.

" Sorry love," he corrected himself. "The three of us have to go back to the pyramid to where we discovered the book."

"Well today is obviously out, at least for me. Suppose we meet tomorrow, say nine o'clock. I should be free for the rest of the day then."

Eric glanced at Violet who nodded her agreement.

"Sounds good pal, see you in the desert. Now wonder woman how about a nice dinner while I do some research with my air photos ?"

"Oh, so now I'm relegated to the kitchen while you play."

"Okay just for that you play in the kitchen while I work at research.."

Violet looked at him confused while she smiled.

Dinner over, both played with the aerial photos. Using the pyramid as a center they further checked for anomalies in the immediate surroundings.

# Chapter 10

All arrived just before nine AM. The words of the riddle were given to Lone Buffalo.

*"Review your past successes and perhaps further your reading."*

"I see what you mean; that's about as clear as mud," replied Dan.

"Which is why we must retrace our exact steps that led to the discovery of the book," answered Eric

As the trio approached the pyramid entrance Mr. Blue appeared, twitched his legs and met them at the entrance.

"I see the king has already been in touch with your friend," joked Dan.

The three of us stepped onto our makeshift elevator, which had been strengthened and fortified by our overzealous teens. We, of course were followed by Mr. Blue. Once we reached bottom, we this time, followed Mr. Blue to the turquoise treasure room. Before going to the middle pile of turquoise, the three of us set about checking walls, floors and stockpiles for any thing unusual to the eye or ear. As expected nothing showed itself. We continued on to the false turquoise pile.

Soon we had the door in the floor exposed. I led the way, but the three of us descended the narrow curved steps. The narrow, low ceilinged hallway, Dan and I had negotiated a few times before but this was relatively new to Violet. I must say though, she handled everything like an expert. It then became very clear to me that she was not fragile physically or mentally. I was able to drop about half of my concerns.

When we reached the stone portal showing the large wooden door, Dove of Spring was fascinated by the Glyphs. She was smiling both outwardly and inwardly. While she studied the Glyphs I proceeded to open the museum door. Dan threw the light switch to illuminate its beauty. Even though we had all seen it before, the history it contained was mesmerizing.  Breaking out of our self made trance, we three all started checking the walls, floors and anything that did not move for any hollow sounds or movement, yet again to no avail.

Dan and Eric looked at each other with the same thought.

"There is only one place left," voiced Eric.

"Where you found the sacred book," finished Violet.

"Which, of course is no longer here," added Dan.

The trio stood there looking at nothing.  Almost in a whisper Violet repeated the kings words.

*"Review your past successes and perhaps further your reading."*

Dan and I looked at her, questions in our eyes.

She looked up at us smiling and said with confidence, "Further could also mean a distance beyond."

All was silent as Dan and I shrugged our shoulders.

"At this point what do we have to lose?" I said.

We fell to our knees looking directly to where the suspense once lay.  Within seconds Violet was also on her knees.  I was about to say something when Mr. Blue jumped into the opening and disappeared under some silk.

"Bingo" I said while smiling across at Violet.  Dan was already on his belly reaching down to lift the silk.  There was no Mr. Blue, but there was a pull handle exposed.

" It's  your turn again,"  as I joined him on my belly. Within seconds Violet was there also.

"Don't leave me out of this."

Dan, dragging out the suspense, hesitated before reaching for the pull handle.

"Oh, you two and your games," said Violet as she reached for the handle.  She pulled upwards with no results.  Without looking at us she studied the pull for a few seconds then with determination twisted counter clockwise and pulled.  A loud thump was heard, as in an unlocking motion.  She pulled, and sure enough it was moved upwards.  At the same time all four sides moved outward into the earth wall that appeared to enclose it.  There now materialized a wide passage that led to more rock stairs ever downward.  As with past experience came a waft of stale air.  I immediately reached for the bandanas and wet them down with the canteen, none too soon either.  The strong stale air was almost choking.  For Dove of

Spring this was her first experience with such matters, yet she just took it in stride. A touch of pride welled up in my chest for such a lady, my lady. Even Dan was impressed with her acceptance of such an instant hardship. After roughly ten minutes of breathing difficulties, all seemed to clear. Their heads were again looking down into this newly discovered world.

The three of us, not moving, just stared, stared at curved, roughly hewn rock stairs. It almost did not equate. We were searching for a lost advanced culture, yet at the same time we were looking at primitive rock steps to get there. Violet was the first to laugh at the incongruity of the situation.

The good news was that we were now looking at an entranceway wide enough for a full grown body. As much as I wanted to be first I looked at Violet and with sincere love stated;

"You uncovered it, so you go first."

With a big smile of acceptance she immediately moved to an entry position. She slithered down slowly until her feet touched the first step. She tested its stability before her whole weight was employed. Dan passed her a hand lantern and she slowly descended. Once there was enough spacing I followed with Dan trailing.

"Keep the masks on," instructed Violet as she paused. We waited for five minutes or so than she resumed her descent. There were about twenty one steps in all. We found ourselves in a round cavern with a ceiling about seven feet high and I would judge about ten or twelve feet in diameter.

As soon as Violet stepped into the circle small lights came on illuminating the room beautifully. Both she and Dan were a bit taken aback while I just smiled.

"I am not unfamiliar with this lighting. I came across it a few times at the lost city in Yucatan. I would say this is a very good example of this advanced civilization. By the way once we are out of sensing range they automatically shut themselves off. This form of power is self sustaining and lasts forever."

Dove of Spring smiled saying, "That is definitely a civilized advancement.

Now that this informal lobby was lighted it showed three magnificent hardwood doors. Each had a distinctive design burned into it An unmistakable Mayan Glyph on one, a definitive Chinese character on a second and on the third an unidentifiable design that the three of us could not decipher.

The ever curious engineering background of Violet instantly showed as she closely inspected each door and frame. Nothing was familiar to her which she readily admitted.

"These are all very interesting, but how do they open ?"

Now sporting a grin Dan replied.

"That's up to wonder man here. That's his forte."

Violet smiled at the reply but her eyes questioned.

"If they are anything like what I experienced in the lost city I may be able to open them," Eric spoke matter of fact.

Violet still questioned with her eyes.

"My friend Carlos had a knack of all the hidden lock mechanisms having to do with his heritage. He's quite a master at it. All I can do is try."

Violet was fascinated by his words. "Okay then, let's try," she prompted.

Eric headed for the Glyph door first. At least that seemed more familiar. He put his fingers to work. He first looked at the floor for scratch marks. This appeared confusing to Violet. Why would he be looking at the floor to open the door. After moving some aging dirt his suspicion was correct. This was a center swing door. Feeling confident he slowly started on the top of the door ledge. At the far right corner he felt what he was looking for. "Gotcha" he mumbled to himself as he let his finger find the indent. Pushing it he finally heard a noise he was familiar with as the door pivoted open at the center with a soft rumble of stone on stone. The stale air made its presence known again as we retied our bandanas. Once more we waited for the air to clear before entry. Finally we dared to peek beyond the open door. It reminded me of the kings pyramid tomb. All was Mayan. Violet and Dan were breathless at what they were viewing, familiar to me but new to them. We were looking at what appeared to be a scroll library. I immediately told of the scroll library, or actually libraries, in the lost city. They were already somewhat familiar with the scroll research they and my Mayan colleagues were conducting in hopes of exchanging valued information.

"These scrolls, I'm sure hold some of the advanced knowledge we are hoping to find. But, I added, "We must be super careful in what we do with this wisdom."

"Don't you start talking in riddles now," Dan threw out.

**I** smiled knowing I didn't want to do that.

"**L**et's sit for a moment. Let me tell you the story of one of my first encounters with Atl and how we challenged each other about advanced knowledge. I lost, by the way, in case you had not figured that out."

**T**hey smiled but urged me on with obvious curiosity.

"**I** have listed some of this in my early journals from my first Yucatan excursion, though I did leave some of it out on purpose. Perhaps this is not the time or place. We have a lot of searching yet to do. Some evening after a great dinner I think would be more appropriate."

**T**hey were both disappointed which showed on their faces but they did again agree on my priorities.

**W**e thoroughly surveyed the room to find nothing but scrolls which as I reminded were themselves invaluable. It appeared that two hours just vanished out of our day.

**W**e moved on to the next door, the all too familiar Chinese characters which we could not translate. We thought perhaps Whispering Wind could since he was so familiar with the old contract scrolls. The door opened with ease using the same technique. This time we were more prepared for the escaping stale air. When we felt the time was safe we entered what appeared to be another scroll library save this one  was all beautifully printed characters yet unreadable to the three of us. Interspersed between were examples of silks with designs and workmanship that is not present in today's offerings. Not that there is anything wrong with the artistry of the present, but what we were viewing now was the Creme de la Creme of silk artistry. Violet could not resist feeling the gold of the weaving world. Actually Dan and I also did our share of touching.

**S**croll after scroll we dared open told us absolutely nothing. Finding the right translator was going to be a job in itself due to the special knowledge they may hold. This in the wrong hands could be devastating.

**T**he three of us were separately looking among the many rows of orderly scrolls.

"**O**h my." came the echo of Violets sweet voice. Turning to where she was also took my breath away. We were now witnessing the painting artistry I was more than familiar with.

"**T**his has to be the same artist." I said out loud.

"**T**he same artist as what ?" questioned Violet instantly.

**I** was so mesmerized by the painting I almost ignored her question..

"Eric, where are you ?" she asked seriously.

"Oh ! What ? Did you say something ?"

Both she and Dan were smiling now.

"How about joining us in our world now." suggested Violet.

Slightly embarrassed, I apologized to both and asked again "What did you ask me ?"

Still smiling now but with love she repeated her inquiry about the painting. More relaxed and back to normal life again I explained, as I had months before, the mural hallway in the kings tomb and the addition painted by Diego that blended in perfectly with the hundreds, if not thousands of years old artistry. I then went on to take a closer look at the art. As others, it evidenced the connection of ancient sailing ships of the then world's powers with more modern  sailing vessels that were so represented by thousands of years difference in time. It wasn't just the subject matter but the orchestration of the actual painting, the detail of which one would only believe that a lens could capture.

"You will know what I mean  when you see the hallway of murals."

Dove of Spring was all smiles now from ear to ear.

"You mean you are going to take me there ?"

"Why of course. Isn't that what we agreed upon ? You, yourself said I can no longer go alone."

Violet rushed to Eric throwing her arms around him.

"Thank you my love," she whispered into his ear.

"Cut it out you two. We still have work to do," reminded Dan.

Red faced but not ashamed of their actions Violet said what Eric was probably thinking.

"Party Pooper."

The three laughed out loud but went about there detailed searching.

Nothing outstanding showed itself, not that they were expecting anything super outstanding. The beautifully executed artistry of the characters was in itself a thing to behold. They almost didn't care about the new evidence they were searching for.

Eric was a little disappointed up till now and was looking forward to the third and last door, or was it ? The three stood there in silence, each trying to understand the design engraved on the door.

"There is something in this scramble of lines that is triggering something in my mind," Violet said softly. This immediately caught Eric's attention. Dan asked her to point out what she was seeing which she willingly did. I looked along with him but registered nothing. As I turned away I caught a glimpse of Violet's face from a three quarter view. It was only a split second but was enough to excite my memory bank. That's all it did though. I could not equate it to anything familiar.

I guess we used up ten minutes or so trying to resolve its meaning. We finally gave up.

"Okay, let's see what's inside," Dan said firmly. I set right to using my fingers again. We had the routine down pat by now. Open door, put on mask, wait. While we waited Dan and Violet continued to discuss the door emblem. Dan forever the clown, asked Violet about her recognition of the old design because she was so much older than he was. Her arm quickly moved to slap his arm just as she did to me days ago.

"Spousel abuse." he shouted with the three of us laughing.


With the air cleared, we slowly entered to a great surprise. The room, the same size as the others was almost empty. We stood there staring at this not expected scene. There was a small shelf about four feet high to one side housing the all too familiar scrolls. A few wooden cartons roughly four or six feet long and about three feet high were placed against the other walls making the room look comparatively empty.

"There has to be a reason for this difference," I posed

"Okay, Sherlock. What is the reason ?" asked Dan.

"If I knew, I wouldn't have posed the question," I smiled back.

"The king must know. I bet this is just another of his riddles," stated Violet in a serious voice.

*"She is really getting to know Atl quite well,"* I thought, *"especially only knowing him for such a short time and the few times that I have spoken of him."*

"You may be correct in that," I answered quietly.

Dan headed for one of the boxes while Violet went for the scrolls. She chose one arbitrarily and opened it carefully.

"Will you look at this," she almost whispered.

I moved to her and peeked over her shoulder. What I saw did not make any sense to me but  it held her attention.  Sensing my presence she slowly murmured,

"These are mathematical formulas,. But not just any formulae. This is a mix of math figures from all over the world. Roman, Greek, Oriental, Mayan and this almost unrecognizable symbol is from early, and I mean very early indigenous people. Long before Navajo were Navajo. To me this sort of confirms what Whispering Wind was referring to when he referred to a lost civilization. A far advanced lost civilization. Almost all was lost at least up until now."

Eric agreed with her saying,

"And we are only now discovering what was lost with our own present advancements."

Violet found a seat on one of the boxes and further studied the scroll. She suddenly became even more excited.

"Look Eric, look here," she pointed. "I only touched on this in my studies, but these equations are some of the basics that make up quantum theories and quantum physics. Yet they are far older than our modern examples."

"Are you sure about this ?"

"Of course I'm sure."

Dan interrupted "Are you two at it again ?"

"I hate to interrupt but look at this."

It was a smaller version of the lamp that illuminated the hallway.

"If we could reverse engineer this we would have unlimited electric power."

Smiling, Eric volunteered,

"You may run into many more intriguing things."

Dan's interest was obviously there.

Eric continued with ,"Just don't get too carried away with trying to get them to work."

Dan looked confused.

"Trust me on this. There could be some inherent danger to these new gadgets."

"How do you know this ?"

"Don't forget I have been with the king for a few years now."

Violet, understanding the king based on what Eric said earlier, suggested he go look with Dan and she would stay with the scrolls.

*"How perceptive,"* Eric thought.

***"A wise decision, my friend,"*** was the echoing fading voice of Atl, for Eric only of course.

The three boxes did not really contain much. Many more of the wall lighting gadgets and various and sundry parts for their make up. Dan thought this would be worth studying. While Dan was looking through the gadgets I noticed a small covered vial with what looked like fine grained sand of various colors. Being as inconspicuous as I could, I retrieved the vial and put it in my pocket.

We spent another two hours reviewing all there was to see and decided we had enough for today. The door was closed and double checked for security, then we exited this newly discovered cavern.

The fresh air was a welcome relief. We all breathed deeply while refreshing ourselves with sips of water.

I noticed a strange questioning look in Violet's eyes, then she looked at Dan and finally turned away. I knew something was bothering her but she chose not to reveal her feelings at this time.

"I guess that's it for the day," said Dan voicing all our thoughts. "We discovered something, but what did we discover ? I personally don't feel as if we gained anything."

"I think we did," answered Violet. "We just don't know what or understand what we saw."

After a long pause, Eric, deep in thought, softly said, "It's time for a session with the king again."

"Do you think that will help ?" questioned Violet.

"I don't know, but we are going to do it anyway."

The three called it a day and headed home. After parting company with Dan, Eric and Violet returned to their own house. Both were rather silent on the way home.

Comfortably settled back at the house, Violet prepared

some fresh lemonade for both and quietly urged Eric to sit so they could talk.

"Sure, what's on your mind," Eric answered cheerfully.

After a very short hesitation Violet began.

"I thought we had an understanding that there would be no secrets between us."

"Yes, and it will always be that way my love."

Violet paused again not knowing how to present her thoughts.

" A while ago, back at the pyramid when we were in the third room I saw you put something in your pocket and you were obviously keeping it from Dan."

Eric smiled, not letting her finish her thought. He reached into his pocket retrieving the small glass vial.

"You mean this ?" he asked holding it up.

"Yes," she replied puzzled.

"Yes, this is and has to be, kept secret. I planned on explaining this earlier but we got carried away with other things and I just plain forgot."

"What's so secret about some colored desert sand. ?"

"Ahhh,! but that's the secret."

"Now you're talking in riddles. I think you have been with Atl too long ," she smiled.

Suddenly becoming serious Eric handed her the vial.

"Just look. Whatever you do don't squeeze it or drop it."

Dove of Spring looked directly at him and sort of smiled.

"You know more of the lost Civilization than you have told us."

"You are correct in that assumption but I am not keeping secrets from you. All that I know, you will eventually know."

"And Dan ?"

"And Dan also. The whole story you will hear, now that I again have this vial."

The ever astute Violet replied.

"This has a hidden purpose, does it not?"

Eric nodded affirmatively.

"And this is the inherent danger  you mentioned earlier

today ?"

Again a positive nod.

"This can kill, can't it ?'

Yes was Eric's verbal answer.

"Such innocent, beautiful beach sand ? It's hard to believe.

"Now for the reason I secreted it in my pocket. Dan as we both know likes to tinker, and that's to his advantage because that helps us all. But tinkering with this....."

Violet, ever perceptive, interrupted,

"Could cause irreparable damage or death."

"Bingo" said Eric. "I will demonstrate to both of you but we must be alone preferably in the desert.."

Violet moved to Eric and kissed his cheek.

"Forgive  me love for my selfish thoughts and now you may take this pretty powder back, I don't want to blow up."

"Oh, you won't blow up, you will just disappear."

"Now you're talking quantum theory's again." she smiled.

# Chapter   11

**D**ove of Spring repaired to the kitchen with thoughts of dinner while Hunter of Stories moved to the outside back deck.  He wanted to contact Atl but this time preferred to be alone.

*"I sense you have a need to converse with me my friend. I am here for you. What is your wish this time ?"*

**E**ric almost did not know where to start.

"**W**e again discovered more hidden doors and objects today.  I assume also that their contents are part of this or your lost civilization."

*"You assume correctly, as always, my young friend.  I realize you cannot decipher these writings, at least not yet.  Do not forget you cannot rush thousands of years of history..  Your patience, as always, will be rewarded."*

**E**ric, just from past experiences, already knew this. One of the few things he did acquire from his relationship with the king, was patience.

*"There is something else on your mind Eric.  Please do not hesitate.  I am here to assist you, not hinder you."*

**A** bit humbled at these words Eric knew Atl was accurate

in his statement.  After a short thinking hesitation, Eric finally spoke with confidence.

"The third door we opened appeared to be of more importance than the others."

The king instantly interrupted.

*"Not actually of more importance, just more physical in nature."*

As usual Eric felt a bit chagrined but continued.

"I know these are all benefits to mankind if accepted as intentioned, but how do we go about such a presentation?  All the things we have discovered to date will be extremely difficult to convince the doubting public, including the scientific experts, as to their existence."

*"The acceptance of change has always been difficult my friend, yet it does happen.  It is inevitable.  Just follow your heart, as I know you will and always have.  I join with Whispering Wind in reminding you of your new life companion.  With Dove of Spring at your side the world is yours.  Do not overlook what she can bring to you."*

Inwardly Eric felt the king's words were prophetic. Quickly continuing,

"I also removed from a storage box a small vial of what looks like your sand used in your scepter."

*"I am not surprised at that my friend.  I did suspect that might occur.  Some of those of my day actually had hope of acceptance by the others of the world, which as we both know never happened."*

Being direct now Eric asked,

"We both know of its inerrant power.  What do you suggest we do with this newly found supply?"

*"You do not need my council on that decision Eric. Do what you know and feel is best for humanity. I trust in your decision as always."*

The last few words of the king were a fading echo all too familiar to Eric. He sat there, staring at nothing and smiling to himself.

"Come back to earth." were Violet's loving words. "And what planet were you on today ?" she asked lovingly.

As I looked up at Violet, I had that tingle yet again. It only lasted for a split second but it was a real thing. A deja vu so to speak. Then it was gone.

"Hello, any body home ?" she smiled again.

I returned her smile, at a loss for anything to say.

"Where were you ? You were with the king again. He always seems to upset you.

"I had to clarify a few things but I'm alright now."

Eric took Violet's hand in his.

"To use the king's words: "With you at my side the world is mine."

Violet felt herself go flush. Eric continued,

"Those were the king's exact words, but I knew that from when I first met you."

Violet was speechless. Eric took her hand leading her to the kitchen.

"I'm starved; what's for dinner ?"

She remained silent but slapped his arm with a smile.

~ ~ ~ ~

Relaxing with his syrupy coffee, Eric easily spoke to Dove of Spring.

"Tomorrow I will demonstrate this pretty sand, and then the three of us will meet with the king again to learn more of his time."

"I would like that very much," Violet quickly replied. "I also want to know more of the Yucatan and when we can go back there. I would like to share in your discovery adventures."

"You're sure about that, aren't you ?"

"Yes.  From now on we do everything together.  You said yourself I could be helpful."

"That life is not easy.  The hardships are never ending." Then with a smile he added, "Besides you will be of great distraction to my Mayan pals."

"More than your Golden Lady ?" she smiled in answer. "I always did like competition but I am yours alone."

"I'm a lucky man, I have you and the Golden Lady."

He then added "Ouch"

"But I didn't hit you yet." she smiled.

~ ~ ~ ~ ~ ~

Atl may not have wanted to meet with me so soon again but I used my best non- pleading  pleading words to make it happen.  Again for privacy we met in the elders council room.  There was only the four of us not counting the king.  Whispering Wind, Dove of Spring and Lone Buffalo and yours truly Hunter of Stories.  I spoke for the group but all received the answers.  To Dan, this method of transmitting thoughts was completely new. You could see his acceptance in his smile but also his doubts and scepticism in his eyes.  Luckily for all concerned he just listened.

***"I am here as you  wished Eric, what is it you want to know ?"***

I was glad he came right to the point without his riddles, as of yet anyway.  I answered as business like as he did hoping he would keep it that way.

"We are here to learn more about this lost civilization.  If I am to further search for your time I would appreciate some additional hints.  There obviously has to be more places than just here under cosmic debris, which as you know is impenetrable."

***"Ever the curious and right to the point. You are right my friend.   You have accepted my challenge for which I am most grateful.  Your knack for***

*discovery has always amazed me and perhaps I can and should assist you more."*

Violet gave a slight almost hidden smile, once again proud of Eric.

*"To the east of here, many hundreds of your miles are certain sights that have not been totally destroyed yet.    They show structures and designs accomplished by my people that are connected to the universe, its planets and stars.   They were built for special purposes which ,of course, the knowledge of such has been long lost.   As attractions as a sightseer you would find them interesting, but that is not where you need to continue your research.    The four major connections to the knowledge that you seek you are already familiar with."*

Eric thought he knew what Atl was referring to but wished it to be further explained for the benefit of the others.  As if reading Eric's thoughts the king smiled and softly nodded his head.

*"The first of the four you are already a part of both by name and by marriage commitment."*

This, of course brought a smile to Violet which she did not attempt to hide.

*"The other three I'm sure you have figured out by now.   The Chinese presence is obvious but the information may not be so easily forthcoming.   You already know of the Egyptian connection, and of course your Mayan research has already opened your eyes to the past.   Had not mankind, as you know it today, been so bent on greed and power, my people could have shown*

*the way to total harmony with benefits for all peoples everywhere. Perhaps, my young friend, along with the assistance of a few faithful followers, you can locate the very basis of our teachings and bring to the world what I and others could not accomplish. Locate the very core of our advanced knowledge and show the world. Your Mayan friends will be of great help, as you already know. The two by your side now already hold the key, as do those at my tomb. You ,yourself know the key. Find the lock for those keys and you will have your answers. Look to the Golden Lady for a very close connection." I know you will find the answer you seek."*

The word seek trailed off to an echo. The king was gone. Whispering Wind was smiling and nodding his head up and down.

*"Your king gives wise council. I will rest now."*

Before a word could be uttered he was gone, his quick pace taking him home.

"You were right." Dan said. "Again with the riddles."

Eric and Violet smiled knowing that they meant something, They both committed themselves silently to the finding the answer.

"I was expecting more, but that did not happen. The king has a funny way sometimes of answering you but not really answering you. I know he is always there when the chips are down but he expects me to discover things for myself.

A little let down and disappointed Eric spoke his thoughts. "I don't know about you two but I am going back tomorrow and look some more."

"No, we will go back tomorrow and look some more." interrupted Violet with a smile.

"You two have at it. I have a field trip with my teens tomorrow which will probably kill the whole day. Have fun but please keep me in the loop."

"Remember I said I was going to demonstrate a few things

but I guess I can put it off another day.  It is definitely something I think you should see," Eric reminded.  "But you're right Dan the young ones education comes first."

The two were happy with this not really knowing what the demonstration was going to be.

**Dan quietly left the council room.**

"Well, Mrs Dexter, I guess we will be researching alone."

Violet smiled " I like the sound of that."

"The sound of what ?" was his reply.

"Mrs. Dexter, silly.  As Navajo we don't have a married title.  We still use our given name but when necessary we combine it with our clan title.  That way our lineage stays with us."

"Thank you for the lesson," Eric said sincerely.  And I would really like to learn some of your language.  Would you teach me ?"

"That would be a most pleasant task ,and I look forward to it."

They headed for Violet's house which was now home to both.

~ ~ ~ ~ ~ ~

Arriving early in the desert, Eric and Violet enjoyed its never ending beauty.  Before entering the pyramid they were joined by Mr. Blue as they silently watched the ever changing colors.  Fifteen silent minutes had passed when finally Mr. Blue turned and headed for the entrance.

"I guess that's our cue," joked Violet.

They followed happily with Eric taking care of the power for lights.  They stepped onto the elevator where Mr. Blue was patiently waiting.

Arriving at the three newly discovered doors, Eric expressed his desire to enter the first because of his familiarity with the Mayan scrolls, even though he could not read them.  Camera in hand they waited a few minutes before entering, the reason, of course, stale air.

Where to begin was a question that showed in both of their eyes.  Violet made the decision for them by pointing to the left for Eric while she moved to the right.  Each reached for as scroll and so started their day.

For quite a while the only sound that was heard was the unrolling of the old scrolls. They were composed of many different materials but all contained the same Glyph script, if script is what it could be called.

"Eric ! Come look at this," ordered Violet in an excited voice.

She held the scroll open as he gazed over her shoulder. He saw what she referred to instantly. The first half of the scroll was all familiar Mayan Glyphs, but halfway down there started Chinese characters. Eric could feel his heart fill with excitement.

"This proves it," he stated not really talking to anyone.

"This proves what ?" Violet asked.

Her voice startled Eric back to real time.

"Huh—, what—, did you say something ?"

She smiled up at him knowing his mind was filled with history.

"I'm sorry," he smiled.

"There have been ideas put forth by some, that the ancient Chinese had at one time navigated the whole globe. These ideas, naturally were put down and discredited by many in authority, saying it was not possible. Yet there is more and more evidence being uncovered yearly as to the validity of such undertakings. Not only the Chinese but also the ancient Phoenicians and the Egyptians. The idea of global navigation by early peoples is just not accepted."

"That bothers you, doesn't it?" Violet smiled.

Eric smiled along with her. "Does it show that much ? I'm sorry, I did not mean to get carried away, but these last few years have certainly been an eye opener for me, both here in the desert and south in the jungles."

"I guess you will want to photograph this. Please let me help you."

Smiling, almost laughing, Eric answered. "As usual you are one step ahead of me. Of course you can help. As a matter of fact from here on out it is required."

Eric set up the camera and tripod, while Violet found a few heavy items to assist in holding the scroll open. The actual photographing took only minutes. Dove of Spring then put the valued roll aside after an identifying mark was placed on it.

      Anxiously now ,the two continued inspecting the hundreds before them.  Violet stayed at the same place hoping there would be others showing dual identity.  After a short while her hopes were realized.  She had uncovered three more rolls with mixed script.  In fact she thought she identified some Egyptian hieroglyphs mixed in on one of the parchments.  She knew now Eric's love for and excitement of discovery.  She, herself, now wanted more.  She understood his drive.  Violet wanted more as she reflected on the Yucatan travels.  She carefully put down the scrolls and moving to Eric, put her arms around him and kissed him saying "Thank you"

      A little surprised at her actions he questioned,

      "What was that for ?"

      "Just because," was her quick answer as she returned to her former place.

      Once settled again she excitedly requested his viewing again. She did not have to point out what she thought was Egyptian, he picked up on it instantly.  Both were super excited now. They again went through the camera routine.

      Back to scanning the scrolls the pair were silent once more.  As Violet removed another scroll from the shelf, she had a small fright.  There was Mr. Blue staring at her.

      "You startled me," she said aloud.

      "I'm sorry." answered Eric automatically.

      "Not you love, your blue companion."

      Mr. Blue twitched his two front legs and reversed direction moving further back in the shelf.

      "Eric, I think he's trying to tell us something."

      I moved to where Violet was and sure enough there again was my furry friend.  He looked at me, turned and disappeared behind some scrolls.  By now Violet was all smiles imagining what may lie ahead.  I noticed her excitement and instructed,

      "Well ! Go ahead, move the scrolls."

      She did not hesitate another second but removed them carefully, treating them as the value they were.  Sure enough, there exposed before our eyes was a small door, roughly eight inches square.  A center knob was stylishly engraved with a Chinese character.  I instructed Violet to open it.  Her excitement showed all over her face.  Her hand was almost trembling as she reached deep into the shelf. Sudden disappointment set in. The door did not open. She tried a second time with the same result. She even attempted to rotate the knob. Her disappointment showed as she looked at me with pleading eyes.

"I guess you will have to use your magic as Dan calls it, to see if you can unlock it."

I smiled in answer as I instructed her to use those beautiful fingers and feel along the edges of the door for any interruption of smoothness. Her smile literally glowed now as she followed my directions. Suddenly she stopped, her eyes sparkling even more, if that is possible.

"There is a curved like dip in the top right edge," she said softly.

"Push it." I suggested in an equal soft tone.

Turning back to the small door she pushed the indent. There was a soft click and the door opened a small crack.. Violet's excitement was now bubbling over as her whole body was moving up and down. She reminded me of a child at Christmas. I did not tell her that, I just let her have her moment.

As she opened the door all the way there staring at us was a large roll of some material not familiar to either of us. Many seconds went by, neither of us moving. In a low encouraging tone I said,

"Well ?"

She looked at me, almost not believing that I was encouraging her to reach for the roll. With an expression of pride and surprise Violet reached and took hold of our mysterious package. She pulled it slowly towards her what seemed like forever. It must have been at least four and one half feet long. She held it like a newborn as if it was fragile glass.

"We can't look at it that way," I reminded with a smile.

Embarrassed now she handed me the roll.

"No," I said. "We do this together."

She obviously approved of that idea. We cleaned a place on the floor and gathered objects to help hold it flat. As it unfurled I knew what it was right away. A world map. Not just any world map. The detail I was immediately viewing foretold of it's accuracy. Once we had the roll flat and secure we were on hands and knees awed by what we were viewing. This was truly a world map before they had world maps. There appeared at first glance that not a thing was missing. All the continents were accurately depicted.  On a closer inspection we were able to see various fine dashed lines throughout the oceans and waterways.  From China, what I judged to be today's Hong Kong, we followed two distinct lines, one to Australia and its surrounds, the second towards the west coast of North America.  This then continued following South America around the cape and on to the African Coast.  There was also a shorter line from the Yucatan area going east and intersecting with lines to Africa.  Now concentrating on the European area we picked up another dotted line from what is now Egypt heading west through Gibraltar to the east coast of North America.  At the coast it split into two directions.  One headed north to the east coast of Canada and beyond.  The second part veered south following the coast to a destination of present day Yucatan.  There were sundry other markings inland on all the land masses we assumed could have been settlements of native inhabitants.

We sat back not really believing what we just viewed.

"This is truly history," stated Violet almost whispering.

I quickly replied,  "Yes, but who is going to believe it."

She gazed at me nodding her agreement.

"Do we tell the king ?" she suggested

"Not just yet but we will show this to Whispering Wind and Dan."

"Are we taking this with us ?"

"Yes.  Then I can concentrate on getting a better quality photo product.  In the meantime I will take some quick shots here in situ.  And if you don't mind I would like to have you in a few of the pictures."

Violet started to object then realized it was serious and necessary for documentation.

She smiled humbly and replied, "What ever you wish Eric."

I then proceeded to tell her of the map find in the lost city, how it showed similar shipping routes from China and Egypt.  The jungle find was not as detailed as this new find; however the intent was obviously the same.  I have photos of it also.  It's just a matter of finding them."

"If you allow me Eric, the spare room at home can be yours to organize and store your journals and research."

I looked at her and again discovered another side of this amazing woman.

"That's just one more reason that proves I need you."

They were quiet again, as both looked at all parts of the map recognizing much of the detail.  This was old, but not that old.

"Now what Mr. History man ?"  Inquired Violet smiling again.

Eric contemplated her question and smiled in return.

"I honestly don't know.  Do we search some more here; do  we look at the other two doors; or do we go home and relax ?"

"As a compromise, why not search some more in this room and then call it quits.  We can do another room tomorrow." was her logical proposal.

Eric grinned widely, "That's why I married you.  You always have your head on straight."

They were both laughing as they continued searching through the scrolls.  Nothing new appeared though they realized they were not reading the actual Glyphs.

By four P.M. they agreed to leave.  They were tired, hungry and breathing was becoming difficult.  The breathing difficulty reminded Eric of the tunnel air stations back in the jungle.  He retold the story to Violet on the drive home.

Home, dinner, and relaxing with a fine Cognac,

"I think I could get used to this life." commented a very content Violet.

# Chapter   12

 

 Violet, Dan and I were at the hogan of Whispering Wind. He was as fascinated as we were with the ancient map.  He smiled as he pointed to certain places as if he were familiar with them.

 

*"You have done well, my son.  Did I not say Dove of Spring would be of great assistance?  Now also you have Lone Buffalo at your side.  This can mean only good things for the future.  This map, as you have surmised, was made by and for great navigators of old. This, that you show me now, I believe is an original of great antiquity, and is complete."*

 

Here he held up his hand indicating we wait a moment.  At a far corner of the hogan, behind many buffalo robes, was an almost hidden leather protective tube, sort of like a large arrow quiver.  From this he pulled a rolled deer skin significantly shorter then our four plus foot map.

With a satisfied look he pulled a rolled map that was a duplicate of a section of ours.  It displayed the same navigation routes from Egypt to Central America and the Yucatan, the basic area that I have spent my last three seasons researching lost and hidden cities.

"I'm sorry to interrupt again sir, but my over curious nature is getting the better of me."

Whispering Wind looked at me with his ever patient smile. I hesitated for a moment trying to find the right words not to sound insulting.

"I realize that you are a tribal elder and possess great wisdom, but this knowledge you have of antiquity puzzles me.  How did you acquire this ancient wisdom ?"

*"Your curiosity will take you far my young friend. One's eyes and ears should always be on the silent alert. Our oral history is a wonderful teacher if you pay attention, which most do not. We, as opposed to others of the world, value our ancient knowledge, because of the lessons they teach, lessons you cannot get from books or a classroom. You, my son, already have acquired much to teach those who come after you. Does that answer your question ?*

He said that with a smile. It was not a chastisement.

Whispering Wind was as proud of what he was showing as I was of seeing for a third time. I had lived in that area. He went on to explain that this chart was handed down to him from countless generations. To me it just proved the valid existence of a lost civilization, a civilization that was truly advanced, yet was destroyed. Destroyed, not by cosmic influences, but by others not willing to listen and learn. We three were as speechless as Whispering Wind was proud.

*"Our native heritage, nay, the world's heritage comes*
"

To me he was almost sounding like the king. I believe they came from the same mold. Come to think of it, that is a good thing.
Whispering Wind continued;

*"Think carefully of the events called history. Think back on what you were taught by the elders of your own heritage. Carefully study these teachings and compare them to today's so- called advanced world. Is there really any comparison ? This question you have to answer yourself, each individually."*

I was about to ask my own question, but looking deep into his eyes I already knew the answer, or did I ?

**W**ith that he turned away returning his map to its Quiver and buffalo robes.  We left silently each pondering the wise mans words in our own fashion. We walked, still remaining quiet.  Once arriving at Dan's office we all seemed to act normal again.

"**I**t's still early; what do you think about that demonstration I spoke of ?"

"**B**ack at the pyramid ?" Dan asked.

"**N**o, I would rather not in case others may be there."

**D**an's eyes questioned where then.

"**H**ow about my rock coffin," I joked.

"**I** don't like to think about that," Violet said seriously.

"**I** understand that but it is far enough away from any human interference and has the proper materials to demonstrate on."

**W**e finally agreed with Dove of Spring, doing so reluctantly.

**T**he three of us rode in one vehicle, though neither of us spoke of our recent session with Whispering Wind.  On our arrival at the sandstone sentry I could tell Violet was still uncomfortable. I put my arm around her shoulder reassuring her that there was no longer any danger here. Dan and I closed and secured all the tunnels and deep pits.  She smiled and hugged me back.  We stopped about twenty feet from the golden mountain. To my captive audience I spun my yarn again of the verbal discourse I had with the king.  He was a walking person then and not a voice in the mind. I went on to proudly list our accomplishments to date and that we were not primitive.  Astronomy, gunpowder, mathematics, internal combustion, flight, underwater travel, engineering, space travel, nuclear power communications and finally computers.

**D**an and Violet were impressed and agreed with my list of our accomplishments.  We have come a long way to be this advanced.  I could tell they were anxious to hear of the kings reaction to my challenge. With out trying to be boring, I restated all the things the king countered with but not in a challenging way; how he quietly reminded me that it was the Maya who invented the use of the zero and how much more accurate their calendar was. He spoke of communications that were simply done with the power of the mind. The king also felt the use of our brain had slowly dwindled away over time because of lack of use. Then he spoke of computers as just advanced mathematics employed by the functions of the brain that were much too advanced for us to understand.

I could tell by their expressions that they too agreed with my challenge to the king of our many accomplishments. I let that settle in for a few minutes and then told of the king's quiet answers. I reached into my pocket for the vial of pretty sand.

"Oh !, now we're into sand painting, are we ?" chided Dan.

"Not quite," I replied. "I transferred some of this pretty powder into this ball point pen housing for demonstrative purposes, the king,s answer to gun powder and nuclear power."

They looked at me curiously.

I pointed to a large boulder over where the mine entrance used to be. With them behind me I aimed the pen and squeezed as the king had done. A small rose colored ray of light emanated from the tip touching the boulder. It just disappeared to the amazement of my companions.

"It is now part of matter scattered throughout the universe."

The mouth open expressions of Violet and Dan were a duplicate of my own and Mario's when we saw the demonstration for the first time.

Once recovered Dan asked the obvious;

"Okay that took care of gunpowder but what about all the other things ?"

"Ahh, very astute my friend. Allow me to answer all those topics with this."

I again showed them the glass vial of colored sand.

"Now watch."

I separated myself again and softly squeezed the vial. Up and up I went, high enough to be almost out of sight. I slowly decreased my hand pressure and descended and touched down to where I originally stood. My friends were shocked into silence. Violet was the first to come around.

"Are you alright Eric ?"

"Of course I am my love. That should just about answer all your questions as to who is more advanced. By the way this also works underwater."

Dan, smiling, his mind working overtime spouted;

"That could revolutionize air and space travel."

"It already has," I replied. "But think about the dark side of such power or sand."

"This could be very dangerous in the wrong hands," Violet suggested.

"Very dangerous," added Dan.

"Right you are, both of you, which is why the king and I agreed to dispose of it. Especially with the shape the world is today."

"Well if you got rid of it, how come you still have some? What is it anyway ?" quizzed Dan.

"We did dispose of it, long ago but this vial I took from the box you were looking at the other day. You know the one with all the gadgets. Who knows, there may be others still in existence around the world. I hope there aren't , because in the wrong hands...?"

"What is it made of ?"

"That I don't know nor did the king share its makeup with me. Actually, I'm glad of that."

"And what are you going to do with that in your hand ?"

I smiled and opened the vial and let the wind take it much to the delight of Dawn of Spring.

"Now that that's over with we can truly concentrate on this lost civilization."

"I like that idea," smiled Violet cheerfully. "Now let's go do some real work."

~ ~ ~ ~ ~ ~

Back to the pyramid they went and to the hidden turquoise pile. Today there was no sign of Mr.Blue. It was almost disappointing to Eric.

"I guess your blue friend took the day off," grinned Violet.

"Well, he earned it," Eric replied a little more seriously. "Okay ! Now for that second door."

Eric moved closer and put his fingers to work. There was no movement. A bit perplexed he tried a second time also with no results.

Feeling frustrated he went through the motions a third and fourth time. Nothing.

"Another Chinese puzzle," wise cracked the never serious Dan.

"That's it," Violet cried out slightly louder than normal.

Surprised by her outburst Eric and Dan turned to her.

"I'm sorry guys I did not mean to shout."

"Okay, but what do you mean by "That's it" Eric enquired.

Smiling now Violet, in a more normal tone cheerfully answered.

"The Chinese puzzles. They have always been known for their tricks and puzzles. Some are hundreds, if not thousands of years old. If I'm not mistaken one of their standards is to reverse the obvious."

Eric, still perplexed looked at her in a blank stare.

"Try the other corner."

Which he did and sure enough the door swung open. For his own satisfaction he continued feeling along the top edge. Sure enough there were two indents for fingertips.

Violet added, " They probably alternate for the opening each time."

Happy and smiling now he turned to her, "Just another reason to prove that I need you."

Dan in his forever humorous mood blurted out;

"Oh will you two cut it out, you're worse than first grade school children."

All three were laughing now.

Once inside they were again taken by the beauty of the silks.

"Okay, a more thorough and detailed inspection this time," instructed Eric.

"Yes sir !" responded Violet as she saluted.

"Get out of here," said Eric as he swung his hand at her purposely missing.

Search they did, ever carefully. Each scroll was opened and examined for anything unusual, unusual to them anyway. Violet scrutinized each and every piece of silk, large and small. She even went so far to check

the shelves and back panel for hidden doors.  The silence of their movement
was a welcome thing to their concentration.

"Hello," came a mumbled remark from Dan.  This instantly
caught the attention of Eric and Violet who moved to Dan.  The scroll he
was holding was longer than any of the others.  This in itself seemed odd.
Starting at the top were what appeared to be the Chinese characters of their
writing method.  In the middle, halfway down was the incongruity.  Staring
back at them were two Glyphs at twice the size of the Chinese markings.
One was definitely Mayan and the other quite obviously Egyptian.  Neither
of which could be deciphered by the three of them.

Eric stared in silence for quite a while.  At last he mumbled,
almost incoherently, "I know this mark."

Of course this caught the interest of the other two.

"I have seen this before," he continued mumbling.  "But
where?"

He continued gazing in silence, then without warning
almost shouted, "The Golden Lady."

Dove of Spring chided, "Oh, now you're thinking of my
competition."

Eric took her remark as it was meant and smiled at her.

"It's always a good idea to have a backup plan."

She instantly swatted his arm.

"Here we go again," said a frustrated Dan to no one in
particular.

"Seriously though, I do remember this somehow connected
with the Golden Lady's throne room.  We will take this scroll with us.  I
think this is something Whispering Wind should see."

They all went back to their self- assigned tasks.  The last
roll had been reviewed along with Violet finishing up with the silks just after
four P.M.

"Okay let's lock up and head home.  I don't know about
you two but I'm starved," stated Dan.  "We completely missed lunch."

"Care to have dinner with us ?" asked Violet.

"Sounds great, but I have a previous engagement."

"Is she pretty ?" teased Eric.

"As a  matter of fact she is; besides you two act too
childish.  I don't want to expose her to that just yet," he smiled

"Your loss," answered Violet

That evening was extremely relaxing while after dinner Eric and Violet enjoyed the cool night air and stars.


The next day Eric took advantage of Violet's offer and moved many of his journals and pictures into the spare room in hopes of making things easier to retrieve. Violet was a tremendous help in organizing things, never one of Eric's better traits. After putting everything in its place, Eric came across the pictures of the Golden Lady. Getting Violet's attention, he mentioned this and invited her to sit with him so he could explain them. Now that he had her undivided attention he went into great detail of the whole discovery and how Diego worked out the fact that this was the real person from Egypt, preserved and painted with liquid gold. Violet was totally taken by the story, and even more so by the Golden Lady herself. She marveled at the results of Eric's professionalism in capturing the lady from Egypt. While she reviewed the many photos Eric busied himself setting his mess in order.

Dove of Spring was mesmerized by the last photo of the lady. It was a three quarter view showing the minute detail of this striking woman. She could not take her eyes from the print. An unknown eerie feeling encompassed her whole being. She was frozen in time with this Egyptian dignitary. It was as if she also was painted with gold. She felt one with this sister of time.

Twenty minutes had flown by, and Eric decided he had pretty much everything in place. Suddenly remembering Violet, he returned to the other room. It appeared to him as if she had not moved, which in reality was fact. He casually mentioned he thought he was finished for the day. There was absolutely no reaction from her. She was frozen with the image of the Golden Lady. He softly called her name a few times. There was no answer. He did not want to touch her to shock her too much. He seated himself across from her slowly making soft noises and talking quietly. He wondered what sort of magic spell she was under. This brought back memories of himself and his four Maya friends being struck the same way but that only lasted a matter of seconds. Looking over her shoulder I saw the portrait of the Golden Lady. The same view that caught every one spellbound in the Yucatan. I again got that funny feeling I had a few times just recently when observing Violet at certain angles. I then placed myself at an angle that allowed me to see both Violet and the photo she was holding. That was it. I don't know why I did not realize it before. There was an actual resemblance between the two. I quickly dismissed this as purely accidental. This type of coincidence has occurred many times throughout history. I laughed at myself for even discussing thinking of the idea.

My lady love was still in the grip of who knows what. I thought it best to leave her be for now. However, within a minute or so Violet was Violet again.

"Have a nice trip ?" I asked jokingly.

Slightly embarrassed she answered slowly.

"I don't know what happened, but something just came over me and I seemed to be in another world. It was as if I knew this Golden Lady."

She looked up at me unsure of herself.

"Please tell me I haven't lost my mind."

I sat beside her putting my arm around her.

"No, my love you are perfectly alright, a little jealous perhaps of my Golden Lady but you are okay."

She cuddled closer in my arms giving out a sigh of comfort. We changed the subject but something in the back of my mind still says there was a connection someplace.

A break for lunch was a good thing. It brought us both back to the real world.

"I know you had a taxing day with the Golden Lady but I was hoping to have another session with Whispering Wind. Care to join me ?"

"You bet I do. Remember we are in this together from now on."

I was pleased by her answer and frankly speaking liked the idea of a companion, especially this one, to share in my work. Who knows perhaps I can teach her some photography.

An early morning call from Lone Buffalo notified us he would be tied up all day and begged off regretfully from our visit to the tribal elder. Violet and I were raring to go but had to wait until mid morning. Whispering Wind was already involved with other tribal matters that morning. I busied  myself further organizing my air photos and journals. Violet worked on some early preparations for dinner, though periodically she was drawn to the Golden Lady's portrait.  What ever was going through her mind she did not yet share with me.  We all need our privacy I thought.

At half past ten, hand in hand, we were on our way joking how Whispering Wind, even at his advanced years walked twice as fast as we did.

*"Enter my children."* we heard in our minds long before we neared his museum hogan.  After closing the buffalo robe door he indicated where we were to sit.  Ready for us was the ever present lemon drink and two cups.

Our host sat on the many robes on the floor facing us.  Looking pensive, he was direct in his thoughts.

*"I sense my children you are curious about this Egyptian connection, the Egyptian along with the Chinese association to our humble native heritage.  We three peoples, nay four peoples, the Maya are very much part of this secret of lost knowledge."*

Already our curiosity was running high.

*"You also now search for the Lost Civilization. You may find it, but first you must know what you are looking for.  Do you know what this lost knowledge is ?  How will you know it when you find it, if you find it ?"*

Now to me, he was sounding like the king with riddles.  I held my arm up with demanding eyes.  Whispering Wind got my eye message, became quiet and nodded his head for me to talk.

Deep in my mind I knew what I wanted to ask, but now in reality I didn't know how.  Three times I tried and three times I sat there dumb.  The elder before me smiled and shook his head slightly.

*"You already have part of the answer, you just have to piece the parts together."*

This meant absolutely nothing to me.  I sat there in total

frustration. Violet saw haw flustered I was and in order to give me time to recuperate she took the vocal lead. She spoke in the Navajo voice, not to exclude me but to give me some rest. While speaking she took the Golden Lady's photo from her pocket and presented it to him. He instantly became silent, his face and eyes filled with alarm and recognition.

*"This is she that you spoke of from your last research excursion ?"*

I immediately answered yes.

*"I know this lady."* he said quietly.

I don't know what magic spell this lady has, but it appears to affect everyone who sees her.

*"According to the history passed down over the ages, she was once here among us. Not here on this reservation, but on our home place of past ages. It is said that she lived among us for many moons before moving to a warmer land. We shared histories and knowledge. Not just the Dineh' but our friends also from many sun rises to the west and across a great body of salted water. You yourself have seen our trading contracts. Our four nations were as one. We learned from each other and shared what was most important in our cultures. At the time we were as one. Please, let me share something with you."*

Whispering Wind moved to the far end of his museum home. He spent many minutes looking at and moving things. Violet and I said not a word, just looked at each other and him with unknowing minds. A long ten minutes passed which neither of us paid attention to looking forward to another of his history legends. He returned to us and refreshed himself with his lemon drink before speaking.

Again he held a tube like bundle which actually turned out to be hollowed bamboo. It was carefully wrapped in both deer hide and a thick furred buffalo wrapping. After a slow process, along with a few mumbled Navajo prayers, an unidentified fabric or animal skin appeared. With great joy and a large smile he unfurled before us a painting of the Golden Lady.  It truly was a masterpiece.  There was no mistaking it for other than the Golden Lady.

Dove of Spring was constantly shifting her eyes from the photo to this painted portrait and back again.  In our minds they were both alike and both alive.

Our lingering hush was broken by our very proud elder.

*"You are the first I have shared this with since it was given to me by my grandfather.  It has been handed down and preserved at the cost of many lives over many years."*

Then Whispering Wind looked directly at Dove of Spring.

*"It is said she was with child sired by one of our heralded warriors long before she moved to the land of our Maya brothers.  Her blood line also has been carried down through countless ages to the honor of our people.  It is our connection to those of the east who grew with us until the total annihilation of that lost civilization."*

The gentle elder at last turned to me.

*"You, my son are now on the quest of these lost peoples and their advanced ways.  You have done well and I'm sure will be rewarded in good time."*

I did not mean to interrupt this great man but I blurted out my request.

"May I photograph this painting.  This must be forever preserved for the world.  It will not be harmed in any way.  It will always be in your presence."

*"I knew that would be your request, and yes you may my son.  Now would be the perfect time."*

**V**iolet was also now smiling and happy for me. I had my camera with me. With permission I opened the buffalo skin cover of the entrance to let in natural light and clicked away. I was ecstatic. I could almost consider my day complete.

**A** very short time later the painting was again secured for posterity.

~ ~ ~ ~

*"Now my young friends, you may continue your chosen work and find the lost knowledge you seek."*

"**L**ost knowledge or lost civilization ?" I questioned

*"Think of your recent discoveries and decide for yourself. Are they one and the same ? Is there lost knowledge ? Is there a lost civilization ? Is it all a myth ? Is it all a dream ? Have you discovered anything new or just rediscovered the obvious ?"*

"**B**ut the Golden Lady is real. I saw her. We, my friends and I saw her. She is far away at the moment, but obviously so is the lost civilization."

**S**miling that "I've got a secret smile," Whispering Wind quietly responded, this time only for me to hear.

*"The Golden Lady may be closer than you think."*

**T**his stopped me for a while. My mind was totally confused. These were all new words, all new thoughts.

**I**t seemed so much simpler in the jungle. I wanted to be back there. I wanted to be back there with Dove of Spring. I wanted to share my symphony's of the night. Life was so much simpler.

**I** gazed at Violet who appeared content for now. I glanced at the elder who smiled knowingly.

*"You will have the answers soon my son. Go now and reflect."*

He paused but before I could say anything I received his message loud and clear.

*"I will rest now and you will plan."*

He nodded a silent good bye to Violet.

The sun almost hurt my eyes as we slowly returned to the compound in silence. I reluctantly accepted the day though questions still felt unanswered.

# Chapter 13

"**W**hat did you think of our little session with Whispering Wind ?" asked Violet carefully knowing Eric's mind was still in turmoil.

**E**ric, reading Violet correctly took her in his arms and kissed her temple.

"**Y**ou are so good for me. You know my mind better than I do. You always know just what to say and when to say it. Thank you. Now to answer your question, which you already know, I really am becoming unsettled with the riddle game."

"**B**ut you handled it so well today. I'm proud of you."

"**B**ack in the jungle Diego explained it to me once about the king and all his riddles. It seems that this was a way of teaching of the Popol Voh. The riddles were a way of making sure the students were thinking. This is from the times of old."

"**I** can't wait for you to meet my Maya friends. I know you will get along well "

"**D**idn't I already meet two of them ?"

"**Y**es, I almost forgot. But that was strictly for a formal occasion. Even they were on their best behavior. I really am looking forward to you knowing them. They are all extremely professional in their fields. That is when they become serious."

"**Y**es, I had a sample of that with their telegram."

"**D**iego is a college chum of Dan. In fact their personalities are identical. Occasionally they can be serious. By the way Diego is an artist extra ordinaire. You will see for yourself when you get to view the mural hallway."

"**A**re you really taking me to the Yucatan ?"

**V**iolet said this with a highly animated expression of yearning.

"**O**f course my love, remember from now on, everything

together. That is unless you don't want to meet your competition, you know my Golden Lady."

As Eric said this he quickly moved his arm away so as not to be swatted again. Violet made no such attempt this time.

Laughing, she said, "See, I did not abuse you." Then slowly added, "This time."

Eric was so looking forward to returning to the jungle he almost forgot about the present situation and the riddles.

He started telling stories of his adventures over his last three years, the good and the bad. He went on non-stop for over twenty minutes till he realized how he was monopolizing all of her time. Sheepishly he apologized.

Violet hugged him saying, "No need for that. I'm just learning more of you and what kind of man I have to love. When do we leave ?"

Eric was more than happy with her anticipation.

"Whoa, slow down girl. That decision is up to the weather. Right now it's rainy season which means we have to wait."

"How much longer ?" she asked with a disappointing pout.

"I don't really know, but I will definitely check with the guys in Arizona."

"How about an early dinner, then we can spend some serious time on riddle solving," Violet suggested.

"Great idea, let me help you."

"No. You run to the store and get a good bottle of wine. I think we deserve to celebrate."

Eric left her to the kitchen chores.

~ ~ ~ ~ ~ ~

The meal was simple, the wine superb. Violet and Eric were having a second glass out under the stars. It was the perfect night for it. A few minutes of star gazing and listening to the sounds of silence. Violet was the first to break the spell.

"How about we discuss the riddles to see what we can make of them ?"

Smiling Eric replied, "I just love your subtle approach to a subject."

"At least it got you to smile."

"Okay then, let's.  How and where do we start ?"

"Let me ask you a question first.  Have you ever not solved the kings riddles ?"

"Well-l-l-l, Noo-o-o, I always managed to pull out some sort of answer."

"I figured as much because that's the sort of person you are.  You don't accept defeat."

Eric felt his cheeks flush slightly by her remark.  Violet ignored this and continued;

"Then I guess your explanation of the holy book did actually solve his puzzles.

"Now even you are confusing me."

"I'm sorry love, it was not my intention.  You are an amazing person.  Don't sell yourself short."

Eric could read that Dove of Spring was being serious.  He indicated for her to resume her thoughts.

"Even today your discussion with Whispering Wind was actually breaking down the riddles.  Perhaps you did not realize it at the time.  Think back to your questions.  Is it really a lost civilization, what are we really looking for. Is the lost civilization and the lost knowledge one and the same.  Your discoveries to date are astounding and have led you this far. I believe you already have the answers in your head and more importantly in your heart.  You just have to clarify a few things in your mind."

She paused here and took his hands in hers.

"Please let me help.  I want to do this with you.  Please allow me."

He squeezed her hands.

"How could I not let you help.  You already have by clarifying aa few things in my mind."

Then out of nowhere came a familiar tingle , a feeling they both felt.  The king's words could be heard by both.


***"The knowledge of the ancients that you seek
is in the texts of the ages."***


The drifting echo now filled the air.  The king was gone.

Violet was all smiles now.  She was privy to the kings words.

"I see what you mean.  Now I know I can help you with riddles," she beamed.

Eric could not help but smile with her, though he also thought he had the answer to this one.  Violet did not let Eric speak.  She excitedly shared her mind.

"We use text books, they used scrolls.  For all intent and purposes they are one and the same."

"You are absolutely brilliant.  I believe you are correct.  Along those lines there are many dedicated people working on the translations as we speak, but we are probably looking at many years before any concrete answer can be formulated."

"What's the hurry after all these years.  That leaves us plenty of time for more jungle discoveries."

I have never seen Dove of Spring look more content and radiant. She was actually glowing internally.

"The world is ours tonight Mr. Dexter."

~ ~ ~ ~ ~ ~

Up early but waiting until nine o'clock, Eric put a call through to Mario in Arizona.  Luck was with him, Mario answered on the second ring.

"And how's the old married man?  Are we ever going to see you again ?"

Eric laughed his answer; "Sooner than you think.  When do you plan on going back to the lost city ?"

"Had enough of married life already ?"

"Not really, she will be coming with me."

"You're kidding, back to the jungle ?"

"She's a strong woman, she will probably out last all of us.  How  would you guys like a couple of visitors ?"

"Are you serious, that would be great.  When are you figuring on ?"

"As soon as we can pack the car." Eric threw back at him. "Give us a few days. There is a lot we have to discuss before we head for the Yucatan."

"Sounds ominous."

"Just the opposite." I replied. "See you soon. Regards to the others."

Eric hung up all smiles now looking at the beauty before him.

"I can be ready in an hour," smiled Violet.

"Perhaps you can, but I can't," answered Eric. "Let's plan on day after tomorrow."

Two days later it was. Eric had arranged for a large SUV, just in case they had trouble booking rooms, at least this way they could still get some sleep.

Soon on their way they thoroughly enjoyed the ride to Arizona. They were headed for a relatively small town called Wickenburg, just under three hundred miles away. They were in no real rush, as much as they wanted to get there they also wanted to soak up the forever beauty of the countryside on the way.

Eric was lucky enough to remember the motel he stayed at during his last visit, which was about two years ago. Again he was able to get a room with a small kitchenette. This would suit their needs just fine.

Upon arrival Eric called his friends but begged off on meeting that night. They would be there early the next day.

Just after nine Violet and Eric entered Mario's office and were greeted by the broad smiles of Carlos, Mateo and Mario. All three immediately rushed to Violet. They went through the usual routine of hand shakes etc. all the while taking in her unforgettable appearance. She was dressed in buckskin top and slacks which only highlighted her long dark hair.

"Don't let this good behavior fool you." warned Eric. They are not usually this well behaved."

Carlos noticed Eric looking around curiously.

"Diego had an early appointment with a student. He should be here shortly."

Violet volunteered how well she knew Lone Buffalo, Diego's class chum and that she was hoping to finally meet Eric's friends. She happily thanked them for looking out for Eric. Then, of course, it started. How much trouble he always got into. How much he interfered with their real research just because he kept finding lost things. Violet went right along with the game but on their side.

"I know what you mean. He is always changing our known history because he keeps locating lost documents and books."

Stunned now by this verbal attack, even by Dove of Spring, he threw his hands up.

"I give up. I'm going back to Vermont and open up my studio again and just take photos of boring people and unruly kids."

"Can we help you pack," offered Mario.

Just then Diego was frozen at the doorway. Carlos saw him first.

"Come on in, don't just stand there."

He stayed at the door staring. "It's her." he finally mumbled. "It's really her, alive."

All heads turned now to Diego.

"What are you talking about," questioned Mario not really having understood his mumbles.

Violet suddenly felt a touch uncomfortable.

Diego stuttered a bit. "It's her. The G- G -Golden Lady."

Eric jumped in now moving to Violet's side taking hold of her hand. Diego finally snapped back to reality and moved to Violet, hand extended.

"You must be Dove of Spring. I believe we met very briefly more than a year ago at your homeland."

Violet moved to him taking his hand, "Yes I remember that was for the funeral services for your ancient countrymen. By the way Lone Buffalo sends his regards. He could not make it this time but hopes to see you soon."

Eric felt better now but in the back of his mind something was still unsettled. He could not put his finger on it.


The rest of the day went well with Violet learning a lot more of the Yucatan research. Because of her engineering background she and Carlos hit it off very well. They even started into the study and reverse engineering of the air vents in the tunnel. She could not wait to see the real thing.

The day whizzed by and all agreed a quiet and not fancy

dinner was in order to be hosted by Carlos.  Pizza was the chosen overall favorite and of course cold beer as the beverage of choice.

Violet was a natural fit to the group.  She more than fit in since she joined in the pick on Eric club.  Towards the end of a most enlightening evening Eric had his revenge.  He went to his rental car and returned with an unopened bottle of Remy Martin Cognac.  The room was suddenly quiet with warm welcoming smiles.

"It's a shame I have to sample this by myself since I am not obviously in the "IN" crowd anymore.  Carlos do you happen to have a single snifter glass that I may use ?"

The room grew suddenly quiet, all eyes on the bottle.  Violet snuggled closer to Eric and in a soft syrupy sweet voice asked,

"Would you like me to help you open this, Love ?"

Carlos automatically brought six glasses from the kitchen.  Smiling he answered Eric's questioning eyes, "I knew you would not refuse such loveliness.  Thanks to you dear lady we all benefit."

Eric filled all six glasses.  Before anyone else could say anything Dove of Spring raised her glass.

"Here's to another successful season at the lost city.  More importantly here's to finding the lost civilization for the benefit of all mankind."

Her words had a sobering effect.  Mateo quietly spoke but it was a reflection of all four Maya friends.

"Don't ever lose that woman Eric.  She is one of us."

Mateo was not known for deep thinking or outwardness yet this time he spoke for all.

A moment of silence followed.  Carlos was the first to speak.

"We all have classes to teach tomorrow, what say we meet at one P.M. at Diego's office."

"Why my office ?" replied a wondering Diego.

"Because, my artist friend, I'm sure the lovely lady would enjoy your art.  It will give her an insight to the mural hallway."

"Oh, right.  That way we get to know her better," Diego replied all the while thinking to himself, *I could do some sketching of her. I will prove to the others how much she looks like the Golden Lady."*

"Sounds like a plan," Eric voiced aloud.  "See you guys on the morrow."

He and Violet said their farewells and headed for the car.

~ ~ ~

Diego had other thoughts in the back of his mind. *"No one really picked up on my Golden Lady comments earlier. Perhaps Eric, but he did not pursue it. I'm glad of that. I'm not ready to show my point just yet. Maybe some alone time with Eric before we return to the Yucatan."*

Eric and Violet did some sight seeing to kill time in the morning. Both were anxious to continue discussion and share information on many topics of joint interest.

~ ~ ~ ~ ~ ~

"This lost civilization you spoke of sounds intriguing. Tell us what you know of it. How did you hear about it ?" questioned Mario.

"Whoa, slow down," smiled Eric in reply. "We," indicating Violet and himself, "were introduced to the possibility by Whispering Wind, a senior elder and holy man of Violet's people. It seems he also knows the king and that he is a chosen one. He is very familiar with their mission of enlightenment for the peoples of the world."

"He must be aware then that this teaching fell on deaf ears," interrupted Mario.

"He is very aware of everything the king has passed on to us, including the riddles. He riddles some things himself."

Violet took over the conversation from here. She related the complete story of the "Keeper of the Past". How we started to dig but ruled it out. Something buried for thousands of years was not going to show itself that easily."

Carlos politely interrupted here.

"This sounds like you are speaking of the period of the end of the last ice age. I believe they call it the Younger Dryas age."

"You are absolutely correct my friend. Actually these people we are referring to lived before that. The end of the last big ice age was really the beginning of our present era.."

"So what you are saying is that the king is from that age,

some twelve thousand years ago ?"

"**I** believe that to be correct."

"**S**o where or how does this Whispering Wind fit into all this ?"

**V**iolet chose to answer this.

"**L**ike your people, ours also respect and honor the oral history of traditions. We feel comfortable with our past and believe it to be factual as do you. We further believe that both our peoples do go back that far and have been connected with trade and sharing since then. This dual past also includes early China and Egypt. If it didn't then why do we have the newly discovered artifacts and trade contracts. Why is the Golden Lady here. Why are there Chinese silks and jade found here in the American deserts."

**E**ric was proud of her participation. She was truly one of them.

**A**ll were smiling now and in an upbeat mood. This documents ancient histories and found artifacts from both North and South America with proof of all their speculations. Proof to them ,yes, but what about the rest of the world.

**A** thoughtful pause took hold of the room. Ideas were running rampant yet were all the same. Dove of Spring feeling quite comfortable now politely garnered every ones attention.

"**G**entlemen, It appears our thinking is all along the same lines, which is obviously a rare thing in today's upside down world. I think we should try to capitalize on this in the way of further research and discovery. While we are all contemplating the situation I would like to put forth a simple idea having nothing to do with the present situation. Allow me to make a traditional Navajo meal if I may borrow some ones kitchen. I personally can't think of a better way to celebrate something this earth shaking than a good meal from the earth."

**B**righter smiles and happier faces could not be found any where else on this planet than right here and now.

**D**ove of Spring was true to her word. Mario volunteered his kitchen and Eric did the shopping as instructed. Diego accompanied Eric with the shopping venture so they could catch up on the news of their common friend Dan a.k.a. Lone Buffalo.

**A**s promised, the meal was perfect. Everyone ate more than their fill, in fact so much so that there were no leftovers at all.  The men did the clean up including washing the dishes while Violet was instructed to sit and relax.  She was generously served a special gold edged glass of Cognac..  Now comfortable and quite content she commented,

"If this is the way you gentlemen spend all your time in the jungle, I'm amazed that you get anything accomplished at all."

Carlos replied instantly, "The Cognac is all Eric's idea.  He bribes us to allow him to learn from us.  We did, however, get some research accomplished in spite of him."

Eric could be heard mumbling out loud, "Here we go again. Eric's turn in the box.  It's always Eric's turn in the box."

Of course there was laughter all around.

~ ~ ~

Getting back to some serious discussion, tell us more of this Lost Civilization," posed Mateo.

Eric was more than pleased with switching topics.

"The king has also urged our seeking the Lost Civilization. As he instructed me, you four are to be part of the search also.  But as you know it was said through his riddles.  He has mentioned more than once the Egyptian and Chinese connection.  The constant theme in his messages is at times confusing.  Are we looking for a Lost Civilization, a lost people, lost knowledge, lost advanced knowledge or all of the above ?  The words of the king and Whispering Wind are never that clear.  Again the riddles."

"Simple, then we will just have to solve the riddles," said Violet without emotion.

Five pair of eyes rolled to her in disbelief.

"Wait gentlemen, before you dismiss me as a total kook, hear me out.  You have already solved other riddles of the king and Eric and I managed to get through one because we took time to sound it out.  I'm not saying it's going to be easy but let's face it you all have been too busy with your real research and sort of put aside the riddles until actually necessary. Am I correct in that assumption ?"

Shy looks of not quite embarrassment took over the room.

Carlos commented quietly; "This woman is much too good for you Eric."

Eric took this as a compliment and agreed with him.

Now it was Violets time to blush before she resumed.

"Let's all write down, as remembered, all of the words of

the king and Whispering Wind.  Enough copies for everyone.  Then we can all consider their meaning at our leisure without interfering with our daily routine.  True it may take a while but at this stage of the game what's the hurry ?"

She let this sink in for a few moments then with a broad smile voiced,

"Okay, now when do we leave for the Yucatan ?"

"Not for another twenty minutes," kidded Mateo. "My clothes are still in the washing machine.'

This did lighten the mood somewhat.  The day ended with the promise of a more productive day tomorrow.  Carlos and Mateo would show Eric and Violet the progress made so far on the scroll translations.  Violet was very much looking forward to this knowing her people were also making some, albeit slow, progress on the contract scrolls.

~ ~ ~ ~ ~ ~

A few most productive days passed when Diego approached Eric.

"Can you spare some time away from Violet.  I have something I want to show you alone."  He emphasized the alone.

"Not a problem pal. She is pretty deeply involved in the scroll translations."

"How about just before lunch ?"

Both went about their own business.

Almost noon and Violet was still enmeshed in the Glyph's translations with Mateo so I made myself scarce. I arrived at Diego's office the same time he did.  We entered and he locked the door.

"Follow me," he instructed as he went to an anti room off his office.  There stood a large artist easel with a covered canvas.

"I would like you to see this," he said rather cautiously.

"Sounds intriguing," I replied.

Diego slowly removed the cover fabric displaying the sixteen by twenty canvas.  There before me was Dove of Spring in all her handsome beauty.  It was magnificent.

"Is Violet sitting for you to surprise me ?"

As I said this I started to get that annoying tingle again yet I still could not identify the irritation.  Diego remained silent looking pensive.  He slowly began to speak.

"This is not Dove of Spring."

It then hit me like a punching glove.  I knew what he was going to say before he said it.

"This is the Golden Lady."

Suddenly the mist in my brain cleared.  All those little annoyances I was having  recently.  This is what it was.  The uncanny likeness of the Golden Lady and Dove of Spring.  I turned to Diego.

"The other day when you first saw Violet you mumbled something.  This is what you were referring to, wasn't it ?  When you first saw her you were looking at the Golden Lady."

Diego remained silent but nodded affirmatively.  Both stood there not moving.  Eric's mind was going wild suddenly remembering comments by Whispering Wind and the king.  Now they were all coming into perspective.

Diego, at last found his voice.

"This sure is a weird coincidence."  He was half smiling now. "I thought perhaps I was losing my mind."

"If you are my friend than I am right there with you.  This is no coincidence.  I believe this is real."

"It can't be real, we are looking at a span of maybe twelve thousand years.."

"You are correct in that assessment," I answered .

He moved to a chair and sat down.

"Now you're really pulling my leg," he said half smiling, yet not quite sure of anything.

"I wish it were that simple.  I don't have it with me but I will bring it tomorrow.  I recently took a picture of a painting of the Golden Lady that has been passed down over eons with Whispering Wind the present keeper.  Your painting is almost exactly the same.  Remember I also have many  photographs of the Golden Lady that I took in the Yucatan."

"Are you saying that Dove of Spring is actually related to the Golden Lady."

"That is exactly what I'm saying."

"Does Violet know this ?"

"Down deep inside I believe she does.  This Lost Civilization is all new to her though, like us, she would like to know more.

I will speak to her tonight alone. I'm not sure how she wants to recognized as such. In the meantime let's keep this just between the two of us."

"I understand Eric, Understand completely. If it was me I don't know how I would handle it."

"Thanks my friend, now let's join the others for lunch."


The afternoon was filled with more study and research to the satisfaction of all six. The newly weds looked forward to private alone time that night. After a quick supper Eric quietly broached the subject of the Golden Lady. With a soft smile Dove of Spring answered openly.

"I was wondering when you were going to get to that."

"I didn't know how sensitive a topic it would be and the last thing I want to do is to hurt or upset you."

"Because of words like that I do believe we were made for each other," she answered softly. "Yes I am very aware and have been for my whole life. It never seemed to be that important until now. Even now it's only a very small piece of very ancient history."

Eric was feeling better now that she obviously accepted what was.

"It has never been of any importance to me, that is until now. This lost civilization thing appears to have everyone excited. I must admit I, myself am looking forward to the discovery of the unknown. Even more so now that I may be part of it."

"How did you learn of it ?" Eric's curiosity was getting the better of him.

Violet smiled now. "The king was right about you. The ever curious Eric."

I smiled along with her. "If you would rather not talk about it, I would respect your feelings"

She answered in a half laugh. "It's quite alright my love. Remember! No secrets. But first some of your delicious Cognac.

Settled again they toasted each other and she began.

"I was born at a very young age, too young to remember too much."

"Now who's being the clown ?" chided Eric.

"I learned from you."

She paused for a sip.

"**W**hen they thought I was old enough my mother and her sister along with Whispering Wind told me the story of this great lady from the far away east who lived with our people for a while.  She brought us a knowledge we did not have.  A knowledge of a far away place in a land similar to ours.  The desert is what she was referring to.  There was a mutual attraction with one of our men and soon they were joined together.  The warrior was killed in an accident and she was left alone with child.  Soon after the birth of a little girl she left to continue her mission of teaching.  What she was teaching no one could remember.  The child stayed with his family.  And so the story continued generation after generation.   There always seemed to be a girl in each generation, so the oral history tells us. I am the last female descendant of the Egyptian visitor.  The whys of her visit somehow were lost in the oral retelling of her visit.  What appeared to be most important was the bloodline.  The girl child and her heirs were revered ever since.  So to put it simply, yes I am related to your Golden Lady."

"**S**o did you feel anything when you first saw a picture of the Golden Lady ?"

"**Y**es, as a matter of fact.  I felt a touch of mystery, but more so, a touch of pride.  I did not want to show it right away. I did not want to appear self centered or consider myself special because I don't think that is my real personality."

"**Y**ou're right, that is not you."

"**H**ow do you feel now that it is sort of out in the open ?"

"**P**ride more than anything else I guess, knowing my heritage goes back that far.  I know others do also, but it is not proved and out in the open for the world to see as mine now is.  Nor do I want it to be. I just want to be plain Mrs. Eric Dexter.  Is that wrong ?"

"**N**o my love, nor would I expect anything less of you."

**E**ric was quiet for a spell.  He was reflecting on the words of Whispering Wind not too long ago.


*"**The** Golden Lady may be closer than you think."*


**H**e mumbled quietly, Well that's one riddle solved."

**V**iolet looked at him questioning.

**E**ric relayed the words of  Whispering Wind that ,at the time did not mean too much.

"**S**ee, didn't I say that we would solve the riddles.  That's just one. We will get them all," smiled Violet.

"**D**oes anyone else know ?  you know about my being related?"

"**D**iego more than guessed it.  Not that you are actually related, but his artist eye immediately picked up on the resemblance, not just a mere resemblance but alike in many features.  Presently he is in the middle of painting a portrait of the Golden Lady.  It looks like a duplicate of the one Whispering Wind showed us the other day."

"**I** would love to see it," Violet said excitedly.  "Do you think he would let me ?"

"**K**nowing him he would consider it an honor, especially seeing the Golden Lady with out the gold."

**V**iolet blushed slightly.

"**I'**m glad you are not gold.  You would be to hard to hold when we're dancing."

"**B**ut we're not dancing," she answered confused.

"**W**e will be as soon as I turn on the radio."

# Chapter  14


Eric and Violet arrived back at the college raring to dive into more research.  When all were gathered Eric changed the schedule slightly.

"Gentlemen let me introduce to you the Golden Lady."

All eyes were on the sculptured beauty of Dove of Spring. Eric resumed his dramatic presentation.

"Standing before you is the living and breathing Golden Lady."

The four jungle companions looked at Eric in their usual way knowing now that he has truly lost all his marbles.

"Seriously speaking, Dove of Spring, my now wife, is truly a direct descendent of the Golden Lady we discovered in the Yucatan. Diego, aided by his artistic eye hit upon this a while ago.  Violet has known this her whole life, but never knew of its importance, at least to her it was not important.  It wasn't until recently, with our discovery of the Golden Lady, that this truth came to life.  I know there is a lot of explaining to do and also more research to do, but the fact is gentlemen this is true.  Standing before you is the living breathing Golden Lady.  Well not the actual Golden Lady but her direct living descendant."

Violet was a touch embarrassed by Eric's theatrical presentation but knew it was all in fun.

"Now my doubting friends, I will let history speak for itself."

Dove of Spring now took center stage.  As she started to speak Eric handed out pictures of the Golden one he had taken at the tomb. Violet spoke confidently and related the same story she had told Eric the night before.  While she was speaking every one was comparing the photo image with the real thing.  They were astounded by the similarities and believed her oral history yarn.  Diego even went so far as to get the portrait he was painting for all to see.  Violet was the most impressed with his lifelike capturing of this Egyptian Lady of history.  Not just her history but now the world's history.  There was no denying the identity of both ladies.

"This does change established history, and quite a bit of it," voiced Carlos, as usual, always the practical thinking one.  "It now more than doubles our problem."

All eyes were on Carlos.

"Is the world ready for such information ?  We all agreed just trying to present our findings to date would be extremely difficult.  And now this lovely lady ? No insult meant Violet," smiled Carlos.

Violet, with an equal smile, politely responded, "No insult taken.  I am who I am.  I can not change that, nor do I want to.  The doubters of the world will just have to grow up and accept reality instead of what fits their comfort zone.  From what I have heard of you gentlemen, aside from the craziness, you are just the ones that can do it.  Whispering Wind and myself, and the whole Navajo Nation are here to aid in that goal in whatever way possible."

Her smile alone captivated the group.  Eric's prideful smile matched Violet's.

Her words were like magic to the group.  An air of positive confidence swept over all.  Violet allowed this euphoria to settle a few moments than added,

"Now can we get back to doing some real research or are you going to be like Eric and just let it jump out at you."

Mateo was the first to answer.

She is one of us, she has Eric's number already but she married him anyway."

Of course this cracked up the whole room including Eric, but he had his own comeback.

"That's okay guys, I can take this harassment, but the next time you accuse me of sleeping while looking at my air photos, I will be.  You will have to discover things by yourself."

Violet, wise as she was, intervened.

"Gentlemen, what would your students think of you acting this way ?"

"She's right again," stated Mario.  Then looking at Eric finished with,  "Hang on to this lady, she is good for all of us."

Eric blushed with pride.

Carlos ended the fun with, "Shall we go to work now ?"

Reluctantly, yet willingly they went to different areas to continue the boring jobs of possibly deciphering the various scrolls, Mayan, Chinese, Egyptian and the Navajo contract scrolls.

Violet  instantly became absorbed in the Mayan scrolls. She had never had direct contact with Mayan Glyph's previously and was fascinated with their artful beauty.  She only wished she knew what they were saying.  However, this did not deter her study.  She read line for line in detail, well not read but studied the script.  She had just finished a particular scroll and was about to return it to its slot when something caught her eye.  Something that was out of place.  She sat down to be more comfortable for further and closer scrutiny.  She stared at a certain Glyph which caught her attention.  A Glyph that did not match or fit in with the Mayan script.  Not trusting her own instincts she called to Eric.

"Look at this.  What do you think ?"

Eric scanned the scroll carefully, then stopped at the spot indicated by Violet.

"This Glyph does not fit in with the others."

"That's exactly what I thought," she returned.

"Let me get Mario and Mateo.  Both have much more expertise in Glyph reading than I do."

Minutes later Eric returned with the experts.

"While you were gone I studied this in more detail and I think I have an answer."

The three looked at her waiting.

"Before I make a fool of myself I want a better understanding of what I'm looking at."

Both Mateo and Mario smiled as she passed over the scroll. They were silent as they studied the document.

"This is going to take some time to translate before we can read this message.  It appears to be some sort of history," Mateo finally put forth.  Violet you said you had a guess.  Do you care to share it ?"

"I do not possess the historical knowledge that you have but I am not ashamed to share my thoughts."

Three pair of eyes now focused on her.  It did not appear to bother her.

"Remembering some distinct study with Whispering Wind

it suddenly dawned on me why this symbol appeared so familiar.  On some of the scroll contracts, the Egyptian ones, at times appeared a cartouche'.  An Egyptian name Glyph or Hieroglyph.  This symbol," she pointed to the area of interest, "Is of similar design.  I believe it is a name cartouche'."

Both Mario and Mateo were now all smiles.

"That my lady can be checked out, and very soon also.  Most likely faster then we can translate our own Mayan Glyph's.  We have a visiting professor whose speciality is Egyptian Cartouche'.  A cartouche' is usually a name or heritage combination.  Perhaps we can get a lead on this and then fill in with our own Mayan translations.

Both Eric and Violet were excited with this idea.

Mateo, who had quietly joined the group expressed his feelings.

"Did I not tell you she was good for all of us.  Now she's just like Eric, finding things that we overlooked.  Now we have two Erics on our hands."

"Yeah, but she's much easier to look at," threw in Mario.

Violet did not blush this time but realized she was accepted by the group.  This made her happy, but even happier for Eric's sake.


The initial excitement over the research studies continued, each to their own area.  Before anyone realized it was past five o'clock.  Even the students had vacated.  Carlos, as usual, took the lead.

"Okay folks, tomorrow's another day, what say we call it quits for now."

There were no arguments.  Eric and Violet chose to return to the motel.  There would be no gathering tonight.

Violet chose a simple meal for them and then relaxing under the stars.  They were content just to be together.

The serenity of the night brought forth thoughts of Eric's jungle serenades.  He proceeded to tell Violet of his jungle music interludes.


"I can't wait," was Violet's excited reply.  "You make it sound so romantic, symphony music in the middle of the jungle."

He also mentioned the screaming monkeys as an alarm clock.

"That's okay, I still want to go.  I want to live what you have lived. I am proud of my heritage and I love the desert, but I have never seen the jungle. All I know of it is what I have read in your journals."

"**A**nd I promise to take you. You just have to be more patient. We have no control over the weather."

"**P**arty Pooper" Violet smiled back.

~ ~ ~ ~

**T**he next few days were the same old routine. Boring but at the same time interesting. At last Mateo called everyone together in the conference room. They were joined by a seventh person. The Egyptian specialist. Dove of Spring could feel a bit of tension building within her in anticipation of his words.

"**G**ood to see you all and in particular you madam. It is not every day one gets to meet living history."

**V**iolet nodded her acceptance of his greeting though still a bit nervous.

"**H**i, my name is Harold Jenkins. My speciality is Egyptology. Well sort of anyway. I have been concentrating mainly on Hieroglyphics and Cartouche interpretations. It appears that you people have come across something we have been searching for, for years."

**T**his caught every ones attention.

"**T**here has always been rumors of Egyptian contact with lands to the west across a great ocean, most of which have been ignored because the earlier beliefs were that trans oceanic voyages were not possible. Even after the Vikings and Columbus many doubts still existed. But your recent discovery of what you are calling 'The Golden Lady' may be the answer we all have been looking for. Yet the matter of proving it to the world is still going to be a rather large mountain to climb."

**T**his, of course, the group knew already.

"**Y**our recent discovery of this cartouche mixed in with your Mayan Glyph's is fascinating. I can see the anxiety in all your eyes, so yes I did manage a partial translation of the cartouche. I almost do not want to believe it myself. We have yet to complete the whole translation but from what we have so far is mind boggling. Not only is this beautiful woman here related to your Golden Lady, But the Golden Lady herself is most likely related to the famous Nefertity."

**V**iolet felt herself flush with embarrassment. She now knew what Eric was going through being singled out as something special.

She leaned into Eric for further comfort.

"I know this may come as rather shocking news but allow me to further explain our findings. As some of you may already know Nefertity was a most distinguished woman of her day. Not just by her beauty but also her actions. Solely she was one of a kind, and in her day that was a rare thing. She, at times, ruled with as much power as a king and was not challenged. But that is getting off the point. She was known to have three daughters. Naturally the daughters had daughters and sons. And so on down through the ages." Looking directly at Violet he continued; "You my dear lady are the continuation of that blood line as your oral history has outlined."

Violet cuddled even closer to Eric. This did not go unnoticed by the others.

"There are still preserved artistic renderings in stone of her beauty. The artists, who ever they were are to be commended for their interpretive artistry. They could match any artist of today. Why I bring this up you may ask. For a very special reason. The actual literal translation of the name Nefertity is 'The Beautiful One Is Come.' Her image, captured by these artists of old, has stood the test of time. In my opinion the genes of that blood line have been accurately reproduced down through the ages. The resemblance of your Golden Lady and Nefertity is unmistakable. And for further update the resemblance of your Dove of Spring to the Golden Lady is also unmistakable and so in the relationship to Nefertity. DNA studies would help us tremendously along those lines. But we also know that is not possible because of the time span. Perhaps with the Golden Lady but not with Nefertity. Remember with the golden Lady we are only talking about a couple of thousand years but the Era of Nefertity was roughly one thousand three hundred and sixty BCE.* That kind of puts us at a disadvantage. Yet with the history we do have available this is more then a good chance that this relationship is real."

He paused here to let this new information sink in.

"Living history, yes, but to what end. We are not living in the age of Nefertity," stated Mario. "To study history is fine. We are all doing it. It is our passion. Why are we doing it ? To date we have not changed anything, only identified it. Is history progress ? Perhaps, but is progress history ? Not really in my opinion. We, as a people of today have not learned from history. Only identified it. If we had truly learned from

* BCE - before current era.

history, the world would not be in the turmoil it is in today."

Nearly embarrassed by his own outcry Mario almost apologized but not quite. He was really not sorry for his thoughts. Carlos, without invitation spoke out.

"Before we get too carried away with our own individual thoughts on history I believe, at present, there is a much more delicate matter we should be considering."

Carlos turned to Dove of Spring cuddled to almost hiding in Eric's arms.

"Openly discussing history is one thing, but ignoring individual personalities is another totally different ball game. This wonderful woman here is a person who has feelings. She has a personal life and she should be able to live it without notoriety. Yes, she may be a part of history but so are we all in one way or another. She is not Nefertity nor is she the Golden Lady. She is Dove of Spring of the Navajo Nation. That is her life and that is her history."

He paused here looking at his comrades affirmative nods

"I agree and think it is a wonderful thing we can trace her bloodline back in time that far but it should end there. Let us keep such a discovery within the confines of our science and technical journals with out actual identification. She and her husband deserve their privacy."

Mr. Jenkins, not seemingly upset by this modest affront, answered professionally.

"I could not agree more Carlos. I apologize if I gave the impression of trying to capitalize on this lady's historical background."

Looking now directly at Violet he offered,

"I'm sorry Dove of Spring if I have upset you in any way. I just got carried away with such a discovery. This is not an everyday occurrence.. By all means I agree with Carlos. This should stay as an aside within the realms of our science."

Violet was sitting upright now and smiling a look of relief yet still holding a touch of embarrassment. Eric maintained a firm warm hold on her hand.

"Let me put a few finishing touches on this and I will let you good people get back to your Glyph reading again. I am personally pleased to have been part of this historical discovery. I will further my cartouche readings and definitely keep you in the loop if anything else shows. My thanks to you all and my grateful thanks to have met this gracious lady of history."

He exited the room in the company of Mateo who returned in less than a minute. By now Violet was beaming with the fact that she was no longer under close scrutiny. She released herself from Eric's grasp and walked directly to Carlos. Taking his hand in both of hers she kissed him on the cheek. "Thank you" was all she said. Mario voiced what all the others were thinking.

"We always look after our own."

She felt herself go flush but was pleased with the acceptance.

Diego, in his ever cheerful mode suggested,

"Okay, if we are all finished playing history, can we go back to work now ?"

Laughing, everyone went to different scroll piles. Violet took her time but finally chose one which Mario immediately took from her.

"Since you chose this one I want a look see first. You and Eric appear to be the lucky ones at finding new things. It's about time the rest of us had a chance."

Laughing she answered, "Okay baby, I'll just pick another one."


The rest of the day or rather week was pretty much routine with no major revelations. There were a few explanations of events but no major reveals. Two weeks rushed by and Eric and Violet finally returned home.

~ ~ ~ ~ ~ ~


They continued working with Dan and Whispering Wind on the contract scrolls with much in the way of new results. They could now prove with dates of contact with both Chinese and Egyptian navigators and traders. Apparently at an earlier time there were Italian trade goods also with the Chinese as intermediaries. Further proof that the Chinese were world navigators in earlier times.

Time went by faster than expected and they received word from Diego that the team was heading back to the lost city. Violet was like a child at Christmas with the news.

"I'm almost finished packing," she informed Eric. "And

I packed for you also except for your camera and equipment."

"What about the other necessities, you know knife, shovel etc. ?"

"That's all taken care of and here's a checklist you can review."

I looked at her with a big question mark on my face. Smiling, she readily answered,

"I about memorized your journals.  I hope I didn't leave anything out."

"Knowing you I'm sure you didn't but I don't think I'm going back this season.  There's so much work to be done on the contract scrolls."

"But you promised." Violet whined.

"Yes I did, and when I do go back you will go with me. Just not this season."

"Then I'll go by myself," she pouted. "And this time you can sit home in the desert and worry.  I'm sure your Mayan friends will look after me."

Here they paused, staring at each other, then suddenly ran to each others arms.

"I couldn't let you go alone," Eric whispered while Violet returned, " I could never leave you alone."

Now that the fun was over I asked about the airline reservations.

"Dan is checking into that for us.  By the way he will not be going with us.  He said his heavy schedule would not permit it.  Perhaps next season."

This was disappointing news to Eric.  He felt Dan would be a good asset to the group.

Plans were finalized and they were on their way with a blessing from Whispering Wind.

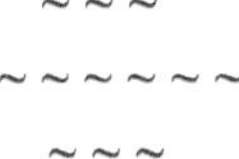

# Part Two

# Return to the Yucatan

To continue the search for a lost heritage.

# Chapter  15


Dove of Spring and I arrived first at the town of Oxtec. Nothing had changed.  I guess because they get so few visitors nothing is worth changing.  We checked into the one and only hotel, the hotel Juarez. We ended up with the same room that I had occupied on my very first visit here. Nothing had changed, not even the people.  I shouldn't have said that. There was a change.  There was a new lock on the door.

"I see they made major improvements since I was here last," I joked to Violet.

The lack of personal conveniences appeared not to bother Violet.  At least the overhead fan in the room was still working.  I knew the others would not be here for another day or so.  To kill time I chose to show Violet the local sights.  Of course that would only kill an hour or so but it at least broke up the monotony of nothing.

While out and about I suddenly heard my name called.

"Sen'or Dexter."

I knew the voice and so turned to look.  I was right, it was Colonel Ramirez.  He actually looked pleased to see me though his eyes went directly to Violet.  I smiled to myself, proud of her beauty.  I introduced them and ever the gentleman he bowed.

"If I did not know better Sen'or I would say she was the living image of the one they refer to as the Egyptian Queen."

This took me a bit by surprise.  I was not aware that her legend was still alive.

"You are a very lucky man Sen'or."

This made Violet smile warmly.  He inquired about the others figuring they would also were due soon.

"I have checked on our lost city a few times in your absence.  All is well, there have been no treasure seekers.  And as per my standing instructions I shall not be far away should you need me.  Good luck in your research Sen'or. And you fair lady stay close to your man. Via con Dios."

Again a bow and he walked away.

Violet was again a bit flushed.

"Get used to it love. Your beauty captivates everyone."

We continued our sight seeing dragging it out as much as possible. I must say though the local eatery served us a wonderful meal and as always the beer was cold.

We returned to the room and immediately switched on the fan on arrival. It was a bit earlier in the season than usual which explained the cool temperature of only ninety two degrees. Mateo felt we stood a good chance for an early start to our season before the rains returned. Even with the extreme heat there was no complaint from Violet.

The night had been surprisingly restful and we were both anxious for the others to arrive so that we could head for the lost city. I spent almost two hours reviewing all the aspects of the lost city and its surrounds and our finds with Violet. She hung on every word. This made her even more excited.

Before long there was added noise in the hotel lobby. My four Maya friends had arrived. Of course along with them were many packs of food and supplies. Enough for six this time. But the biggest surprise of all was that Lone Buffalo had joined them.

"I thought you had too many other obligations," I asked.

"Well I finally was talked into joining you. You will never guess who took over my class so that I could come."

Both Violet and I looked puzzled.

Whispering Wind," offered Dan. "He said that you two would need watching in order to protect our Mayan friends."

Diego joined right in with, "Boy, he sure has the both of you pegged right."

Dan continued with;

The kids were thrilled to have Whispering Wind. Shows you how much they think of me."

Smiling, Violet soothed him with;

"That's not true and you know it. Any one would be thrilled to have Whispering Wind as a teacher and that includes us."

"I know you are right, I was just trying to get people to feel sorry for me."

**B**y now it was one big laugh fest.  We finally quieted down realizing we were disturbing others.

**A**ll turned to in getting all the boxes and equipment in order for our journey.

**W**e finally settled and had a wonderful dinner of local food and spent the evening reliving our past adventures both good and bad, much to the delight of Violet which even built her interest even more.  A sudden thought overcame me.  Her presence here was going to be a positive one.  Both the king and Whispering Wind were correct in their assessment of her.  She would definitely be an asset.  Not only to me but to the whole group and our discovery efforts.

**I** don't know what the delay was but we had to hold over another day before our water taxis could meet us.  The day was well spent though in planning our next steps.  Violet was the most eager of us all.  Her enthusiasm was contagious.

~ ~ ~ ~ ~ ~

**S**even in the morning and we were all set to go.  For a few dollars we were able to get a horse and wagon to transport our luggage and supplies down to the river. Our water transportation was waiting.  Again the same boatmen.  There was, however, out of necessity, another long boat because of the two additional people and added supplies.  During our trip up river we realized a problem existed with the extra supplies.  How do we transport everything to our camp.  A couple of us would have to make a double trip.
Dove of Spring suggested we ask the boatmen.  For an additional fee of course.  Mario did the negotiating and with success.  The fee agreed upon was even less than we were willing to go.

**I**n just under eight hours we were at the old dock looking at the old broken shelter that would again be our hotel for the night.

**W**e turned to as always, as a group and before you knew it our cots and mosquito netting were in place.  Violet did more than her share and with a happy smile.  The newbie this time was Lone Buffalo, who of course, took a constant ribbing from all, Diego in particular.  A quick supper and we all hit the hay, or should I say hit the cots. Violet did whisper to me how she liked the night time serenade.  I assured her that once we got in land the symphony would really prevail.

"I can't wait," she bubbled.


Four instead of the usual two dugout canoes were waiting for us as we finished breakfast. In a matter of minutes we were on our way again upstream. Five plus hours later we were at our destination. At least as far as the water travel was concerned. Dove of Spring was fascinated by the animal life, as was I on my first trip. She took particular interest in the caymans and did not show any fear of their obvious awesome power. Dan, on the other hand was a bit apprehensive.


All in all the trip was uneventful and we safely reached our drop off point. Dividing up our load we set off for the lost city. It was worth the extra money for the two boatman to help carry our life blood for a few months. Concerned, yet proud of Violet for carrying her share of the load without a complaint. One overnight in our hammocks and we were on our way at a good pace knowing we would make it before dark. And that we did though we were a very tired bunch.

Violet stood there in awe.

"This is just as I imagined it. The threat of difficulties and trying times of the jungle but still living in harmony with it. Today's people appear to want to control what is free for all. I envy the people who live here."

"Isn't this pretty much as your people live ?" asked Eric. "You live with nature and all that it provides, unlike most of the world."

A seriousness came over Dove of Spring.

"What ever happened to us as a people. I mean globally. Where did all this need for power and greed come from.'

"Even if we knew the answer to that, how do you go about changing that way of thinking."

They stood there, hand in hand, each in their own thoughts, just staring at the pyramid tomb.

Mario softly brought them back to reality.

"There will be time enough for that later. We have to get home set up before dark settles in totally."

The instant yet unwanted mood change had not embarrassed Eric or Violet and they joined the others in establishing home for the next few months. Diego assisted Dan in setting up his hammock just as he did Eric years ago.

All helped in setting up private dressing quarters for Violet. It truly wasn't much but it did provide her the respect and privacy she deserved.

Once satisfied that home was now complete they turned to quick MRE's for dinner. Dove of Spring was so thrilled and happy she could not stop smiling about everything. She even enjoyed the super quick meal.

Eric spoke up before the others, "Before I get picked on because of my neglect, I think it's time for a toast to a successful season." With that he held up a bottle of Remy Martin Cognac much to the delight of all.

Violet could not pass up the opportunity as she spoke in a very scolding tone.

"Here I am believing all of you so called scientists were her to do research, not to party. No wonder your seasons take so long."

All looked at her in semi shock until they saw the start of a smile cross her face.

"If this is what you call research, fill my glass first," as she held up her cup.

Toasts all around ended with yawns. It had been a long day. Each drifted to their own sleeping area. Eric and Violet were slightly further from the others for privacy granted them by the group. Each in their own hammock but close enough to hold hands Eric gently whispered.

"Listen, my love. It is just beginning."

He meant , of course, his jungle symphony. Neither said a word but she squeezed his hand a little tighter. No words were needed. The music of the night gently put all to sleep.

# Chapter  16

The aroma of freshly brewed coffee wafted over the camp as if it were the alarm clock.  Eric awoke to  the familiar scent only to find Violet not in her hammock.  It was she who brewed the syrupy elixir.  Cups were lined up for all.  She sat alone at the table with a smile of satisfaction as she mentally photographed the surrounding jungle including the king's pyramid tomb.  She even chuckled aloud at the chattering screeches of the howler monkeys.

She was startled slightly by Diego's voice from behind.

"One of these days we're going to have monkey stew, then maybe we can get some sleep in the mornings."

Violet laughingly scolded,

"This is their homeland, not ours.  We are the intruders."

"Now you sound like Eric," he returned with a smile.

"I'll take that as a compliment," Violet answered.  "I believe this is your mug, shall I fill it for you ?"

"That would be great, but we don't need to be spoiled like that, thank you," he said as he poured his own.

Eventually the others joined the early birds.  Conversation was light as they mutually spoke of general plans for the season.  Carlos suggested that Eric and Diego show the basic sights to the new comers.  All agreed and then breakfast as usual as if they had never left the jungle.

Violet was excitedly anxious for the beginners tour.  Dan, also anticipating but not physically showing his eagerness.

Breakfast ended with a quick cleanup by all.  Carlos and Mario left camp first to open the pyramid tomb and then head off to the jungle.  It was Mateo's turn to stay in camp and look after dinner.  Diego and Eric with Dan and Violet slowly walked straight to the tomb. Violet could not wait to get there.

Upon entry Eric and Diego paid honors to the king and in turn to Frank Thurber. Violet and Dan stood mesmerized by what they were viewing. They too were taken by the spell of the ages. So much so they dared not speak. Startled back to reality by the normal toned voice of Diego and Eric they felt a bit embarrassed. It was not overlooked by the seasoned researchers having been in the same quandary many years ago.

"Who knew a place this old and basically constructed of rock could be this beautiful," whispered Violet.

Diego was pleased with her respect for his heritage but instructed that it was okay to speak in a normal tone. Dan accepted the same instruction.

Diego suggested they split up in pairs. He with Dan, Eric with Violet for the grand tour. They would meet again in a few hours or so.

Eric hand in hand with his love went straight for the scroll library.

"Why are we stopping here," she questioned. "It's just a blank wall."

Without saying a word Eric touched the hidden key and the wall opened. Violet stood in total disbelief at the magic before her. She was now viewing what Eric referred to as the scroll library.

"These scrolls contain lost knowledge of who knows how many years or even centuries," Eric said quietly.

He let her have her silent time of review.

"May I touch them?"

"If it were anyone else but you I would say no. Yes, of course you may look at them. They are not as fragile as they appear," Eric smiled in answer.

Without further hesitation she gently removed a scroll and opened it. She was instantly taken in by the history she was viewing. She studied it as if attempting to decipher it. A few long minutes passed and Violet returned to the real world.

"I'm sorry Eric," she softly apologized. "I guess I was just completely taken away. This beauty, this history, this unbelievable moment."

"I know my love. I went through the same thing my first time."

"And you photographed all of them ?"

"Yes, and many others else where."

"No wonder you spent so much time here," she laughed.

Dove of Spring viewed a few more to completely satisfy her curious appetite.

They exited and Eric closed the wall. This again fascinated Violet because once closed, the wall appeared seamless.

Eric pointed out other interests then started for the mural hallway.


Arriving at the door to the murals they met Diego and Dan.

"You are not going to believe this. That's all I will say," volunteered Dan as they walked away.

Violet was already excited but after Dan's words she became more so to the point she was actually pushing Eric ahead.

"Hey, slow down. They are not going any place."

Chagrined at her own childish attitude she apologized to Eric. He smiled knowing her anxiety. Once in the actual hallway she froze at the first painting inspecting every detail, covering every inch. With a little coaxing from Eric she finally moved to the next painting repeating her detailed inspection.

Violet's tour in this short hallway took about forty minutes. Eric could not believe the time she spent at each work of art. He figured she must have every square inch memorized by now, but in kindness remained quiet and let her bathe in the beyond beautiful art. Not surprisingly she even picked up on what she thought looked like a submarine. Eric said he would explain later. At the kings portrait she stood in awe. So this is Atl. He looked the part of a king. She then commented on the king lack of aging.

"For something this old, I would think he would be shown more youthful."

Eric smiled and explained that this was done only a year or so ago. She looked at him eyes questioning. He further explained it was the artistry of our own Diego. Violet almost could not believe it. She kept remarking how stunningly beautiful it was and exceptionally life like.

"He did it from the real subject. Atl was still among us then."

"But the colors, they all seem to match all of the other painting."

"Probably because he mixed his own colors from the existing materials found in this natural environment."

Violet was too enthralled to say anything as she reviewed all the murals again and again.

Begrudgingly she finally relented and gave in to Eric's nudging that they should move on. Tomorrow they would have to do their part in the actual research. She, of course, knew he was correct. The next stop was the treasure room. Yet again she was amazed at the collection of priceless treasures. Right away she identified some of the various items and the parts of the world they most likely originated. She could not, however, be exact about the date. The fact that they were all quite dated was obvious.

Dove of Spring was so enthralled and into everything she was shown that they completely missed lunch. They were alone when they returned to camp. They each grabbed a piece of fruit and took off again to see the river where they would normally fish. There they met Dan and Diego. The four were reviewing all that they had seen so far. Violet brought up the tunnel and air vent system. Both she and Dan had their interest peaked.

Together Eric and Diego described their good and bad adventures in the tunnel. Violet, for some reason or another was extremely interested in the air vent system. They went into as much detail as they could remember, both inside and outside. She could not wait to actually see the system particularly the out side. Diego went on to further discuss the false tree cover that actually hid the air vents.

I promised a tunnel visit among the hundred other must see places. I guess she wanted to see it all in a short time though it took us three years to discover.

They returned well before dinner time and chose to fix supper for all which, of course, was greatly appreciated by the others of the real working crew. The four touring crew were the brunt of harassment for the balance of the evening. Plans for tomorrow would be discussed tomorrow at breakfast.

Eric's symphony of the night took everyone to dream land.

~ ~ ~ ~ ~ ~

A cool ninety two degrees greeted the group the next morning bringing hopes of a productive day. Plans were discussed while they ate. As much as Violet wanted to see the Golden Lady, that would have to wait. She fully accepted that their time was regulated by the rainy season and their research must continue.

Violet was paired off with Eric on further study of the tunnel air vents.  She was actually looking forward to this.  She felt her engineering background could be put to use.

Dan was to accompany Carlos on a yet to be studied structure Eric had spotted on the aerial photography.   The others were to continue the routine of recording measurements etc.

Breakfast cleanup finished quickly and they all parted in their chosen directions.  Diego was assigned to camp for the day which met with his approval.  This would allow him more sketch time to aid in the final presentation.  Also in the back of his mind he could go fishing and prepare a nice supper.


Eric and Violet headed off on the now familiar trail following the tunnel above ground.  Dove of Spring was loving every minute of this jungle life.  Eric could not believe how child like she had become at times.  He laughed to himself and was happy for her.

Finally reaching the end where he and Diego had marked and studied I showed and explained to Violet the false tree cover that hid the air vent system.  Anticipating her question I answered no, we had not dug down to the tunnel yet.  Time did not permit last season.

"Good," she stated excitedly.  "Perhaps I can take on that chore.  This vent system is intriguing."

"You're serious about that, aren't you."

"Of course I am.  I'm here to contribute in any way I can, and because I love you is the best reason of all."

Eric felt himself blush but tried to hide it.

Dove of Spring just smiled inwardly.

They spent quite a few hours studying  what they could with no real answers.

*Yet, anyway,"* Violet thought to herself.  With plans and ideas already crowding her mind Violet and Eric started backtracking to home base.

Violet never stopped looking with every step they took.  The return was actually taking longer, but Eric did not mind.  Though it was slow going, they were heading back to camp.  He was content to be with his love that he hoped for, for so long.

"**W**ait, I want to check something out," paused Violet as she wandered off our chosen path.  She did not go very far.

"**C**ome look at this Eric," she directed.

**A**ll I saw was the normal jungle growth.  I turned to her with a question showing on my face.

"**H**alf of these trees are fake, just like the ones by the air vents to the tunnel."

**N**ow I was the on who felt foolish.  I should have recognized this.  I passed this way numerous times.  Then it suddenly dawned on me, this was not any where near the tunnel we already explored. *"Could it be?"* I asked myself. *"Another tunnel and if so from where to where."*

"**L**ooks like you have done it again my love.  Now I know how the others felt whenever I would discover something new."

**W**e both looked into more detail to make sure this was real.  It must have been.  Everything we came across was exactly the same as the details of the air vents of the known tunnel.  This, of course sent my mind haywire.  If I was correct in my thinking this area was at least a mile away from the one we investigated.

**W**e searched the surrounding area in as much detail as we could but found nothing else that we could actually connect.  I took a GPS reading that I could use on both the topo maps and the air photos.  Obviously I missed something somehow.  So much for my expertise.

**W**e continued on our chosen way following GPS directions to what I thought might be some structures I saw on the photos.  It took another half hour of hacking and slashing with our machete's to finally reach our goal.  Structures there were.  At least I felt somewhat better, I wasn't wrong on this one.  There were three structures or at least once were structures.  Time and the jungle had taken its toll and it was obvious some stones were moved on purpose. Most likely the Spanish hauled them away to be used for another purpose.  The buildings were rather small and appeared insignificant anyway.  My guess was for storage or supply elsewhere  in between points of highway or travel.  There really was not much to see or report but we could add it to our plot map as part of the expanded city.  I took a few photos for the record along with GPS readings for plotting.

**W**e headed for home base with Violet's eyes recording every detail of every step.  I thought I was curious.  She had me outdone ten to one.   We were the first ones back to camp with Violet excitedly telling Diego of her find of another air vent not connected with the already known tunnel.

**W**hile they were comparing notes and ideas I moved to the plotting table to record our finds.  I was correct in my first thoughts.

This new air vent was no where near the known tunnel.  This really cued my interest.  I immediately went to my air photos.  It took a while to find the right coverage because of my lack of orderly filing.  Perhaps, I thought, I could get Dove of Spring to organize things for me.  If I did I would have to be prepared for her verbal ribbing, and rightfully so.

**O**nce I located the right aerials I then set about finding the matching topo maps.  At first glance the topo maps revealed no hints of possible tunnel directions, if even there was a tunnel.  My last thought triggered my brain.  Perhaps there was no tunnel, but an underground room or vault or hiding place.  There I go again with my overactive imagination.  As soon as I ended that thought my mind instantly went to Whispering Wind and his lost civilization story.  Why I don't know, but I suddenly felt that there was a connection between these two peoples, and obviously the Egyptians also.

**T**he soft voice of Violet brought me back to reality.

"**W**hat world were you in this time ?" she chided.

**I** smiled back admitting that I really didn't know. " My head won't turn off."

**S**he took my hand lovingly saying,

"Perhaps some dinner will help."

**I** looked at her in total surprise realizing I had lost track of time.

"**E**veryone has returned, the only one missing for dinner is you," she offered.

"**I**'m sorry," I replied.

"**N**o need to be.  I like you in your own world."

**P**ulling him by the arm she smiled, "Come, let's go eat."

**A**t dinner, Diego was the first to cheerfully tell of Violets discovery of a new air vent.  He went into all the detail that Violet had shared with him.  When there was a pause Mario spoke up.

"**O**h great.  Now we have two Eric's.  Let's face it guys, from now on we just stay in camp and let these two discover every thing for us.  All we have to do now is write the report and get all the glory.  We don't have to work any more."

Eric politely countered with, "If I'm that busy doing all the work, who will get and serve you the Cognac."

"I didn't think of that.  Okay, I guess we can do a little to help.  But don't expect too much."

"You guys are worse than kindergarten kids," Violet threw in.

"What do you mean by that ?  We are kindergarten kids," answered Mateo.  "We just act grown up once in a while so we get paid."

"Is it like this all the time ?" asked Violet smiling.

"Oh no !" answered Carlos  seriously.  "Sometimes we even act like children."

In the meantime Dan mumbled under his breath, "And I thought my kids were bad."

The rest of the evening was just relaxing fun.  The night time symphony called all to their hammocks.

# Chapter 17

Breakfast found a quiet, sunny day with a very cool temperature of eighty eight degrees.  Even the local birds and animals were relatively quiet on this day.  The monkeys were conspicuous by their absence.  Mateo, remembering old stories of his youth commented on th absence of the noise.

"Something is in the air and the jungle is reacting to it."

"Oh, great," commented Mario.  "We really don't need any trouble now."

Mateo was quick to answer;

"It doesn't necessarily mean trouble.  There are times that it indicates good things."

All remained quiet for some ten minutes or so including the people at breakfast.  Then as if on signal the birds resumed their musical chatter and were soon joined by the monkeys until all the jungle was sounding normal.

Mateo was now all smiles .

"Probably just some large jungle cat rambling through," he said matter of fact.  "Anyone for more coffee ?"

This , of course, reminded Eric of his run in last year with the large Jaguar that he never told the others about, but he did not appear concerned or alarmed.

Breakfast conversation turned to the day's assignments.  Carlos suggested they all go to Violet's find of the air vent and continue the search outward for others.

This pleased Violet that she was taken seriously and felt truly accepted now.

Mateo volunteered to do camp duty today with fishing also on the back of his mind.

By nine  o'clock the band of six took off following Eric's

GPS with Violet's eyes continuously searching. Dan was also now into the searching mode finding the jungle not to be as scary as he thought.

Finally attaining their goal, Carlos, together with Violet thoroughly studied the newly found air vent. He confirmed and agreed with her find. As planned the six moved out in different directions towards points in a weaving movement so as not to miss anything. And so began the boring, slow moving trek outwards. The further they moved away from each other they remained in touch with voice calls. They were to continue that until the distance became too great to hear each other. Eric was at first concerned for Violet but slowly comforted himself about her abilities and her own self confidence. He realized how lucky he was and how truly happy he was to be back in the jungle.

Voice contact was now fading so their return trip was started after marking their ending spot. One by one they returned to the air vent. Carlos was the first, soon followed by Eric, Mario and Diego. After another five minutes or so Violet showed all happy and smiling. They were all discussing their individual treks and suddenly realized Dan had not returned yet. Diego, Dan's long time friend, took off immediately in Dan's direction.

He soon found Dan sitting and resting on a stone like throne in front of a small, almost pyramid shaped stone structure. It appeared to be about a seven foot square oriented to the cardinal points of the compass. Intricately carved on one of the stones at eye level was a cartouche, definitely Egyptian.

By now the remaining four caught up to Diego. All were stunned and frozen in place. Violet slowly whispered;

"I know that symbol. I can not read it but I have seen it before."

"Me too," added Dan. "Oh , and yes I did find another air vent. It's on the other side of this mini pyramid."

All but Violet went to view the Air vent. She remained fixated on the cartouche feeling a strange, not quite a chill, run through her. Dan had followed the others to view the air vent.

Dove of Spring was now alone enveloped in a mystical cloak of silence but not a silence in her mind. She was hearing calls but not understandable. She was completely frozen in place eyes fixed on the cartouche.

Eric noticed Violet's absence at the air vent site and returned to the other side of the stone structure. Violet remained steadfast, eyes fixated on the inscribed stone. Eric was still taken by her classic beauty. Not wanting to frighten her he quietly cleared his throat. Violet still had not moved. Eric then moved slowly and quietly up to a position between the building and Violet. This finally broke the spell she was under. He moved to her and enfolded her in his arms. She clung to him willingly. After many seconds passed she softly spoke.

"I'm alright now. I guess I got too caught up in the moment."

Eric respecting her inner thought privacy did not pursue the topic. He knew she would eventually open up to him. Yet he did wonder what power this Egyptian writing had over her. He then heard the familiar voice of the king.

*"As you have taken on the search for the lost civilization, my friend, so has she. It is her destiny as it is yours. Whispering Wind has often related to you the value of Dove of Spring at your side. Embrace his words and together you will succeed,"*

The usual fade away told Eric he was alone again. Alone with his life love. He unconsciously embraced her tighter. Violet raised her head a little and lightly kissed his cheek.

"Thank you," she whispered as she broke the embrace.

The others were returning. Eric mentally relayed to Violet

"We will talk later."

She answered with a quiet smile.

Mario voiced what everyone was thinking.

"This adds another confusing piece to our puzzle."

Everyone lightly laughed.

"Not necessarily," Eric offered.

All eyes instantly turned to him.

"We," meaning he and Violet, "already spoke of Whispering Wind's wishes and desires to locate the lost cavitation. It was physically impractical to search the site on the reservation. Yet his oral history does make the connection of his people and the Maya and their predecessors.  That's part of the reason Violet and Dan are with us now. To find clues to the location of this civilization of old.  This just validates the Egyptian connection also.  How else do we explain the emergence of mathematics, astronomy, medicine and art and other knowledge concurrently in all our peoples. At almost the same time?"

"Of course," said with a big smile, Dan voiced.

"You know for a white man you sometimes make sense."

This, of course, brought laughter all around.

"Don't spread that around too much, it will hurt my reputation."

Level headed Carlos took over the conversation from here.

"You know, Eric may be right.  To date we have only been looking for clues of our own heritage which Eric has helped with tremendously.  We have been ignoring other ties to other peoples.  His lost civilization hunt makes real sense.  We already know we are going to have a hard time against today's paradigm, so why not go all out and follow Eric's lead.  We will still be studying our own heritage but will actually learn more of how we ourselves developed.  This Navajo and Egyptian connection must mean something.  So let's find out what that something is. There, I've shot my mouth off, so I'll leave it up to the rest of you."

"I couldn't have said it better myself," chimed in Mario. "We will still be doing the same work, just looking a bit deeper into our roots."

Diego lightened the mood with everybody in agreement when he said,

"I'm hungry, let's go have lunch.  I think better on a full stomach."

Back to camp and lunch.

Eric and violet trailed the group holding hands but not speaking.  They were again content just with each other.


Lunch was carefree and slow.  The group felt as if they had already worked enough for the day and decided on a leisurely afternoon to discuss how to go about the season now that there were new things to try and identify.

Mateo returning from a productive fishing day was surprised to see everyone.  Of course, it was his turn in the hot seat for not having lunch ready but when they saw his bountiful catch he was forgiven. Dan and Violet volunteered to help prepare this wonderful dinner.

The afternoon was quietly passed discussing this new slant on their history. Dove of Spring was an active participant in the idea formulations but did plead her case for wanting to see two things, the tunnel and the Golden Lady. She was assured the tunnel would be no problem but the Golden Lady did present certain complications. Carlos and Diego explained the hidden entrance and what they had to go through to re-hide the entrance.

Disappointment showed on her face but she did accept their reasoning. Eric promised he would take her to the trapezoidal structure that housed the Golden Lady. Of course she wanted more but at least this was a start. The next day Eric headed for the tunnel with Violet and Dan while Mario and Mateo returned to the newly discovered mini pyramid. Carlos and Diego were to finish updating records and notes on the overall city to date.

The walk to the tunnel was uneventful except for the ever curious Violet. She was excited at seeing everything. On the way Eric reviewed the tunnel discovery and the cave in that nearly took Diego's life which, of course, lead to extra caution and warnings to Violet and Dan. The tunnel itself was fascinating for the two newcomers. They also wondered how it was constructed so well without the modern equipment of today's world.

Walking the tunnel the Glyph markings caught the immediate attention of Dove of Spring. She had already guessed that they marked the placement of the air vents. Without access to ladders or climbing aides there was no real way to study this engineering marvel.

After a few hours of tunnel viewing the three started their return trip. Dove of Spring fell back a bit her curiosity aroused.

"Dan, Eric come look at this," she instructed.

They retraced their steps to Violet who was already running her open hands up and down the wall.

Eric, who had been through the tunnel countless times could not imagine what would catch her attention.

Calmly, but obviously excited Violet pointed to the wall she had just been touching.

"Look Eric, it's probably nothing but this section of the

wall does not match the rest.  It's only this six foot section compared to the rest.  The texture is totally different.  It really is smooth here as if it was done on purpose."

Knowing how level headed Violet was Eric agreed to look at what she was indicating.  He ran his hands, as did Dan, over the subject area.

*"She's right."* he thought to himself.  *"I'm surprised I missed this."*

Ignoring his two companions he concentrated on this new anomaly.  *"Violet was right. The smooth area is just under six feet."*

Turning his attention to the others he instructed,

"Come here, look at this.  To me it actually looks like they, or whoever, tried to rough up the surface to match the rest of the wall.  This was definitely done on purpose, but why ?"

Eric stepped back a little staring at the floor.  Then he was on his hands and knees wiping the floor with long sweeps of his hands.

"What are you doing that for ?" questioned Dan looking confused.

"Looking fo scratch marks," Eric mumbled not really paying attention to them.  "Yes !" he said almost in a shout startling Violet.

"I'm sorry." he apologized, "But look at this."

He pointed to obvious scratch marks on the floor.  While Dan and Violet were looking Eric was on his feet again applying his fingers to the edge of the wall.

"He's trying to find the door trigger," Dan whispered to Violet.

"I can't reach high enough." Eric complained to no one in general.

Violet  responded, "We passed some loose rocks a short way back.  Would they help ?"

"I guess they would." Eric smiled.  "That is if we can move them."

"We won't know  until we try," offered Dan already walking that way.

They were too heavy to lift but between all three they managed to tumble them end over end to the supposed door area.  Precariously balanced on the large boulder with the assistance of Dan, Eric attempted his finger magic again with zero results.

Frustrated, he did not want to give up. Next he went to the one edge of the six foot span and instructed the others to do the same.

"Now look for what may be a seam or line between the two different wall sections."

The three worked silently for almost ten minutes. Violet spoke up quietly;

"I'm not sure what this is but there is a definite difference here on the lower wall."

Eric rushed to view for himself. He brushed, rubbed and blew at the section indicated. Suddenly stopping he stood and kissed Violet.

"You have done it again, my love."

Smiling, Dan commented quietly,

"I'm glad it wasn't me that found it."

Violet laughed, "I'm glad it wasn't you also. Okay big guy, what do we do now ?"

Eric was quiet in thought for a few seconds finally responding,

"We go back to camp and rest."

"What !" shouted Dan. "We find something new and you just want to go and rest ?"

Eric smiled, "We have to check with the expert on door openings."

"You mean Carlos, don't you," asked Violet.

"How do you know that ?" questioned a confused Lone Buffalo.

"I really, really studied Eric's journals."

The three turned and headed to camp.

~ ~ ~ ~ ~ ~

It was early afternoon when they neared home base. Almost at the same time Mario and Mateo appeared from the opposite direction. They seemed to be excited as Eric.

Carlos and Diego were a bit surprised at the early return and met all at the coffee pot. Eric and Mario both started talking at the same time. Now everyone was laughing as Carlos held up both arms. Eric politely pointed to Mario.

"Go ahead my friend.  You seem to be quite excited about something."

Thanking Eric with a head nod Mario started right in.

"There is more to this little pyramid than meets the eye. There are a number of Glyph carved stones scattered about the nearby jungle.  On quick readings, and not very accurate ones I'm afraid, they indicate that this may be a special place or holy place.  The stones themselves fit certain places on the sides of the pyramid.  We are guessing they were removed and thrown away by the Spaniards.  You know that pagan worship stuff."

Mateo continued the conversation from here.

"We believe this mini pyramid is something special. What, we don't know, at least not yet, but suspect it may house something, perhaps other information.  Mario and I decided we need your expertise to really check over the structure."

"Sounds quite interesting.  Now let's hear from Eric and then we can decide what to do," Carlos put forth.

All eyes turned to Eric who was sipping at his favorite black syrup.  He excused himself and started with;

"This pretty lady has done it again."

This caught every ones attention.

"She found something in the tunnel that we all missed."

He paused here watching all the friends expressions change.

" A possible other door, again with the center pivot."

"A door to where ?" asked Carlos immediately.

"We don't know.  I couldn't open it, but I would say it heads off to the west.  I tried everything you showed me but I could not find a trigger point."

Carlos looked at Violet saying, "Thank you for your sharp eyes.  We could have used you three years ago.  We would possibly be finished by now."

Violet's eyes glowed because of his recognition.

"Okay, now we decide what to do first.  The tunnel or the mini pyramid."

Diego was the first to speak,

"I say we do the tunnel first.  If we can open the door then a few of us can follow it while you use your magic on the pyramid."

Smiling Carlos replied,

"Oh, I see you just want to be part of another cave in and get our attention again."

"Okay, you figured out my plan, so we do the pyramid first," Diego pouted in answer.

"Actually your plan makes sense.  So it is agreed then, we go to the tunnel first thing in the morning.  Now that we settled that we still have time this afternoon so we can all turn to on the recording information Diego and I were working on."

All agreed without question except Violet.

"Since I'm unfamiliar with your records, at least for now, I'll go ahead and work on dinner preparations."

This, of course, drew many smiles from the group.


The recording work went smoothly and quickly with all pitching in.  Dove of Spring put together a wonderful meal of mixed everything.  The jovial mood carried on into the evening until nature's symphony called everyone to their sleeping areas.

# Chapter 18

Yesterdays joviality continued through breakfast. Soon Carlos with his magic touch, accompanied by Eric, Dan, Violet and Diego headed for the tunnel. Mario and Mateo stayed in camp but were anxious to go to the mini structure, their curiosity slowly building.

Eric reviewed as much as he could with Carlos on their journey to the tunnel. All the things Carlos was suggesting Eric felt he had already tried but to no avail.

"Well, keep your fingers crossed and hope I will have more success. It sounds as if you did all that I would have done though."

As usual Violet was non stop with her eyes taking in every tree, bush, leaf and stone. Eric noticed that Dan appeared to be occupied with the same task.

Reaching the tunnel entrance Carlos stopped with a quick word of caution to Violet and Dan of the dangers of such an old tunnel.

In they went and in less than an hour arrived at the wall section in question. Carlos stopped standing about five feet away and studied the wall. Within seconds he spoke.

"You made me come all this way for this. All you had to do was use the door knob."

Eric and the others looked dumbfounded until they saw the smile slowly creep across his face.

"You had me going there for a minute," laughed Eric.

The others joined in.

Carlos found the seams and like the others ran his hands up and down and across the different sections. He carefully checked both top and bottom and just as Eric did looked for floor scratches. Feeling helpless the other four started looking closer at both walls not really knowing what they were looking for but it did pass the time.

Almost a half hour of silence was at last broken by a soft utterance from Carlos.

"You are right Eric. I also believe this is a door but I'll be damned if I can figure out how it works. It's almost embarrassing. This one is going to take some time and patience. Tell you what. Why don't you folks head out for something else to find and just leave me here to cuss quietly at the wall until I get it to open."

They were all reluctant to leave him alone but he finally convinced them he would rather be alone on this.

~ ~ ~ ~ ~ ~

The four silently left Carlos to do his own magic. Once back to the open air Eric made a suggestion much to the delight of Violet.

"This would be the perfect time to show you the trapezoid structure, the house of our Golden Lady. Perhaps we can still accomplish something and leave Carlos to his own world."

Diego joined with that idea.

"Perhaps," he put forth. "We can get these two outsider opinions of the function of the mystery building."

Violet was all smiles suggesting; "Well let's not stand here, let's move."

The three men all answered the same.

"Yes Boss."

Eric led the way holding Violets hand lovingly, of course, to the gentle harassment of Dan and Diego.

During their trek Eric and Diego outlined what ever they could about the odd shaped building. Forty minutes later they reached their goal. Dove of Spring froze in place taking in its rustic beauty. Deep inside she felt a sudden emotional pull but kept this feeling to herself.

The four of them then proceeded to walk the perimeter studying all four sides which Eric and Diego had already done many times. Returning to their starting point Diego suggested they climb to the top to take in the beauty of the whole structure.

Curiosity overwhelming her Violet asked about the entrance to the Golden Lady. Diego was now sporting a wide grin.

"Why are you so happy, all I did was ask a simple question?"

Eric now also smiling answered for him.

"Diego was mainly responsible for the elimination of the hidden entrance. I guess he's just proud of his hiding efforts. We passed it when we circumnavigated the structure.."

Turning to Diego Violet congratulated him.

"Not only a talented artist but an accomplished magician. I saw no hint of an entrance."

She let her words sink in but again deep inside she felt that same unexplained tingle when passing a certain spot on their walk. Again this would remain her secret for now.

Eric, looking around asked, "Where's Dan ?"

"Perhaps he doesn't like heights," quipped Diego as he walked to the edge calling his name. Dan answered saying he would be up in a minute or so. He wanted to check something out.

Violet was given the complete tour of the top platform including being shown the four different design markings at the center of each side. She naturally was asked if she had an opinion of the use of this raised platform.


It was some twenty minutes later when Dan finally joined them on top. He took another five minutes or so to familiarize himself with the surrounds. Innocently he put forth a question to Eric and Diego.

"How well or in how much detail did you study the outside ground dimensions of this unique structure ?"

Eric and Diego looked at each other confused. Diego answered,

"We certainly did not do a professional survey job, but the five of us went over the outside pretty well. Why did you ask that ?"

Rather than answer right away Dan posed another question,

"Are their any unique markings up here on top. You know, out of the ordinary stones or scratches ?"

Again Eric and Diego gazed at each other confusion still showing in their expressions. Even Violet became interested in Dan's remarks. Eric finally spoke out.

"Okay, I give up. Just exactly what are you talking about ?"

Realizing he was confusing everyone Dan explained what he was referring to.

"I did a lot of studying of the desert pyramid back home and also reading the studies of the Egyptian pyramids.  The sides at ground level are almost exactly the same measurements within a fraction of a foot."

Eric and Diego again glanced at each other waiting for further information.  Dan now sporting a slight grin continued.

"All four of these sides are significantly different in length, not really noticeable in the normal perusal when walking."

Diego admitted they never really measured the length of the sides.

"In addition to that the upward angle of the four sides are also different."

Diego, now almost laughing asked, "Where were you when we discovered this a few years ago."

Eric interrupted. "Why did you also ask about any different markings here on the top ?  As a matter of fact there are.  One in the middle of each side.."

"Can you show me ?" asked Dan.

Eric led the way to all four inscribed designs.  Dan now took his time studying those designs.  He was silent for close to fifteen minutes as he kept returning to one particular side.  He at last returned to the others.

"I am no Maya expert by any means but I believe we are standing on a celestial observatory."

Again both Eric and Diego just stood there, their mouths partly open.  Violet also looked amazed yet proud of her fellow Navajo.  Dan let this sink in for a moment then spoke again.

"Here let me show you."

He pointed and walked to the side he had studied a few times.

"It's true I cannot read this Glyph or cartouche or whatever it is, but if you look carefully at this design you can see, or at least I think I can, the star pattern of the constellation Orion."

He knelt down and pointed to the pattern as he saw it.

"I would stake my reputation on it.  This is definitely Orion's belt, etc."

The others could not help but agree with him. Dan resumed his reasoning.

"The angle of the slopes of the wall I believe will point to the constellation itself at the appropriate time. I am assuming the other sides will also direct you to a specific heavenly cluster. At least that's my interpretation."

He paused to let this all sink in.

Diego's artistic mind was in full gear now.

"It just so happens I have a book on constellations back at camp. Obviously our next trip here it will accompany me. I'm sure I will be able to match these designs to a cluster some how."

"Aren't you glad you came along now ?" Violet posed to Dan.

The excitement of the find was obvious with renewed interest by all. The decision was made to return to camp but not before showing Dove of Spring the hidden entrance to the Golden Lady. Even Diego himself was amazed at how well his efforts worked. He almost did not recognize the actual spot.

A strange inner tingle ran through Violet again as they neared the well hidden entranceway. She froze in place staring at the ground, a feeling of belonging filled her whole being. The only one to notice was Eric but he chose not to interfere. In fact he shielded her with his own body from the others who were discussing how well Diego's plan worked. Within a few minutes Violet sheepishly was standing next to Hunter of Stories mentally saying thank you. Eric ignored her mental note as if nothing had taken place.

With in minutes the group were headed back to camp anxious to relay the discovery Dan had made. The usual joking took place on the return trip and naturally Eric was the brunt of all remarks. Even Violet joined in lovingly.

They arrived back at home base not realizing just how late it was. Mario and Mateo had supper ready and waiting.

Typical Diego spoke out for all to hear.

"No wonder I'm hungry. We missed lunch" He turned to Dan continuing, "It's all your fault. If you had not discovered new things my stomach would not be growling at me."

"What new thing ?" Mario was quick to question. Then followed with, "Where's Carlos ? I thought he would be back by now."

While getting a drink of water Eric explained their time in the tunnel and how they ended up at the Golden Lady's home.

Eric, now looking a bit concerned voiced, "I'll go to the tunnel and check on him."

"I'll join you." added Mateo as they both headed in that direction..

Barely reaching the jungle's edge they were met by a very tired looking Carlos.

"What's for supper ?" he smiled.


All were relaxed after their long awaited meal and Eric could no longer contain his curiosity.

"Well did you find the door opening ?"

Carlos smiled his answer. "Yes, but only minutes before I quit for the day from sheer exhaustion."

This statement from Carlos  now  piqued everyone's interest.

"Well tell us.  If it was that difficult, then tell us," pleaded Diego.

His statement was echoed by all.

Carlos slowly took a sip of coffee and sat back smiling.

"I would rather show you then tell you. Tomorrow we can all go to the tunnel." Looking directly at Eric he furthered. "You will really get a kick out of this."

Mario asked if he followed the opening.

"No. By that time I was to exhausted, frustrated and hungry. But, yes there is a tunnel.  To where, your guess is as good as mine.  We will just have to wait until tomorrow."

With that Carlos finished his coffee and excused himself. "I really am tired,"  He headed for his hammock.

The others did not push any more and quieted down knowing the man was truly tired.

Conversation was light after that knowing they would have to wait for their exploration to the unknown.  One by one they all headed for their own sleeping area leaving Teller of Stories and Dove of Spring alone. This solitude was rare and they cherished these moments.  Words were not spoken nor did they need to be.  Each knew the others heart.  The symphony of the night played to their shared love and they were content.

Breakfast was a happy event each anxious to move to the tunnel discovery.  Mateo volunteered to stay in camp this day.  He was anxious to do more fishing which he promised for supper to every ones delight.

The trek to the tunnel was uneventful with the usual humor and sarcasm, of course directed at Eric.  Even Dan and Violet joined in.

"Keep this up and I'll retire from discovering anything new."

"That's okay." said Mario.  "We now have Violet and Dan to do that for us."

Eric, pouting now retaliated with; "I think I'll go back and go fishing with Mateo."  Although he kept on walking as he heard a soft voice say, "I still love you." in his receptive open mind.

Arriving at the hidden tunnel entrance the groups serious side took hold.

"Okay, now show us this frustrating entrance." stated Mario.

Smiling now Carlos went through his usual motions of finding the trigger mechanism. The floor, the walls, even the ceiling showed marks of his scratching.

"Finally." Carlos exclaimed, "I gave up out of frustration and stood over here and leaned against the wall to rest my weary bones."

With that he leaned against the wall.  Suddenly there was that familiar sound of stone on stone as the wall pushed open.  Of course they all moved back allowing the stale air to escape.

Violet was even more excited than the others at this period of discovery.

*"No wonder Eric loves  the jungle so much.  Discovery by day and symphonic music by night,"* she thought.

Carlos, turning to business again stated the obvious. " Okay, not everyone will enter at the same time for safety's sake."

Turning to Dove of Spring  he politely followed with; "Since this was your discovery my lady, you shall have the honor of first entry." He then added with a smile, "And you might as well drag Eric along with you.  He seems to like tunnels."

Mario volunteered to join them.  Dan and Diego remained

with Carlos as emergency backup.  Their turn would come later.

Violet was both honored and thrilled to be first in the tunnel.  After fifty yards or so they spotted a Glyph marking the wall.  Eric reminded her that it was identifying an air vent.

This beginning part of the tunnel was far from being straight.  There appeared to be slight curves to the left.  Suddenly there again was a solid wall.  Both Eric and Mario applied the finger technique to no avail.

Violet quietly spoke.  "Try pushing it."  Which Mario did only to hear it slide open.   "It just seemed logical since the main door opened that way." she added as the men looked at her.

Embarrassed, both Eric and Mario just smiled as they stepped back because of the stale air.  But with the air vent system the bad air build up was not serious.

The three continued on again with many turns, both left and right.  Neither could figure out why this zig zag path.  Eric was sorry now for not having been plotting this as they went along.

*"Oh well,"* he thought. *"I'll just have to do it at a later date."*

In their wanderings, which so far was approximately an hour and a half, they came upon two more doors along with many turns, both ways.  It was almost built as a maze for what reason none of us speculated at this point in time.  The only guessing they could do was regarding the many doors.  This they assumed was meant to be a deterrent to the Spaniards who may have stumbled upon the entrance.  But so far it looked as if that did not happen.  The real question bothering them now was where was this leading.  They all voiced their own speculations of this quandary while resting.

Eric glanced at Violet who appeared to be disturbed by something yet was hiding it well.  Not to embarrass her he mentally connected.

"Is there anything wrong my love ?"

Violet outwardly smiled while answering.

"Oh no, I just felt a twinge of something.  I'm Okay," she fibbed.

Eric for some  unknown reason did not really believe her but  accepted her answer while telling himself to keep a closer eye on her.

The resting period did renew their energy but on further reflection they all agreed on calling an end to the day.  It was getting late and if they wanted to be back at camp by dark it would be wise to start their return trek now.  Violet was a bit disappointed but knew these experienced jungle researchers were correct.

Carlos was surprised yet not surprised to see the return of the tunnel searchers.  He knew how level headed both Eric and Mario could be when necessary.

The tunnel hunters reviewed their day with Diego and Carlos on the walk back to camp.  Violet more than willingly expressed her excitement of returning the next day in hopes of gaining an answer to this maze mystery.

As promised Mateo had a successful fishing day and they all literally stuffed themselves not having had any real lunch.  Again Eric voiced his opinion that the energy bars did not really cut it on a physically taxing day.  There were no arguments.

The evening was laughter and fun with both Dan and Violet thoroughly enjoying themselves.   As the hour grew late Dan commented on how he used to feel sorry for Eric working twenty four seven in the jungle heat, physically wearing himself down just to look at a few fossils.

"No wonder he did not want Violet or I to come with him just to see how hard he wasn't working."

Violet readily agreed with him furthering with, "Now that Dan and I are here perhaps this group could get some real work done . By the way Eric did you bring any more Cognac ?"

This all against Eric night at last came to an end with the jungle serenade calling to all.

# Chapter   19

Breakfast was quick but filling with the group anxious for an early start.  Dove of Spring, of course, being most eager to return to the tunnel.  Today Carlos would join with them while Mario along with Dan would unite to further study Dan's find of the mini pyramid.  Diego chose to stay in camp for further sketching saying he would take care of dinner.

All was set and they were on their way as Diego was already buried in his sketch pad.

Little more than an hour passed when suddenly Diego realized he had visitors.  There was a group of five men standing by the archway entrance.  He instantly recognized them because two of the men were brandishing the Spanish lances.  On closer viewing he was familiar with a few faces from their group meeting last year. These were the ancient ones still living the way of long ago.

Diego's mind was open as always, but was yet startled at hearing the king's voice.

*"Do not be alarmed my young artist friend. They mean you no harm.  Hear their words and make them feel comfortable as I know you will.  Their mission is a peaceful one.  Communicate only with a good heart and listen to their request.  Judge not their intentions."*

As the way with Eric, a hollow echo followed. Diego knew he was alone again.  He laughed to himself remembering Eric"s sometimes frustration.

Making eye contact with the group he bid them enter the encampment.  Almost fearful they declined signaling for Diego should join them.

$\quad$ **W**illingly and with a smile he moved to the group just outside the archway.  Diego knew he was not the linguist that Mario was but he did manage the gist of their visit.  Within fifteen minutes, he guessed, they disappeared into the green jungle looking satisfied on a successful mission.

$\quad$ **S**lowly returning to his sketch pad Diego was deep in thought pondering how to tell the others of the visit.

$\quad$ **A**gain ATL tuned into his thoughts.

> ***"Fear not my friend.  Their request is perfectly normal for a people who have lived as they have for so long.  Your group would do the same if you were in the same situation.  I will alert Eric but not the others.  Do not concern yourself, all will be well."***

$\quad$ The drifting echo signaled Diego was alone again.

$\quad$ **F**or a while he just there staring at his sketch pad, his mind totally empty.  The sudden screech of a monkey shook him back to reality.

$\quad$ **"W**ell, there's nothing I can do now.  I'm not going to go chasing through the jungle or tunnel only to find the others not there.  I will just heed the king's word that all will be okay and wait till they all return this afternoon."

$\quad$ **T**his he said aloud to himself.

$\quad$ **D**iego actually felt better and he continued his sketching.

~ ~ ~ ~ ~ ~

$\quad$ **I**t was well before nine AM when Mario and Dan reached their goal, the mini pyramid.  Although it had been viewed by all earlier the pair slowly walked all four sides again.  Dan, as he did on the trapezoidal structure paid particular attention to the length and angle of all four sides.  They all appeared to be relatively equal.

$\quad$ **H**is concentration was broken by Mario's voice.

$\quad$ **"I** think there is more to this then meets the eye," he directed to Dan who returned his gaze with questioning eyes.

$\quad$ **"H**elp me dig a little and I think I will be able to show you

-150-

what I mean."

The two reached for their folding shovels and immediately went about uncovering the angled wall on one side.

"This is just like the digging Eric and I did back in the desert. This wall goes on and on. Digging in the sand had its advantages."

Mario suddenly stopped digging and looking at Dan said,

"This is just what I suspected. This is most likely a full sized structure, and  from the looks of the dirt and rocks it was most likely buried by volcanic disruptions who knows how many thousands of years ago."

Smiling now Dan commented, "Oh if I only had my back hoe now."

"That would be great," commented Mario, " but how do we get it into the jungle ?"

Both agreed digging, at least now, would be fruitless.

Mario furthered, "We'll just let Eric do his thing with the GPS and photography so that it can be plotted on our master map."

"Now what ?" queried Dan. "We still have half a day ahead of us."

"Let's take a closer look at that air vent as long as we are here and have the time."

They moved in the direction of the vent area with Mario suddenly slowing down. Dan said nothing but could see Mario's expression questioning something. Speaking softly, almost mumbling Mario was heard to say.

"This may not be an air vent, at least not only an air vent."

Turning quickly to Dan he followed with directions.

"Come on, we are about to do some digging again."

Dan readily complied. Being the new kid on the block  he did not want to question the decision. They did not have to dig too long either when they jointly heard the shovel hit what obviously was wood. They were both smiling now but for two different reasons. Mario held the grin of satisfaction because his hunch was right.  Dan was smiling remembering the similar occurrences with Eric back at the desert pyramid. He mentioned these magic moments to Mario and spoke of their many exciting finds.

"Then let us hope your luck is still with you,"replied Mario.

They eagerly returned to digging and soon their efforts

rewarded them. There before them was a wooden door, handle and all.

"How did you know about this ?" questioned Dan.

"It just didn't make sense to have an air vent this close to the pyramid unless there was an actual need for it."

"Well you guessed right on this one," Dan smiled in return. "Your guess, so you do the honors."

Dan waved his hand at the horizontal door. Mario, expecting problems they were so used to on their discoveries was extremely surprised when his effort on the doorhandle was met with an easy open to reveal stone steps going down to who knows where. Both stood there, mouths open staring down into darkness to a depth unknown at this point. Again familiar feelings returned to Dan as his mind drifted to the desert once more and the finds he shared with Eric.

"Let's not hesitate my friend, unknown history awaits"

Mario cautiously tested the first step, then proceeded down into darkness. Within seconds Dan followed sort of thinking out loud about not having a flashlight. He no sooner finished his statement when a wall torch illuminated a large cavern. This underground room appeared to be about twenty feet square with an overhead roughly ten feet high. The room was basically empty save for a single wooden bench along one wall. They guessed its length at seven feet. There were grass woven baskets underneath four of them. All were empty but one. A lone scroll apparently made of a tanned hide of some sort of animal was retrieved from it. As gentle as they could they unrolled this mystery material. Engraved on the smooth interior were groups of symbols. What caught their eyes most was the writing appeared to be gold. Whoever designed this unreadable message apparently used liquid gold.

Dan and Mario continued to study the document to no avail. Neither had seen these symbols or writing before. It seemed obvious to both that it contained a message or story or a warning perhaps.

Being ever so gentle they carefully recoiled the document and returned it to the basket. In doing so they nudged the bench slightly and behind it a small section of the wall opened. They were now viewing a narrow hallway that went on into darkness. It could not have been more than thirty inches in width.

Dan looked at Mario, "Do we dare without a light ?"

"Hold on a minute," answered Mario. "There were some old tree branches I noticed outside. Perhaps we can rig up a torch of some kind."

"Good idea, I do have a lighter with me," Dan followed.

Mario returned topside   and was back in less than five minutes.  Now set with their makeshift torch they stepped into the darkened hallway.  Dan was first with Mario following with the torch.  They could not have gone more than ten feet when the entire tunnel was illuminated.  They were both laughing now because of the extra time they spent rigging up the torch.  They managed to extinguish the fire but kept the wooden stump with them just in case.

"Shall we go on ?" inquired Mario.

"Why not, we still have a lot of day left," was Dan's reply.

Slowly they moved through this narrow corridor both amazed at the smoothness of the walls and overhead.

The magical illumination continued about every forty feet or so.  Their pathway now started taking on turns, both to the right and left.  With each turn the walking width grew.  It wasn't long when they found themselves walking side by side.   There were a few inclines now and then, but nothing that presented any hardships.

The lighting continued as did the turns in the tunnel.  They stayed on their trek not really paying attention to time.  Mario suddenly realized the passed time.  He paused reminding Dan they had been walking for more than an hour and a half.  They both sort of laughed again.

"What a life we lead," stated Mario.  "But it's better than being in the classroom."

Dan heartily agreed.

They mutually agreed to go on for another half hour.  If nothing showed they would return to the jungle and to camp.  They would just have to continue the search another day.  This would be right up Diego's ally anyway.

"Do we even know which direction we are going," asked Dan.

"I haven't the slightest clue," was the answer.  "We have taken so many turns by now we could even be in Europe for all we know," Mario joked in answer.

They continued on for another ten minutes when suddenly they came to a dead end.

"Where is Carlos when you need him ?  There must be an opening here someplace.

Mario and Dan instantly set about using Carlos's technique with their fingers hoping to find a trigger mechanism to open the wall. After five minutes or more of frustration they decided to quit and return through the narrow tunnel. They froze in place suddenly aware of a voice. Not physically speaking but in communion with their minds.

*"Do not give up so easily my friends. Seek and you shall find has been of great assistance to your colleague, the Chosen One. Continued pursuit will gain you your goal. The obvious is often overlooked."*

A drifting echo was all that remained. Mario and Dan gazed at each other. This was the first for Dan. He had not been privy to the king's mental messages before, yet was familiar with the fact that they existed. Mario, however was very familiar having been privy to the kings lessons in the past. Now he understood what Eric had mentioned about the king's riddles.

"Obvious to him, but what about us," mumbled Dan.

Half smiling they both turned to the wall yet again sort of wishing it open.

"I need a rest," Dan said as he sat down leaning against the adjourning wall. As he did so a low rumble could be heard as a section of the wall pivoted open.

"The obvious is often overlooked," smiled Mario. "We should have realized a turn rather than an end."

They stood back to let the air clear feeling a bit embarrassed.

"I guess we go on now," voiced Dan. "We have got to see this through."

They traveled slowly for almost another forty five minutes when they heard voices. Throwing themselves against the wall they froze and listened. Smiles slowly grew as they realized the voices were their fellow tunnel searchers.

True enough, another short walk revealed the tunnel hunters to each other with much surprise. Carlos appeared to be the most surprised of all once he heard the story of how Dan and Mario found this new tunnel. He was abruptly quiet wearing an expression of deep thinking. Slowly pulling himself out of his thinking world a slight smile was crossing his face.

"This is all beginning to tie in quite nicely."

This, of course, drew many different quizzical looks from the gathered. Fully awake now Carlos continued.

"This lost civilization idea seems to be more and more real all the time. At least to me. We will have a lot to discuss tonight my friends but for now, to the business at hand."

Each discussed with the other referring to the many turns in their travels. Dan and Mario also confirmed the same findings.


Further wanderings found them facing another wall or doorway if you will. Carlos voiced what was on the minds of the others.

"It's already mid afternoon, I think we should perhaps retrace our steps and head back to camp and dinner. We can finish this up tomorrow when rested."

There were no real objections from the group. Violet suddenly but friendly, though politely, suggested her desires to go on. This shocked everyone including Eric, although he chose not to interfere. Violet looked at all the shocked faces realizing she was talking out of place.

"Please bare with me on this. It's a feeling deep inside. Please, we must go on."

Her demeanor was totally different than it had been up till now.

"Please," she pleaded again. "I know it's the right thing to do at this point in time."

"Who can argue with such a lovely lady, said Carlos. "Gentlemen, on we go."

On they went, all six of them with Carlos in the lead followed by Dove of Spring, then Eric and the others. Eric was of course a bit concerned for Violet but did not want to question it just now. He was aware of her tingles, as she called them and knew how she wanted to follow them through. He followed silently.

It was not long when they again were facing another wall. This one however was marked with a cartouch. Violet instantly cried out.

"This is it ! This is your Golden Lady's home. I just knew it was here," she said in a most serious tone.

Everyone viewed her with serious doubts.  Even Eric had doubts while his concern for grew.

Feeling their doubts Violet softly repeated so that all could hear:

"This is her home gentlemen.  I just know it is and I must see it, please."

She quietly, but with purpose walked to the cartouch and ever so gently touched three letters with three separate fingers at the same time.  Slowly stepping back she watched along with the others while the wall door pivoted open exposing the majestic Golden Lady in all he beauty.

Violet took a step forward and bowed her head in total respect.  The others remained silent in amazement for what they were viewing.  The classical meeting of ancient and modern history.

### *"A new world is now open to all of you."*

This was the voice of the king to all.

*"You have done well my daughter."*  whispered the voice of Whispering Wind heard only by Dove of Spring.  *"Now you can bring the lost civilization to all.  Eric and the others will assist you."*

Violet remained frozen in place staring at the Golden Lady, her long lost ancestor.  She spoke not a word nor moved a single muscle.  It was almost as if her breathing had stopped which ,of course, was not the case.  He five male companions let her have her time alone.  Eric felt a certain pride for her knowing her connection to the ages was now fulfilled.  He chose not to disturb her for as long as it would take.

The men drifted away slowly almost feeling themselves to be a small part of her connection, wishing they could learn more details of the Egyptian, Navajo, Maya  relationship.  They did all realize though that would be something they would never be privy to.

Eric, although at a distance kept a close eye on her.  It might have been his imagination but he thought he saw Violet bow her head now and then as if saying yes, she understood.

Eric let his mind and imagination wander.

"I wonder if she also is connected with the ancients.

Perhaps we can learn more of this strange connection of different worlds."

~ ~ ~ ~ ~ ~

Twenty minutes had dragged on when Dove of Spring finally left her trance like state.  She turned to the more than anxious group sporting a large smile.

"Thank you all for putting up with my fickle behavior. I don't know how but I just knew your Golden Lady was here. I am usually much more grounded in my actions.  With all these new and strange happenings I'm a bit at a loss for words.  Please bare with me a while longer.  I promise I will return to normal.  I just need to rest a spell."

She moved to a bench and seated herself.  Eric joined her taking her hand in his.  He chose not to speak.

"Thank you," was all Violet said to him with her eyes.

The others moved about viewing the doorway and tunnel in more detail.  Violet eventually joined them and with her winning smile asked,

"Can we go home now ?  I'm starved."

It appeared all was normal again.

# Chapter 20

The return trip was routine and without incident.  The mood was essentially somber except for the unanswered questions of all the zig zag turns.  Why was the underground pathway constructed so.  Violet appeared totally her usual self although Eric detected an even more upbeat demeanor.

They just entered the archway as the last of the sun was swallowed by the jungle.   A slightly concerned Diego greeted them with his usual clowning.

"I was just about to call the State troopers to send out a search party.  Here I am alone, slaving away over a hot stove all day preparing a super dinner only to find that you guys ate out."

"What's for dinner ?" asked Mateo.

"Reheated MRE's.  I ate all the good stuff myself."

Everyone just pushed Diego aside and headed for the table.

"You may now serve us," directed Mario to the delight of all.  Near dinner's end Carlos said the obvious.

"It's been a long and exciting day, I suggest we put off our days discussion until morning when we all have clearer heads."

There was no argument.

Dinner cleanup took only minutes as the hammocks called to each.

Hand holding and a few hugs satisfied Eric and Violet as they tuned into the symphony of the night.

Eric noted that Violet was fast asleep within a few minutes.

*"I guess she had a full day of excitement,"* Eric justified to himself.

As he lay his own head down he detected the familiar echo of the king.

*"Your assessment of your desert queen is correct my friend.  Do not push for her inner feelings.  All will be revealed at the proper time.  Your Carlos is coming around to the lost civilization thinking.  Encourage this and work with him.  The results may surprise all, though the world is not ready for this."*

The symphonic sound of the jungle once again took over Eric's being and he to became part of the night.

Dove of Spring was the first awake and raring to go.  She prepared the syrupy coffee and set all the mugs at the table before arranging a delicious display of fruit and berries for all.  She laughed at herself wishing she could prepare a real hearty Navajo breakfast.  Sitting alone sipping her own coffee admiring the new world of trees and ancient structures she was mildly startled by the soft voice of Carlos.

"It is beautiful isn't it.  I never tire of my homeland."

"Nor I of mine," replied Violet.  "I do hope that you were not too put out with my behavior yesterday.  I apologize if I did so."

"On the contrary dear lady.  Where would science be today if not for the unexpected intrusions.  Eric also has rewarded us many times with the unexpected and sometimes unwanted disruptions.  Don't ever back down from your beliefs or inner feelings.  If we all did that there would be no discoveries or advancement."

"Flirting with my lady now," came Eric's voice from a distance.

"Why not ?  You weren't here to protect her," Carlos threw back.

One by one all slowly reached the breakfast table.

"We have to increase this lady's salary.  She's spoiling us too much," recommended Mario.

Violet felt truly at home.

~ ~ ~ ~ ~ ~

With appetites now sated discussions of yesterdays new finds started.

"Oh by the way, I also have some new things to present, but I will wait until you sort out your great day," stated Diego without emotion.

The tunnel story was rehashed over and over until all were satisfied with their findings. The new entrance to the Golden Lady of course was foremost with all eyes and many thanks to Dove of Spring.

Diego took advantage of the verbal impasse.

"I have some news of extreme interest to us all," he began.

Of course, this drew the attention of all, especially when they knew Diego was alone here at camp yesterday.

Knowing he had their total attention he continued.

"We had visitors yesterday. Five of them."

Here he paused eyeing all the shared expressions.

"They were from the ancient village. You know the ones who wanted to sacrifice Eric last year."

As an aside he added that apparently they have been watching us all along unbeknownst to us.

"They still believe that the Chosen One is among us, which is why they have not entered our compound."

Everyone was truly paying heed to his words now.

"Well apparently one of their watchman has seen the living Golden Lady."

All eyes instantly went to Violet. She showed no emotion but smiled inwardly.

"Now that she has been seen and confirmed that she is among us all again, their wish is that they have and have requested a visit from her."

Instant objections were thrown out. The most vocal was Eric.

"No way. My wife has been through enough already because of this Egyptian connection. Carlos said it quite succinctly in defense of her before that Egyptologist, Harold Jenkins. I know she is proud of her connection to Nefertity but how much can we ask of this private woman. We will have to placate these humble people another way."

Mario echoed Eric's statement repeating that she has been through too much already.

It appeared all were in agreement. They decided another visit from the Chosen One would satisfy their needs. Everyone was now talking all at once in defense of Violet. This went on for another five minutes. At last the table was silent and remained that way for a bit.

Dove of Spring, in a cheerful and confident voice shocked all.

"I think it is a wonderful idea and I know she would approve. After all, these isolated people have been waiting a lifetime, several lifetimes for a fulfillment of their dreams and their life's purpose. Why not show some compassion for them. You have all said yourselves how fortunate they have been not to have been exposed to our world, especially over these last few hundred years. Who are we to deny them a small bit of happiness."

Here Violet stopped but kept a smile and eye contact with all.

The long silence that followed was finally interrupted by Eric.

"That gentlemen is why I love this woman."

Mario, trying not to be too serious offered,

"It's not going to be easy you know. It will take some planning."

"I know that," smiled Violet in answer, "But that's what you men are for."

The mood having been lightened somewhat they all decided a day of rest was in order. Rest yes, but planning for the visit to the ancients would continue. Mario and Diego volunteered to visit the old place to prepare for the visit of both the Golden Lady and the Chosen One.

# Chapter 21

"Are you sure you want to do this." Eric quizzed Violet.

"I'm very sure. I meant every word I said before. So far the hazards of your jungle that you are always trying to protect me from have not been hazzards at all. In fact they all been pluses to us individually and to your work as a whole. Yes I am very sure. These people deserve to have a dream fulfilled and that is something I would very much like to be part of."

Eric accepted this without any more questions.

I have to find some more appropriate attire. I'm sure this will mean a lot to these humble folks."

"I'll bet the others will be able to help along those lines. Especially Diego. He has a flare for the artistic side of things. Come to think of it, there are some silks stashed away in the king's tomb."

Violet sort of ignored Eric, her mind obviously concentrating on something else.

"Now who's in another world," Eric joked.

Smiling, Violet refocused on Eric mumbling something about the Golden Lady's cone shaped head. She wanted to be as realistic as possible.

"There again, that's where Diego fits in. I'm sure he can come up with something realistic."

Looking around to make sure they were absolutely alone Eric, in a serious mood, put forth a pertinent question that he almost did not want to ask.

"Ever since you met the Golden Lady you appear a bit different. More pensive perhaps. Are you sure you're okay ?"

Looking directly at Eric, Violet smiled.

"I didn't think it showed. Yes, you are correct in your assessment. I don't know what it is myself but I definitely felt a strong attachment to her which convinced me that I am truly a descendent.  It was as if she was attempting to give me a message.  Exactly what I do not know, yet I did feel a definite association of minds.  A melding so to speak."

"You did appear to be in another world for a spell.  Believe it or not, after my many dealings with the king I think I understand."

Violet moved closer and gently lay her head against Eric's chest whispering,

"You are the perfect man for me."

Just as quickly she stood apart.

"Back to reality," she spoke out smiling.  "Let's go find Diego."

The day was occupied by all, making necessary preparation for the royal visit.


With everybody turning to for Violet's benefit she graciously volunteered to prepare dinner.  This dinner turned out to be an actual feast  Dove of Spring had outdone herself in arranging this special thank you meal.


~ ~ ~ ~


The next few days were occupied with preparations of the up coming visit with the ancients.  These were the real world people as viewed by the Mayan researchers.  They were not doing their normal research of history but felt this was more important for the time.  This was unknown history.  Unknown to the world, today's world and the world past.  The original four Maya scientist considered themselves lucky to have been exposed to this factual link to the past.  To convince the historians of today of the validity of their findings they knew would be a difficult task, yet they also knew this was the real path of truth.  In the end they knew the real truth would survive.  The world would just have to adjust to a new reality.

Those few days passed quickly in the operation of turning Violet into her Egyptian ancestor.  When all was said and done the only detectable difference was that Violet was breathing.  She was truly looking forward to this meeting.  She did not feel that this little charade was being deceitful.  This was to the benefit of both parties.

*"You are correct in your thinking my child."*


**S**lightly startled at hearing the kings voice she looked around to see if anyone was looking.

*"We are quite alone my Egyptian lady,"* continued the king.  *The advancement of knowledge is always beneficial when used properly.  Your heart is true as is your chosen life mate.  It will always keep you focused on the right path.  Prepare yourself for new knowledge.  Learn from these innocent ancients.."*


**D**ove of Spring was suddenly aware of the distant echo Eric had spoken of so often.  She shared her meeting with the king with Eric who acknowledged his pleasure for her.  He truly felt this mission would be a success.  Deep inside he was quite proud of her and her non selfish participation here in the jungle.

**T**wo days later the royal entourage left camp just after seven in the morning for their three plus or minus mile trek to the ancients. Eric was again dressed like Atl, scepter and all.

**E**very now and then he sensed a presence.


*"You are correct as usual Eric, but fear not.  They are here as guards for your trip but choose to remain hidden.  There is no danger."*


**T**he fade away words were all too familiar.  He chose not to say anything about his feelings but continued to follow Dove of Spring in all her splendor.

**A**s they neared the village their unasked for body guards showed themselves, Spanish lance heads and all. No one appeared surprised by this. In fact, as was later found out, they all expected it.

~ ~ ~ ~

And so the play acting begins.

~ ~ ~ ~

Although the women of the village possessed no formal attire they were however all clean and neat. Each had adorned themselves with their most valued trinkets of jewelry, valued for their beauty not a monitory expression. Dove of Spring was amazed at the jewelry. These were no fake costume trinkets. These were the real thing. Gold, silver, emeralds, both blue and green turquoise and even unidentifiable red gems. The women appeared to be in awe of the Golden Lady they knew so much about, though had only heard of her from their oral history traditions.

As Violet passed each one they would bow, their eyes cast to the ground. This bothered her a bit so she would extend her hand and bid them to stand upright.

The children were more curious than shy and would approach Violet with out stretched hands to touch her flowing silks and then run away all smiles. Finally deeper into her play acting she stopped before the biggest pyramid, turned and motioned for the children to approach. Their hesitation was obvious but with further encouragement they did slowly move closer. Violet then indicated the women do the same. The women approached even more shy then the children.

At last Dove of Spring was completely surrounded. She, without hesitation advanced to each child and gently caressed the cheek of each girl and touched the head of each boy. The children's expressions of fear completely disappeared as they were touched. Smiles replaced the awkwardness. Some giggles, as only children can make, replaced this unwarranted fear.

The women of the outer circle also harbored smiles for the gentleness shown their children.

Though Mario was the better spokesman for the old language Violet signaled for Diego to join her because of his natural childlike nature and more than winning smile. She bid him to entertain the children while she attempted to befriend the women. Mario joined her in this effort.

-165-

In the meantime Eric did as he did the time before and slowly toured the village. All the village , near and far. A group did follow him yet not too close. He had no fear this time even as he approached the sacrificial alter. His thoughts did, however go to the poor souls in the past who lost their lives for who knows what reason. Eric extended his touring to allow Violet all the time she needed.

The overly sure of himself head man timidly approached the Golden Lady bowing before her. This time he was without his scepter. Most likely remembering it would not match the unknown power of the one possessed by Atl. Carlos, Mateo and Dan did stay within reacting distance to Violet just in case.

After his bow he spoke to Violet in a soft and respectful manner. The translation by Mario explained the head man's request. He wished for her to accompany him into the main pyramid. Apparently he wished to show her something. Mario looked to Carlos who nodded his approval as he moved to join them.

Some disappointment showed on the leaders face but he chose not to challenge anything. The group of five entered the pyramid. It was similarly designed as the kings tomb back at camp. A master bench commanding the attention of the smaller benches scattered about. A polite hand gesture indicating for Violet to sit was made which she chose to refuse. Mr. Importance bowed to her wishes then indicated a narrow passage way asking her to follow. Carlos chose to go first just after the head man. Violet and the others followed suit with Violet totally protected both front and back.

A short distance found them in a large room filled with scrolls not unlike the kings tomb. The far wall was filled with cut outs, large cut outs to house larger items. A huge box constructed of wood commanded the attention of all. The ancient leader went directly to it. Opening the apparent locking mechanism he lifted the top half and put it aside. Reaching in he retrieved a large book. He carried it to the Golden Lady setting it on the main bench.

"This, my queen is for you. We have been keeping it safe for your return."

Mario quietly translated. Violet smiled and nodded to the Ancient one. He mumbled something pointing to the book. Mario did not understand and told Violet so. She smiled quietly thinking to herself.

*"Mario did not understand but I did. They were Navajo words*

Mario asked the leader for a translation but was told he did not know what he said.  These were words passed down through the ages regarding this honored book.

Not wanting to break her identity Violet again thought to herself,

*"You may not know but I do."*

She reached out her hand and touched the sacred book. Again feeling a simple tingle she turned the cover revealing unreadable Egyptian glyphs.  Yet in the lower right corner was the familiar Navajo symbol she recognized from the contract scrolls.  She turned her head slightly so as not to give away her recognition. Re establishing her queens poise she turned the first page.  More unreadable Egyptian markings. She again turned another page, and another, and another.  Here she paused staring at many number glyphs.  How did she know they were numbers? She had seen this before.  Back in her university days at M.I.T.

*"Do not give yourself away my child."*

This was the voice of Whispering Wind. Violet immediately  collected herself and closed the book.

*"You will have time to reflect on your thoughts later.  Continue being the Egyptian Queen."*

She looked at Mario mentally instructing him to pick up the book. She followed with a swing of her head towards the book.  Mario bowed in obedience.  Before he actually lifted the book he asked for a covering of sorts to protect the relic. Not really sure what to do the village leader looked hesitantly at Violet.  She bowed her head affirmatively while again gently pointing.

Dan, unnoticed slipped away to find Eric.  He located him at the sacrificial alter surrounded by a group of men intently watching.  Eric in a stately fashion pointed his scepter at the alter while shaking his head in a no fashion.  Dan's appearance drew the attention of all.  He bowed before Atl whispering, "We are ready to go."  Eric nodded and turning to the group withdrew the scepter and cradled it in his arms indicating for Dan to lead on. After a low bow Dan started for the main pyramid ignoring the group who again parted allowing passage.

Arriving at the main village they encountered the Golden Lady exiting the pyramid.  Stepping away from the structure a short distance she stopped and turned facing it.  It was obvious she was studying the building as she looked to its top and both sides repeatedly.  At last smiling at the leader she nodded her approval and followed Mario towards the jungle.

Near the exit pathway was a post as if guarding the entrance.  Here, and with great flourish she removed one of the silk scarves and draped it over the post while looking at the gathered children.  With a final smile she turned and again followed Mario.  Mateo fell in line behind her.  Atl guided by Dan fell into the column with Dan and Carlos taking up the rear.  As expected the lance guards walked along side but at a great distance.  The villagers watched in awe as the jungle swallowed the royal visitors.

*"You have done well my child,"* repeated the voice of Whispering Wind.  *"There will be no trouble."*

This was followed by the king to all.

***"As I expected all went well.  The Golden Lady herself could not have done better.  You will learn much from this book.  Treat it as the gold that it is.  I give you my greatest admiration Dove of Spring.  You played your part well.  You have given the world a great gift. Remember your past always in your future."***

The welcome jungle sounds renewed their vigor as the group wound their way home each immersed in their own thoughts.

# Chapter  22

As the now happy research group drew nearer the entrance portal Mateo and Diego fanned out, doubling back on the trail they just left. Just to make sure the unasked for guard had returned to their own village.

Once inside the archway all let loose with smiles and their thanks to Violet.

"Coffee first, then we will talk," said Carlos as they headed for the kitchen canopy.

Eric could not contain himself any longer and crushed Violet in a loving hug while whispering,

"I love you more now than before if that's even possible."

Violet sunk herself deep into his arms not saying a word, just content with the moment.

"That's not fair for you alone," said Carlos.

One by one they all took a turn at hugging Dove of Spring. Slightly embarrassed but happy she finally managed to say,

"The coffee is burning."

~ ~ ~ ~ ~ ~

The group returned by mid afternoon.   Although the day was not physically taxing the stress showed on all.  All that is but Violet. Deep inside she felt she did some good for this isolated village.

The coffee hit the spot but all it really did was make them realize they had not eaten since early morning.  The quickest thing would be MRE's to which they all heartily agreed.

The meal was finished in short order and all were relaxed. It was now time to review the day.  Violet was anxious for this but allowed the others to have their say first.

"**N**ow my Egyptian Queen we shall hear from you," directed Carlos.

**N**ot at all shy this time Violet took center stage.

"**W**e have a lot to show the world, that is if they will accept it."

**H**er hand touched the book they returned with.

"**T**his book, gentlemen, will give us many answers.  I believe more then we can anticipate."

**A**ttention was now piqued.

"**I**f you recall their leader gave a name to this book."

**M**ario interrupted;

"**Y**es, he said some words but I did not understand them. It must have been a dialect from a very old form of Yucatecan, our language of old.

"**I** would not have expected you to understand," Violet put forth.  Smiling she continued.  The words he used were Navajo.  Words of old but still Navajo.  The rough translation is "The Book of Secrets"

**Y**ou could almost see the mental questions flying through the air.

"**T**his, my friends lends credence to the myth of the Golden Lady.  She did come from my homeland and apparently I am her living decedent."

**T**his she stated proudly.


*"There should never have been any doubt Dove of Spring.  Carry your head high.  You are history."*


**V**iolet, for a second took on a distant look, then inwardly smiled after the fading echo.  Eric detected this yet remained silent.  His eyes met with hers momentarily.

**V**iolet composed again continued,

"**I** have not reviewed much of this gift but I do know there will be many answers to as yet unasked questions."

**M**ario jokingly put forth, "Now you are talking riddles like the king."

At least the laughter broke the tension that was building.

"You have teased us enough.  What else have you discovered in this history book ?" Carlos asked.

Laughing in answer, "I cannot read your language but I do know the references to higher math."

Puzzled queries appeared on the faces of her audience.

She humbly answered, "I hold a Masters degree in engineering from M.I.T."

"Will this woman ever cease to amaze  us?" remarked Mateo.

"My degree is not the point.  The point is the obvious higher math used by these so called backwards people.  The same math shows up in regards to the pyramids in Egypt also."

Again questioning glances.

"I'm sure you are all familiar with the mathematical term "PI".  Well according to these writings PI was used in designing the pyramids, both here and in Egypt.  Our more modern teachings say this was only introduced by Archimedes in the third century BC.  How is it then that these totally separate structures were built involving the mathematical constant of PI some two thousand years before.  I am willing to say gentlemen this may be or is part of the lost civilization."

Here Violet stopped, feeling she had gone to far on this too new subject.

"I'm sorry my friends.  I tend to get carried away sometimes.  Please forgive me."

The more than interested companions were silent for a few minutes contemplating the words just thrust upon them.  Carlos, at last interrupted the hush.

"Today has been a stress on us all and in particular our gracious guest.  I say we just relax for the rest of this evening, forget about work and all get a much deserved sleep tonight.  Tomorrow we can nit pick everyone's thoughts and make a plan for moving forward.  Remember, we still have to continue research here in our new lost city."

There was no argument.  Violet was particularly relieved. She was unaware of how stressed she was.

Dan, although new to the group, was accepted even more when he advertised,

"To follow in my leaders footsteps I did manage to secret

some cognac in my pack.  I believe it would be in order about now."

Not a word was spoken but they all held up their cups.

The evening was total relaxation.  It was as if they went back in time to their childhood.  Stories were willingly relayed of their early years, both comic and tragic.  It appeared that no matter what their background was or where they came from their childhood stories showed a common theme.  They were one big happy family.

The music of the night was slowly pushing the daytime sounds away.  Every one paid attention to the gentle change over and casually drifted to their respective sleep corners.  Eric and Violet were the last remaining cherishing there private moments.  Sleep eventually dictated their moving to their more private sleeping area.  The symphony seemed even more special this night.

# Chapter   23

**A** normal one hundred degree plus day greeted the now rested adventurers.  Diego in his normal kidding mood asked Dan,

"**W**hen you get your coffee would you turn on the air conditioner?"

**D**an's answer was in keeping with the mood.

"**I** was going to do that before but someone cut the plug off."

"**N**ot again!  I guess I'll just have to order another one."

**A** long lazy breakfast and two cups of coffee later they all gathered as comfortably as possible.  Mario took the lead.

"**O**ur quiet research into a lost Maya city, thanks to Frank, has now turned into a turn the world upside down wonder.  The only ones around here who have knowledge of this lost civilization from their passed down history are our friendly alarm clocks who refuse to communicate with us."

**T**he smiles all around were expected.

"**S**o I guess it will be up to us to start this uphill battle which, of course, will be like talking to our monkey friends.  Who knows they might understand better than our own kind.  Okay, to get serious now, let's pick up where we left off yesterday."

**H**e said this while looking at Dove of Spring.  Here Eric put his hand on Violets to signal his interruption.

"**B**efore, our Queen speaks to us again let me bring you up to date a little on this "Lost civilization" thing.  We all know of our king and his reference to being a chosen one.  He and a few others whose efforts fell on deaf ears.  Prior to our coming here this year I, or should I say we, had some very serious discussions with Whispering Wind.  Bare with me for a short time longer and I will relay his words to you all.  I have thought of them so often I have them just about memorized.  Dove of Spring was witness to some of these words, as was Dan.

*"As you well know, we too have had contact with the distant Egyptian culture, but again no one wants to believe our words.  I now have something to share with you that will, if ever believed, change history and the way modern man believes and thinks.*

*My friends, as old as our history is, there is yet a civilization older than ours.  Your king, Eric, as I'm sure you have already surmised, is from that civilization.*

*I am in possession of some information regarding that ancient civilization which I am now going to pass on to you Eric.  As your king has already chosen you, I too am choosing you.  You are true to your heart, and if anyone can find any remains of this historical epic it is you. You already have two others who are also worthy.  You have a knack for finding lost history.  I have faith in you to also find our lost past.  Not just the Navajo past but of this whole continent , if not the whole world.  In the words of your king, Eric, you truly are a chosen one.  My full trust is in you, knowing that you will succeed*

*Oral history has been passed down for many hundreds if not thousands of years.  Too many to really count.  We were once a mighty nation and a proud people, as were others in this land.  This was long before the European conquest.  The best I can decipher is long before even European advanced civilization, there existed a technology that was far advanced from today's so called modern world.  Even with that advanced knowledge, we still lived in harmony with the land and its other creatures.  I know you are aware of some of those powers that were harnessed by the ancients.  Your Mayan king enlightened you to their wonders.  They were meant to help all mankind without exception.  These ancestors lived in a world of untold peace with all nations on all continents.  Disagreements, the few that there were, were handled by those of clear minds with fairness for all.  War was all but forgotten.  It was just a word from the past.  Mutual respect and sharing ruled all without disagreement or prejudice.  The world was as it was meant to be and as it should be. "*

Here Eric stopped to let his words register with his four Maya friends.

"I didn't mean to be so long winded, but I thought you should know what is behind my motivation. Or, I should say our motivation. Back at the desert there is a link or non passageway to this lost civilization, but because of a cosmic conflagration eons ago it is buried by thousands of feet of earth's accumulations. I, or should I now say we, have been directed by both the Atl and Whispering Wind to find this past epic of man. This latest gift, the book given to Violet, is just one of our first steps toward our goal. Now, and I'm sure to every ones delight, I will shut my mouth."

The noise of quiet could be heard by all. Even the jungle itself became silent.

"Then where do we go from here oh Chosen One?" questioned Mario smiling.

Natures melodies picked up again as the smiles did for the group.

"I would humbly suggest we let Violet continue her commentary of yesterday and then we all hash out our thoughts and ideas."

Much more at ease than the previous day Violet did not hesitate in resuming her observations of the book.

"I will need a lot of help in the translations of this Book of Secrets. Most of it is in glyphs I do not recognize or Mayan writing and actually many other languages. But the math formulas and presentations do stand out. We, gentlemen, by comparison are newcomers to design and mathematics. I would be willing to bet even more secrets have disappeared over the millennia. I believe in a lost civilization. Proof of such an existence is all around us and has been all along save for that which has been destroyed by ignorance. This ignorance that still exists may never allow us the full understanding of our ancient history and its superiority to what we have today. All we humble few can do is to continue to search and discover and present to the world a truth they will not want to believe."

She could see from the faces that many questions or remarks were forthcoming so Violet added a closing sentence.

"But in a final conclusion this by no means should deter your present work on this absolutely beautiful lost city of your own ancestry, or which could be everyones. Who knows ?"

There was a very slight pause before Carlos spoke.

"Talk about getting right to the point. This lady knows our minds. You are absolutely correct Violet. Our present work is also really part of the lost people search. I'm sure it all ties in some how, whether here, in North America or Europe, Africa, the Pacific or both poles. I'm sure the connection is there and always has been. Now that we have some more concrete evidence we can in time string it all together. So, Lady and Gentlemen we shall continue with our normal work while letting Eric and his two desert friends pursue our antiquity."

"Coffee any one?" asked Mateo.

Diego asserted himself before the breakup.

"There is one more very important item remaining which I believe to be also part of this years research work."

Confused question marks covered all faces while Diego took his leave returning with a veil covered object.

"Hollywood has its Oscar while the Yucatan Jungle has its Oscarette. This years winner is the legendary "Golden Lady" as performed by Dove of Spring. Her unequaled performance has rewarded us with invaluable information of our heritage."

He removed the silk veil from the quickly put together figurine of the Oscarette. He graciously bowed as he handed it to Violet. The others respectfully applauded.

A truly embarrassed woman, blushed her acceptance not knowing what to say. Each in turn kissed her hand.

"Now, coffee anyone?" repeated Mateo with a broad grin.


The unnecessary weight now having been lifted from every ones shoulders all appeared to be normal again. They discussed assignments for the day including Dan. Eric and Violet chose to be camp watchers. Violet wanted to do more studying of the Book of Secrets while Eric photographed the book in detail for validation.

Dan, Carlos and Mateo went on to further study the astronomical alignments at the trapezoidal building with Diego's constellation book in hand. Mario and Diego headed for the new tunnel entrance to further study the buried pyramid.

Eric, as was his norm did appreciate the alone time even more so on this day with the presence of Dove of Spring. Just being near her satisfied his whole being. He felt it made his work easier.

Violet was deep into her studies of this book, even as Eric was photographing it. Blind to the translations, yes, but math is math no matter how you display it. These relationship formulas are not identified or named as Pi per se but are the mechanics of Pi nonetheless. Some of her thinking was done out loud whether Eric was listening or not. He really surprised her when he admitted that he was listening. He just did not understand what she was so excited about.

"Here let me show you," she willingly explained. "Remember yesterday I mentioned Archimedes is credited with the discovery of Pi as a mathematical standard. That was in about 200 BC. Yet these pyramids, here in South America and the ones in Egypt were constructed 2000+/- years before them all using the basics of Pi as a standard measure. This Book of Secrets is truly that. These diagrams show that to be fact. The relationship of the square and circle drawn here for the design of the pyramids are in fact using the theory of Pi. I'm sure as we study this further we will find more proof of just such knowledge. This is a lost people. Who knows how many eons ago they flourished. Most likely before the last ice age as spoken of by Whispering Wind. Much was obviously lost and only rediscovered to bring us to where we are today, yet not as advanced."

Violet smiled as she apologized.

"Forgive me. I do get carried away sometimes."

"As we all do my love," replied Eric. "What you are saying all fits in with our recent discoveries. We will bring this up again tonight at dinner Perhaps we can get this written down in a much more explanatory way for society to understand and accept. I'm sure we can eventually get backing from other scientists, archeologists and professionals from around the world. There is proof all around us all over the globe of this advanced technology. We just have to overcome the reigning paradigm of beliefs."

Smiling now he added,

"In the meantime we should both consider what's for dinner for our hard working comrades."

They both reluctantly pulled themselves away from the book. Violet carefully re-wrapped the silk covering and set the treasure aside. The pair did the best they could to prepare a full meal. Violet set the table as fancy as she could in thanks for their respect. She even prepared a special fruit bowl. She had discovered the kings special place on her own. Eric had managed to catch a few fish which Violet prepared her own special way.  This beautiful feast was finished just as the two teams of weary researches returned.  The two teams were obviously anxious to report today's findings.  Dove of Spring used her charm to convince them of dinner first.  There was no real argument.

**D**inner was slow and much appreciated but you could feel they were all anticipating the upcoming discussion. Eric and Violet decided to be the last to speak.  Carlos took advantage of the lull while coffee all around was doled out.

"**D**an was absolutely right about the constellation alignments and thanks to Diego's book we were able to ascertain the correct constellation for all four sides.  There is even the possibility of two corners alignment.  To what we do not know yet.  One very interesting possibility did show itself however.  Because of planetary precession over the years the alignments are not perfect any longer.  But on the good news side once we can get an Astrol-archeologist to review our findings we can put an age on the structure.  This, Eric, fits nicely with your lost civilization theory. Getting an actual date on this trapezoidal pyramid will be most helpful to all our present studies.  We can go into more specifics after we get today's findings written down properly."

**T**urning to Mario and Diego he asked, "You two look like you also have something to share."

"**T**hat is absolutely correct," answered Mario.  "Thanks to Dan's discovery of the so called mini pyramid we not only found the second tunnel to the Golden Lady but on further study today we did find an entrance to the pyramid.  And yes Carlos this is a full sized structure. Because of limited equipment and time constraints we did not get to study much."

**D**iego took over from here.

"**T**here is much to study.  This building is unlike any other pyramids that any of us is familiar with.  There is much art work.  Some painted directly on the walls and some as separate pieces which can be carried. There are books, scrolls and many Glyph markings to be studied."

**M**ario spoke up again.

"**T**here is a problem though which could hinder any serious study.  At least for now.  There is no air.  There are no air vents as such as those in the tunnels.  Probably because they were not needed when this was built.  Which is another subject altogether.  This, as mentioned by Carlos earlier was a free standing structure above ground.  But now with ninety percent of it buried it is not a workable breathing situation.  We will have to overcome that before any real studies can be done.  This could be a very promising find.  Again leading to a lost or forgotten peoples."

"Looks like we have had a very full and promising day," stated Carlos.  " Now lets hear from today's cooks and bottle washers."

Eric smiled answering, "All I did today was photography but the lady here may be able to provide some information."

Violet, now also laughing stood up.

"Gentlemen, I will try not to be as long winded as I was yesterday.  I did a lot of study of the book again today and I am convinced of its authenticity.  The advanced math being used we are only using now.  I'm sure upon further study there will be astronomical observations also.  We may call these people lost, but they were anything but, education wise.  My personal opinion is that these people were far better off than we are today.  They had this advanced knowledge of math and the sciences yet still chose to live in harmony with nature.  They nurtured it, not destroyed it as we do today.  I know we are not exactly certain yet what made them disappear but we can only hope to learn from them, which we obviously have not done yet.  Our collective findings may never go any further than this jungle but at least we do know the truth of how to live.  I will bore you no longer."

With that she sat down and reached for her coffee mug.

Much to her surprise they all began to applaud her short wording of the apparent truth.


The rest of the evening was enjoyed just relaxing.  No business was discussed.  There would be time enough for that tomorrow.  Eric and Violet took a quiet stroll to the kings tomb to revel in the night.  The night time serenade followed them.  They returned shortly as the others also were readying to retire.

The night was exceptionally quiet with a full sky of stars unusually bright. The symphony adjusted itself to the occasion.

# Chapter 24

A mood of total satisfaction appeared to have settled over the entire camp.  There was no urging of "must do" in the air.  There was some discussion of things to do but no real push of importance.

Breakfast was every man for himself, or herself as the case may be.  Carlos was the last man up this lazy day.  As he relaxed with his black syrupy coffee Dove of Spring quietly approached.

"Mind if I join you, there is something I would like to discuss."

"You are always welcome Violet. What can I do for you ?"

"It's about the buried pyramid.  You seem to be the one with engineering experience so I thought between the two of us we could come up with a plan to get air into the buried building.  I have not yet studied the air vent system but perhaps an adaptation could be made.
Or even an in and out pump system.  Enough to allow for further probing to what may be vital information."

"I was thinking along those lines myself.  You may be right. With your background we may be able to rig something, temporary though it may be, it may be enough to aid in our study."

With that, Carlos signaled for the others to join them. When all were gathered and the jokes died down Carlos presented Violet's idea.

"Great thought.  You name it and Dan and I will build it," volunteered Diego. "We did a lot of that in college."

Dan filled in with, "But nothing ever worked."

"It will this time because we are not designing it," answered Diego.

"I guess that's settled then.  Eric you can take your lovely lady to the outside air vent and allow her to study it.  The rest of us will goof off with our paper work."

$\qquad$ **D**an volunteered to join them on their trip into the jungle.


$\qquad$ **B**reakfast over the three desert people, or in reality two desert folk and one New Englander took to the jungle trail to the air vent above ground with machete and shovels in hand.


$\qquad$ *"You are doing well, my son.  Did I not predict Dove of Spring would be of great assistance.  Allow her, her own mind and you will be rewarded."*


$\qquad$ **T**hese words of Whispering Wind could only be heard by Eric.  He did not share the message but willingly accepted its content.

$\qquad$ **T**he day was perfect for their jungle trek and sooner than expected the trio were looking at the false tree cover. Dan was the most fascinated by the artificial tree bark.  It did not take long for Violet to start her reverse engineering thought process. Without asking for help she started the digging function of her study.  Actually not shy about asking for help she addressed her male companions.

$\qquad$ **"I** really need this excavation to be at least six feet down. Would you two care to give me a hand," she humbly asked.

$\qquad$ **A**lmost embarrassed for not helping sooner they both helped her up to level ground and proceeded to dig to a seven foot level. They themselves were surprised at what they uncovered.  Here before them was a downward vent, obviously to the tunnel, but what fascinated them most was a fan system operating on the slightest breeze from above.
This pulled air from above down into the tunnel.  Violet was already lost in her study of the workings of this age old system that was still functioning. This possibility was going round and round in her mind.  She was so deep in the thought process that Eric and Dan no longer existed.

$\qquad$ **T**he fan design was unique yet at the same time wasn't.  She likened it to a child's four leafed toy that spun with the wind.  But, as she observed, it was self lubricating with the dew of the jungle night air.
The spoke it spun around was of the jungle yet did not show the wear of ages. Natures self lubricating process was far beyond anything our so called society had to date.

$\qquad$ **T**otally ignoring her two male companions Violet was swimming in a new world of nature's dynamics.  The natural lubricants she found to be produced by nature itself.  What we today throw away was the precious self lubricant from the flowers of the grasses and stems of the many thousands of plants around us.  That annoying stuff we ignore and throw away.

After close to an hour of uninterrupted study Dove of Spring looked up at Eric and Dan and with a broad smile stated,

"You may help me up now."

They rushed to the hole and gently assisted her up tp ground level.  Her face appeared to them as one from heaven.

"The advanced simplicity of these people, who ever built these things, is a miracle of intelligence.  We are almost backward by comparison.  Gentlemen we can now provide air to the buried pyramid.  Thank you for your indulgence."

Once totally on stable ground she gently hugged each of her two male companions.  Eric especially.  He heard her say, *"Thank you my love for bringing me here."*

"I am now convinced there was an intelligent world long before us.  By comparison we are not modern at all.  Only modern to the greed controlled  so called leaders of the world.  If only they knew or would accept reality.  I'm sorry.  There I go again getting carried away.  I'm beginning to sound like you now Eric."

"One Eric is enough," joked Dan.  "Though at least you're prettier."

"Never mind that now.  Do you think we can build an air supply ?"

"We can try," was Violets answer.  "Let me look around here for a while for the necessary natural materials."

While Violet scanned the surrounding area Eric and Dan descended into the hole to look closer at what Dove of Spring had been studying.  They wanted to touch and feel but dared not in fear of spoiling so perfect a device.  They puttered around till they heard a voice from above.

"If you gentlemen are finished playing now we can start back for camp.

Once on the trail back Dan, out of curiosity questioned Violet.

"Do you really think you can duplicate the air system ?"

"Yes, eventually with more study, but not now.  It is much to intricate a system.  We can, however, based on that design rig up something that I believe will work."

**A** half hour into the return journey Eric stopped.

"**W**e forgot to cover up or fill in the hole."

"**I**t's not like there are a lot of tourists running around here." Dan answered.

**V**iolet joined with, "That set up is extremely vital to all of this research.  Not to mention someone getting hurt by falling into a hole in the middle of the jungle."

"**Y**ou go on ahead, I'll run back and cover up the best I can" proposed Eric.

**D**an touched his arm to stop him.

"**M**ay I suggest something else.  It most likely will be okay for just this one night.  I will return tomorrow with Diego.  He can do his magic then.  It will also give us some together time to catch up on times gone by."

**E**ric hesitated while Violet seconded Dan's proposition. Eric thought for a few minutes then finally , although reluctantly, agreed. They continued on the journey home.  They arrived back at the camp archway shortly before normal dinner time.  Violet immediately joined Mateo in the preparation.  Camp was basically quiet with journal updates.

**O**pen discussion as usual during and after dinner.  The main topic this night was Violets study of the air vents.  She went into as much detail as possible with Carlos hanging on every word.  This particular topic ended with all in agreement and that they would try to manufacture an air device of their own for future use and present use with the buried pyramid.

**T**hat settled for the moment Eric spoke out.

"**I**'ve been doing a lot of pondering lately."

"**H**ere we go again," interrupted Mario smiling. "We don't have time for any more discoveries.  We can't even keep up with what we have now."

"**O**kay.  You may be excused and go to your room, but no T V tonight." returned Eric laughing.  "As I was saying," he continued, "This lost civilization thing.  There must be something to it.  Please follow me for a few minutes. First we have the king.  We did not want to believe this in the beginning yet look how far we have come because of his influence. His chosen one status so far has been proven time and time again.

At least to us."

"**Y**et fell on deaf ears of those immediately before us. They considered the jungle  uninhabitable.

"**E**xactly my point." Eric went on.  "Then we have Whispering Wind, though not a chosen one, has related to us from eons of oral history, a more than convincing study of just such a people.  A lost civilization.  Then we have here Dove of Spring, an actual relationship to someone from ancient Egypt, which according to today's beliefs is not possible.  Next we have proof of actual trade contacts and contracts world wide.  Again by today's rules was not possible.  All of these things brings us to where we are today.  Here in a jungle considered uninhabitable. Yet look around.  We are surrounded by proof of a society that once thrived here thousands of years ago.  Possibly even more advanced than the one believed at the beginnings in Africa and Europe.  We are stuck in a paradigm belief system that does not want to change history as it was written of old, no matter the proof being exposed on a regular basis world wide.  Just look at the construction of large walls, temples and buildings from around the globe.  Right here in South America we have Sacsayhuaman with walls of individual cut blocks of stone, some weighing  in excess of one hundred tons.  Yet cut at different angles and fit together interlocking like a jigsaw puzzle.  No mortar of any kind was used, nor will any of the joining seams accept a piece of paper into the joint.  It is many tens of feet high.  How was this accomplished ?  This was built by backwards people?  I think not.  I could go on and on with structures just here in Central America not to mention what has been found globally all dating to many thousands of years before our so called intelligent civilization.   To me there is no doubt of a lost civilization and I believe we are viewing some of it right here.  We as a people in general call ourselves an advanced intelligence.  We have built nuclear  weapons  whose  only  use  is to destroy our planet. Is that intelligent ?   We are controlled by the greed and power of a few which again will only lead to our own destruction, but yes "WE" are an advanced intelligence."

**H**ere Eric paused to take a breath and calm down. Looking at his silent audience he sincerely apologized.

"**I**'m sorry my friends.  It's just that sometimes this world we live in has a tendency to get to me.  I have got to learn to control my mouth."

**Vi**olet reached out and gently took hold of his hand squeezing it with her love.

**E**ric, my friend," stated Carlos, "And you are among true friends, none of us here has any quarrel with your words or feelings. In fact I'm sure we all agree with you one hundred percent. All we have to do is convince a few billion others."

**H**e smiled with his last words.

"**N**ow I do believe it is time for another Cognac." offered Dan.

"**Y**ou've been holding out on us," commented Diego.

"**N**ot really, I've just been waiting for the right moment such as this," was Dan's answer.

"**B**efore we call it a night I might suggest that we all think about what Eric has put forth. We should continue our work as usual but consider how we may include in our findings this lost people idea. We few believe it. Now let us prove it to the world."

**M**ario's thoughts were agreed upon.

"**N**ow that I've had my say, where's the cognac."

**A**s they all relaxed sipping their favorite elixir a calm came over the surrounding jungle. The king's voice invaded the minds of all.

*"My friends, I am well pleased with what I have witnessed tonight. It is obvious that you no longer need my assistance. This group, with Eric's guidance can and will continue the work of the Chosen Ones. In your quest for the forgotten peoples do not lose sight of their standards of living. Peaceful co-existence with all, preservation of the environment and sharing of the same with and for the animals who are your brothers. True happiness is not the gain of material things at the expense of someone else. Nor is it, as I have said before, technological advances. These kind of advances do not necessarily mean happiness or advancement. Look around you right now. Are you not all happy, yet you do not have your computer or electronic world around you. You are at peace with your jungle surroundings. You love one another and co-exist according to your needs.*

*Is that not contentment.*

*I am also content. Now I will go to forever rest knowing my purpose has been fulfilled. Remember, your future is really from your past. Live in peace and harmony with all my friends. I shall sleep now forever more."*

The familiar fading echo signaled the jungle to reawaken. The songs of the animals were suddenly more beautiful. The sounds of the jungle more gentle. The night air was more comforting. The world, at least this jungle world, was now at true peace.

Not a sound could be heard from the seven researches. Peace reigned in all hearts.

Dove of Spring enfolded Eric in her arms knowing how he felt. It was not really his thing to be singled out for anything let alone the weight of the world suddenly being thrust upon him. He buried himself in her arms, holding back tears and very mixed emotions. Happy to be able to show the world the truth of history yet sad and upset at such an obligation thrust upon him.

"I am not a Chosen One," he mumbled into Violet's shoulder.

His five colleagues chose not to say anything at this moment and one by one silently drifted away to their sleeping areas.

The symphony of the night was the most beautiful he had ever heard in his three years of his Yucatan visits. Just as abruptly as his emotional breakdown he revived his positive outlook. Still in the arms of Dove of Spring he commented on the beauty of the night, its music and his love for the woman holding him.

They remained in each others arms, unmoving, engaged in the sounds of the night for uncounted minutes. Automatic mutual consent had them slowly moving to their sleeping area. The jungle put them to sleep.

# Chapter  24

Eric and Violet  were the first up and the coffee prepared as the others slowly rambled to the table one by one.

Eric was his usual old self and knew he owed an apology to his friends for his actions of last night.  He waited till all were gathered.

"I wont drag this out but I wanted to beg your indulgence for my actions of last night.  I know you are aware of my feelings, particularly this Chosen One status but there was no excuse for my behavior last night.  So if you all just forget it then we can concentrate on what we came here for.  Now what are our plans for the day."

Everyone just smiled and routinely stated the day.

"As promised Diego and I will go back to cover up the air vent," stated Dan.

Carlos mentioned that Eric should go back to the air photos and see if we can finalize the size of this newly found city.  He and Violet would work on a design for an air supply to be used at the buried pyramid. Mario and Mateo would do whatever they thought pertinent to the overall study.

Eric was internally happy with the plan for the day.  This would give him some alone time to sort out his mind.  Besides that the air photos is what he did best.

All appeared normal again.  Even Violet was happy here. Eric was happy for her. He put the king's words out of his mind, at least for now.

Scanning the high altitude photo coverage a certain shadow caught his eye.  He was surprised he had not seen this before.  He located the Topo maps of the same area which really did not show him anything. Moving some things on the table he made room for a total spread of his photos.  Finding the low altitude air coverage he aligned it up with the others.  Sure enough there was the same anomaly.  He silently berated himself for not catching this earlier.  It took a few moments to locate the stereo glasses but eventually settled himself down for a more detailed look.  Sure enough, he convinced himself, this was a man made feature.  Not just a pathway from building to building but an extension into the jungle.

"First we have to locate it.  Second, follow it.  Third, study it in detail."

"There you go, back to talking to yourself again."

Carlos's voice slightly startled Eric but seeing Violet turned his whole demeanor.

"When you talk to yourself it means you found something, which in turn means more work for the rest of us.  Will you ever give us a break ?"

"Why should I.  You have to earn your money some how," Eric smiled.

Violet glowed for Eric.

"Okay, on the serious side, what have you found ?"

"I'm not exactly sure myself yet.  But in detection a major roadway.  Long and wide.  As usual though, the jungle is protecting her own."

"Is it far ?" was Carlos's next question.

"I really don't know yet.  You came upon me just as I recognized it."

"I'll leave you alone with this lovely lady.  I will join Mario and Mateo to see if we can find certain material with which to build an air fan.  This lady is quite an engineer."

With out time for a return comment Carlos turned and walked away.

"Let me get some coffee and then you can show me your discovery.  Perhaps I can be of assistance in mapping it out.."

Eric looked at her grinning.

"Please," she followed with.

Who could resist such an offer.  I knew she actually meant it.  I know she truly wanted to learn more about aerial photography and the interpretation of it.

*"Why not?"* I thought, " It will give me more time with her and that's not a bad thing."

"Okay," I answered. "But only if you fill my coffee mug also."

"Yes master," she quipped back.

The rest of the day was quite a production. Violet being of more help than I expected. She caught on to the use of the stereo glasses immediately. We plotted what, or thought was a roadway, until we ran out of photos. The only air photo coverage we had to work with was only one of this immediate sight. Obviously we would have to wait to continue this road way study.

We then discussed the actual walking of this highway. She and I and possibly Dan could take on this chore which would leave the other four to resume their regular study of this rather large city. This of course would have to wait for tonight's debriefing.

Once satisfied with a base map and direction we agreed to take care of diner for the guys. I found it amazing what this woman could do with nothing and make it look like a sumptuous meal. We took a short romantic walk around the compound while waiting the return of the others.

At dinner I put forth my proposal of following the roadway that we think we found. There appeared to be no objections. Dan even seemed to look forward to the possible discovery walk.

I checked over my camera equipment to make sure all was in order. Dan put together the other necessities: machetes, water, power bars and of course our faithful GPS. We three made ready for an early start.

Up and on our way before seven AM. We were extra quiet so as not to wake the others. We had an easy trek for the first hour. We slowed a bit and made use of the GPS to find where we thought the start was. The next forty five minutes were frustrating and dis appointing. We could find nothing of such a roadway. We rested a bit while I double checked our hastily made map. While Dan and I pondered Violet drifted a little just studying the beauty of the environs. Disrupting the quiet we heard

"Damn !" followed by a loud "Ouch."

Dan and I rushed to the sound. Violet was sitting on the ground with an embarrassed but smiling face.

"I should look where I'm walking. I was too busy looking up at that blue, red and yellow bird, when Boom and here I am."

Naturally my first question was, "Are you alright."

"Yes thank you, only my pride got hurt."

"Is that why you're sitting on your pride?" clowned Dan.

Dan and I helped her to her feet. As we did so Violet semi shouted, "Look at that. That's what tripped me."

The three of us were staring down at a large pavement stone. It was approximately two feet square. I was immediately on my knees, digging with my fingers to clear the dirt and leaves. Dan soon followed suit exposing another flat stone.

"You guys shouldn't have all the fun." said Violet as she too was digging away.

Not a further word was spoken for the next ten minutes. Soon we were viewing an actual roadway. It had to be at least twenty feet wide with the flat stones fitted well together despite its obvious age and being subject to who knows what kind of weather conditions.

All three of us were now sitting and grinning.

"Looks like you have done it again Eric," Violet put forth. "Your Mayan friends are not going to let you look for things any more."

"This looks just like the pathway we found leading to the Golden Lady, only that was not as wide."

"You mean there are actually more man made roadways here in the jungle ?" asked Dan.

"Well they have not yet been actually mapped out but that seems to be an actuality. I have read many articles on just this very thing. Both here in Central America and also throughout South America."

"That sure does add credence to the lost civilization theory," added Violet.

"I agree, but how long is it going to take before the world will accept a change in their history?" Eric asked rhetorically.

"Who cares," said Violet in a serious voice. "We know the truth, so let's continue to pursue it. Not just for us and today's people but in respect for the Chosen Ones and Whispering Wind."

"That's my girl," smiled Eric.

Dan, ever the clown put in, "Ahhh, let's not get mushy now."

Both Eric and Violet threw a hand full of dirt at him.

"Enough rest for now," directed Eric. "Let's follow this to

who knows where."

It was not as easy to follow as they anticipated due to the jungle reclaiming what she thought was hers. Yet follow it they did. It curved both ways, went both up and down with the terrain, but was solid. Dan a bit perplexed, wondered out loud why such a beautiful highway if they didn't have or use the wheel. "At least that's what I have read."

"That appears to be the general belief," answered Eric.

"Just imagine the work that went into these roadways," put in Violet.

"We civilized people could take lessons from such minds," Eric added sarcastically.

Dan joined in. "I find this land amazing. First we have tunnels beyond imagination. Now we have major highways in a land that is hard to walk in. Who built them ? Why and how ?"

"Welcome to the world of Archeology and Anthropology." laughed Eric. "We may discover things, questionable things. We know the truth of what we see but it goes against present history. Right or wrong it never changes. Why ?"

"People are comfortable with what they think they know. The unknown frightens them, therefore why change?" were the common sense words of Dove of Spring. She added, "It is almost three in the afternoon and I already finished my power bars. When do we head back ?"

"Oh if I only had my truck now," Dan laughed.

On the serious side Eric mumbled, "This roadway could handle such a vehicle but that's another study. You're right my love, we had better start back if we hope to make it before dark."

Pictures and GPS readings recorded the trio started for camp.

They had only traversed a half mile or so when Eric signaled a halt and put his finger to his lips indicating quiet. They all froze in place. True enough they could hear sounds of movement. It appeared to be all around them. They waited silently, each looking in a different direction. Within minutes they could see men dressed in camo clothing appearing from the surrounding jungle, each brandishing a semi-automatic weapon. Eric and his two companions were totally surrounded. The three were showing surprise but not fear. A voice rang out from behind the armed men.

"Ahh!  Sen'or Dexter.  It is nice to see you again.  To tell the truth we are very happy to see you.  We have had enough conflict over the past week."

Eric showed a look of concern as he gazed at Colonel Rameriz.

"No need to be concerned my friend.  Those that we have been following are not a worry any more."

He did not go into any further detail.  Colonel Rameriz turned and gave a slight bow to Violet.

"My regards to you Egyptian Queen.  Your beauty only complements the beauty of my jungle."

This time Violet did feel herself go flush.

To cover for her Eric introduced Dan.

"I see you are also Navajo my friend.  Welcome to my home." the Colonel said as he offered his hand.

Dan took the offered hand with genuine warmth.  Rameriz picked up the conversation again.

"I told you we would always be close by to see your work was not disturbed."

Eric acknowledged this with a shake of his head as the Colonel continued.

"I see you have discovered our roadway."

Eric again showed surprise.

"No my friend, we are not spying on you.  One of my scouts came across you earlier.  That roadway you were inspecting is only one of many throughout this land."

Rameriz again detected the look of surprise in Eric.

"We are a proud people, my friend.  We have an extremely long history.  Long before the Europeans came and all but destroyed us."

Turning to Dan and Violet he added,

"As they did with your people also.  Our connection goes back many centuries."

This statement surprised the three.  Eric had no idea that the Colonel was so knowledgeable and he wanted to pursue this in minute detail.

"You already knew of this roadway ?"

"Yes Sen'or, and all the others it connects with."

Eric, Violet and Dan were excited now that information such as this could be so easily had.

"I can tell I have your extreme interest now. I did not mean to upset you Sen'or. You see for many years I did what you and your colleagues are doing for my government. Our history goes back farther then even I realized. It is a great history," he said proudly. "In researching our ancient background I came across many who would destroy it even more just for monetary gain. I then realized I was more suited for protecting my history than just researching it. Alas, here I am my friend. Making sure you are safe while you find the truth and background of my people."

Eric was stunned by this revelation.

"Do you think you could spend some time to talk with my fellow investigators. I feel you could be of invaluable help. It may even cut our time to find the final answer. I know you would be most welcome into our camp."

"You honor me Sen'or, but I have my duties and obligations."

Eric was determined. Violet could sense and feel this in her favorite man. So without any preliminaries she spoke out.

"Most honored Colonel, down deep inside I know how you feel. I myself am of the same mind set. Just to confirm your suspicions, it is true, I am a direct descendent of your Egyptian Queen even though I have been raised with my Navajo family. I am here because of that relationship. Please Sir, for the benefit and learning of both our peoples please share with us your knowledge. Our aim is not for personal accomplishment, but for enlightenment of the world. The world which has been blinded by greed and personal self satisfaction."

"I bow to your reasoning my Queen. Allow me to make the necessary military arrangements. I shall see you within the week. My time will be limited so please understand my position."

Dove of Spring answered in a positive manner.

"A mere moment would be invaluable to our research."

The Colonel now looked at Eric with a smile.

"You are a very lucky man Sen'or Dexter. This woman is not only beautiful but charming and intelligent. Who could refuse such a request. I shall see you in a few days. Adios for now."

He turned and disappeared into the greenery surrounding

them.  His armed band followed.

**D**an half laughing remarked, "Remind me never to argue with you two.  No one stands a chance against you."

"**W**hispering Wind was so right about you." Eric mumbled to himself while looking at Violet.

**T**hey continued their journey back to camp in silence.  Just before entering the archway Eric felt a disturbance in his mind.  He concentrated on this and was answered.

*"**I** knew you were the one to follow in my stead. Your success is already evident.  Love your Dove of Spring. She will always be at your side in any venture.  Go and rest now my son."*

**E**ric's mind was now clear and he smiled inwardly as the three passed through the archway to their anxiously awaiting friends.  He mentally thanked Whispering Wind but did not mention this message to anyone.

**A**ll three attacked their already prepared dinner without a word.  They were left to themselves until dinner had been totally devoured.

**O**nce the table was cleared Carlos quietly asked,

"**A**nd what have you three delinquents been up to all day while we wore ourselves out doing paper work and recordings?"

**W**ith the carefree tone having been set Eric slowly outlined their whole day.  Violet and Dan added their input when they thought necessary.  An extreme positive mood overcame the gathering.  Dan added, proudly. Dove of Spring's plea to Colonel Rameriz followed with, "I do believe this woman could charm even our jungle jaguars."

**T**he symphony of the night called everyone to sleep.

# Chapter 25

Not knowing exactly when Colonel Rameriz would join them they all stayed close to home, no more than an hours trek away from camp.  Even with their self imposed restrictions their work and study never ceased.  Progress was being made by Mateo on the stele translations with the assistance of Dan.  Together they found common glyphs to both the Navajo and Maya.  This was no longer a surprising first, what with all the global contract scrolls they were now familiar with.

Dove of Spring, of her own accord, took to the stereo glasses once again to see if she could improve on her interpretation skills.  Eric was preoccupied with photo work but was ready to assist if she so needed.

"Eric, come look at this." she asked not moving her head from the glasses.  "I found some of your air photo's of the back side of the kings tomb.  Please take a look and tell me what you see."

"What am I looking for?" he asked routinely.

"That would not be fair to either of us.  Just tell me what you see."

Eric adjusted the glasses for his eye spacing and made himself comfortable.  His first quick glance showed nothing but after a slight movement to his right he stopped and studied carefully.  Raising his head up he mumbled to himself.  "This is the high altitude run, lets find the low altitude run."

Half smiling Violet helped sort through the now better organized photos.

Still mumbling to himself Eric voiced, "Okay, now  let's see what we have."

It took less than five minutes and he zeroed in on the subject location.  He studied this for quite a while and finally asked Violet to see if this was what caught her attention.

As they switched places again Eric was smiling inwardly. *"She caught on quite fast."* he thought.

"This is exactly what I saw in the high level photos."

"Okay Miss Interpreter what are you seeing ?"

Looking quite proud she quietly answered, "A possible roadway.  Just like the one we discovered yesterday.  This one ends at the king's tomb."

"BINGO" uttered Eric rather loud.  "I guess what the good Colonel was saying is exactly correct.  There are roadways all over the Yucatan."

Violet added enthusiastically. "Roadways no longer used and have been reclaimed by nature, just as this stone structure has been swallowed."

The excitement of this discovery was openly loud. Enough to draw others' attention. Carlos was the first to join them.

"What has got you two so excited ?"

As Eric explained Violet's find the others had joined the gathering.

"Good," voiced Mario.  "Now we no longer need Eric to look at pictures and fall asleep all day.  He can be our permanent stay at home chief cook and cleanup man."

"Now you're getting nasty.  No more Cognac for you."

"Now who's getting nasty," quipped Mario in return.

Smiling, Violet corrected,

"Now children behave or I send you both to your rooms."

The light and airy mood continued for the rest of the day congratulating Violet on her success at the photos. Diego, in his ever happy mood, brought to every ones attention.

"And now we don't have to go very far to study this roadway."  As he pointed to the kings tomb.


Just before the working day actually started Colonel Rameriz appeared at the archway with two others, both armed.  Of course they were most welcomed with Mario the first to greet them.  In turn all seven expressed their pleasure for his willingness to share his history. Eric and Dove of Spring felt honored by his presence.

The colonel then explained his comrades. They were not just for protection but also were well versed in their ancient history and were exceptional in the Maya language as well as English and Spanish .

Diego was already deep in conversation with one of the associates naturally discussing the art of old.

After coffee and breakfast had been offered Carlos got right down to business questioning the recently discovered roadway. Rameriz smiled and offered what he knew. The roadway in question was more than familiar to him

"When you spend as much time as I and my men traveling this amazing land she eventually gives up some of her secrets. You may not be aware my friends but this is not the only access road. This land is criscrossed with many such avenues. I am not in possession of the actual figures, nor is anyone yet, but an educated guess would be many hundreds of miles of these byways. That would be just here in Central America. If you were to consider the total of South America we are most likely looking at many thousands of miles, all connecting both large and small cities and villages."

The research group was surprised, yet not surprised. They did believe in ancient civilizations but were not quite aware of so large a population.

"As you know our jungles have reclaimed what was theirs originally even to the point of wiping out most of the scares of the raiding Europeans. What you are finding now and studying are just a few remnants of our magnificent past.

"This may sound like a stupid question, but why so many highways when it is known that we did not even possess the wheel in ancient times ?" asked Mateo.

Colonel Rameriz thought for a minute before answering.

"In a way I believe it is obvious. The wheel did not create the need to travel. As in all peoples everywhere the need to travel was for survival originally. Hunting, food gathering, sharing of ideas this was the need. Small groups settled in distant places so naturally a pathway was made from place to place. As our peoples grew there were differences in how we lived and what we possessed. Eventually as with all peoples, rivalries began and warring factions started. Better roadways were necessary for traversing the jungle. Labor for building these avenues was shared by all. So this intricate highway system was forged over eons. Then with the influx of the European conquerors came dissent and out right decimation of our peoples."

Here Rameriz paused.

"I'm sorry my friends. Forgive me for getting carried away. My history means a lot to me and I am proud of my people. We at one time lived in harmony with the land and with each other, but that was before the white man came."

Here he paused again and turned to look directly at Dove of Spring.

"There were some, however, who came to us to share and teach as our queen here represents. Also the people who raised her as witnessed by these two among you. Their ways of life were the same. They lived in total harmony with the land and nature, sharing equally with all."

Violet felt a sudden sense of pride that her past was portrayed in such a manner.

*"Wouldn't it be wonderful if the world could live this way?"* she thought.

Eric was looking around at the gathering sensing they were all thinking the same thing as he.

"Now my friends, enough of lecturing. I came here to help in your research not to preach. I see at your map table some aerial photography. Who is the specialist and how are you using it."

Violet was proud to answer as she clung to Eric's arm.

"This is the guilty person here Colonel." she said smiling.

"In the early days of my studies we were introduced to aerial coverage. At the time it did not appear to be of much use because of the jungle canopy. We did see a few things but they were obvious to anyone."

Carlos willingly answered.

"Eric has made our quest much more successful with his interpretations of the air photo's. And recently we found out he has been acting as a mentor to this gracious lady in the same art."

Now Violet was blushing again.

"Ahh, beauty and brains. What a combination. You are a very lucky man Sen'or Dexter. But enough of that, we three must leave before dark so let us get to the nitty gritty and see how we can assist you."

All agreed and they broke into three groups. Carlos and Mario with the Colonel, while Diego and Dan met with one of the other men, leaving Eric and Violet along with Mateo with the third. This group walked to and behind the king's tomb to the newly discovered possible road. This knowledgeable soldier, whose name was Juan, was a fountain of interesting information which he freely shared. They followed the almost non - distinct roadway away from the pyramid. Juan was non stop in pointing out ground and tree features to look for. That would guarantee a roadway despite the reclamation of the jungle. He shared and answered any and all questions with what information he possessed. His enthusiasm for our research studies was genuine.

"I like and am proud of the work I do in protecting our heritage and its value. I believe it is important to safe guard our past. If I get to the point that I can no longer do my present job I would most like to join you in your research and discovery."

"And you would be most welcome," answered Eric.

After a most enlightening couple of hours they returned to camp. It was obvious that the other two groups were as successful. Just before five o'clock the Colonel and his companions bid their farewell to us all along with his respectful bow to Dove of Spring.

The camp was basically quiet while they all prepared dinner. There was much to discuss at dinner, having been enlightened by the three visitors. The feeling of a successful season already overcame the group yet they still had many weeks to go.

The serenade of the night quietly encroached signaling rest. Just before Eric and Violet kissed good night she quietly mentioned,

"The way everybody treats me I'm beginning to really feel like a queen."

She blushed at he own vanity.

"You will always be my queen," whispered Eric as he settled beneath his mosquito netting.

Violet had barely settled in her hammock when she again felt a minor tingle.

*"It is good that you recognize your destiny, my child. A queen does not necessarily have to sit on a throne. It is how you teach and look out for others that makes your reign successful. Accept your future with gratitude as I know you*

*will."*

**D**ove of Spring smiled peacefully cherishing Whispering Winds words. More so this time than ever before.

~ ~
~ ~ ~ ~ ~ ~
~ ~

**A** new day, new goals and renewed enthusiasm. The unexpected support from locals was a welcome boost to the moral of the dedicated researches. Information gained from non professionals was invaluable. Basically, it was eye opening. A source they had not tapped before, but would follow up in the future.

**T**he jungles of Central and South America had achieved very little in the way of archeological studies due to the difficulties the land presented.

**T**he mornings conversation at breakfast was based on just this problem. Carlos put forth the idea to further study the legends and oral history in the future. Not that the work of archeological and anthropological study was not important. It definitely was, but added verbal and oral history would be more enlightening to the overall study. It would give more meaning and understanding to the architecture we were uncovering.

**T**here was no doubt in any of the minds now that a lost civilization did exist. When and where and for how long was the question to be answered along with why it disappeared.

**W**hispering Wind mentioned a catastrophe. That theory has been questioned by many scholars and so called authorities, yet there appears to be more truth of this being discovered all the time.

**W**e all agreed with what Carlos put forth.

**F**or now though we should and would continue with our normal work. This, of course, was uncovering and mapping the present complex we were studying. It was not just a lone pyramid discovered by Frank Thurber. This was apparently a large city or complex that included many small outlying villages. What we have mapped already covered a vast area of the jungle, although because of the jungles reclamation, was not obvious to the naked eye. Nor was it that obvious through the aerial photo coverage.

Eric was aware of the new LIDAR system which was having success registering disturbances despite the protective reign. What would actually be done with this newly uncovered information remained to be seen. It, too, would also attack the dominant paradigm of thinking. Changing history as written is an extremely difficult thing to accomplish.

To start the new day Dan and Diego, as promised, began on the air vent system to allow study of the buried pyramid. Violet stayed in camp for any engineering assistance the college friends may need. Mateo joined me in returning to the jungle to re-bury the air vent system Violet so throughly studied. Mario and Carlos were off to who knows where to possibly follow up on the highway mapping to determine a destination. They actually planned on an overnight and carried adequate supplies to allow for that.

Mateo and I returned to base by late morning satisfied with our cover up job. Diego and Dan appeared to be making great headway under Violet's guidance. Mateo returned to his translations while I buried myself in the aerial coverage to see what I could make of the roadway finds.

The rest of the day was pretty routine. Supper was quiet and of course the absence of Mario and Carlos just added to the non-discussion evening. Though thinking back on it was welcome by all. A night of total ease and relaxation. We all purposely avoided any business conversation.

It appeared my love for the jungle symphony had become contagious. Unknowingly I had won over the whole crew. I no longer had to explain the music I was hearing. The serenade captured us all. You could almost equate each individual creatures sound with a known instrument, hence the symphony. It would match any known artist of the classical era.. Our waiting hammocks called us individually and no one refused the invitation.

Violet and Eric remained alone for a while. Words were not spoken but their love was shared nonetheless.. Sleep finally called them also.

# Chapter 26

The next morning found the lazy camp still resting in their hammocks around eight in the morning. A rather unusual event.

Carlos and Mario, in the meantime, were up, packed and ready to continue on their roadway mapping, taking note also of the tree and vegetation growth both near and away from the paving stones. They thought this may be of further assistance to Eric with his interpretation work.

The two road mappers suddenly found themselves surrounded by seven dirty looking and smelly men. Most carried weapons of different sorts. It was quite obvious who and what they were. They had come across drug cartel members before, but were able to avoid actual contact. Prepared ahead of time for such a confrontation they only spoke the local dialect of Mayan. This was, of course, a protection for them, they hoped.

One man took the lead and spoke in Spanish. Both Carlos and Mario pretended not to understand. The leader then spoke in English which again fell on deaf ears. Mario uttered a few words in the Maya tongue. One of the uninvited guests caught on somewhat but was limited in the conversational use of the Maya language.

Carlos, using basic hand gestures tried to explain they were following the roadway. Both factions were becoming frustrated, each with the other. The cartel group leader finally commanded in Spanish that they be brought along with them after their hands were tied. The other men tore apart the packs and took what they wanted. What did not appeal to them was thrown into the underbrush. They did remark disappointment though for not finding any money.

Mario suddenly recalled Eric's time on the sacrificial alter. He instantly concentrated on mentally sending a message to the others at camp.  Eric was the first to tune in followed by an alarmed Diego.  Eric returned that their call for help had been received.  Diego, without hesitation spoke up.

"I know where the Colonel's camp is and I'm on my way right now."

Eric did not try to stop him.  There was an expression of alarm on Violet's face.  Eric using a comforting tone voiced.

"Not to worry.  They will be okay. You and Dan stay here. If you need to, go to the tomb and lock the entrance.  You will be safe there."

Without waiting for a reply he and Mateo took off at a run and disappeared into the green curtain.  Dove of Spring mentally wished Eric her love and his safe return.  Of course she was concerned but not overly upset.  She knew Eric to be a resourceful man with great survival skills.  He seemed well adapted to the jungle and its hazards.

Dan looked suddenly lost and upset.  He did not like not being able to do anything to help.

"You may not think it much but you are helping by watching the camp.  It takes a worry away from the others," suggested Dove of Spring.

Dan realized she was right yet it did not relieve all his concerns.  Even Violet knew this.

Dan, not having been privy to telepathic messages before was slightly startled at hearing the voice of Whispering Wind.

*"Your concern and desire to help is admirable. I would expect nothing less of you.  Heed the words of Hunter of Stories.  All will be well.  Care for our Egyptian Queen."*

The voice in his head slowly faded away.

Violet smiled inwardly having guessed what  just took place.

Eric and Mateo knew they had a long way to go yet forged on without hesitation.  They had decided to travel on through the night if necessary.

Diego was having better luck having reached Colonel Rameriz in just over two hours.  After giving whatever information he had he rested a bit with some supplied water while Rameriz contacted some patrols via Radio.  The radio signal did not carry too far in the jungle but he always had men posted close enough to relay messages.  In less than ten minutes Carlos and Mario had been located.  The news was relayed to the Colonel, who, with quite a number of men set out immediately.  Diego followed but paid strict attention to Rameriz's orders.

By night fall the drug camp had been located and was immediately surrounded.

The Colonel approached Diego with a sly grin.

"I know of your telepathic capabilities."

Diego was stunned by the Colonel's straight forwardness.

"There is no time to waste.  Contact your friends and tell them to drop to the ground at the sound of the monkey cry."

Knowing the Colonel was serious and knew his job Diego obeyed instantly.  The Colonel and his men stealthily crept closer to the camp, weapons at the ready.  When at touching distance the monkey cry was sounded.  Carlos and Mario hit flat on the ground as gun fire rang out.  Within seven or eight seconds all was quiet again as the Colonel's men wound their way among the bodies making sure there were no survivors.

But there was one.  The cartel leader had made it to cover behind an old broken rock structure.  He was slowly backing into the cover of the trees when he heard a familiar click.  The special noise of someone pulling the hammer back on a pistol.  It was Colonel Rameriz himself.

"Going someplace Sen'or ?" he whispered.

Shock and fear crossed the face of the Colonel's target.

"Do not fear, Sen'or.  Your time is not yet up.  I suggest you cooperate and perhaps you will be spared your comrade's fate," smiled Rameriz.

Mario and Carlos were now standing with Diego more than happy to see their artist friend.

Colonel Rameriz approached the trio gently prodding the surviving leader.

"I am sorry you had to witness this scene my friends.  But my governments orders are quite firm and I know they have the backing of other governments also.  We must rid the world of this curse if we expect to live in harmony as my ancestors did."

The cartel leader just sneered at all.

"Your work is very important to you as it is to my people.

I am here to protect you so that you may have success in your research. And to that end I am having a few of my men escort you back to your camp. I wish you a safe journey. I will take this one back to my headquarters for further questioning. My government is working very hard to put and end to these drugs. Via con Dios my friends."

The two groups parted to their respective destinations.

The trip to camp was uneventful, though some additional information was received referencing the roadways. This was passed on by the accompanying escorts

Eric and Mateo intercepted the returning group about two hours away from their encampment. With all safe and sound the mood went back to happy joking again.

It was not quite dusk yet when they passed through the archway much to the relief of Violet and Dan. Violet was not ashamed to show her emotions with a big hug for all the returning men with a little extra special for Eric.

The escorts were invited to stay for the night but chose to return to their own camp.

At dinner the day's adventure was rehashed in detail. The crew realized how lucky they were to have Colonel Rameriz as more than an official guard. His friendship made the relationship more meaningful. To cap the night off Violet explained that the air flow system would be ready by mid morning unless the men decided to go drug dealing again.

"I do believe gentlemen that this will work. It is not meant for long term use, but for four to six hours at a time it should prove more than adequate."

After the excitement of the day they all chose an early trip to the hammocks. They looked forward to tomorrow being a better day.

~ ~ ~ ~ ~ ~

Breakfast mood was upbeat with all looking forward to a constructive day. The excitement of an air system for the buried pyramid had everyone anxious for an early start. Mario chose to be the one to stay in camp. This would give him time to catch up on some translation work.

Dove of Spring was the most anxious of the group looking forward to being the first to explore an unknown find. Her great expectations were quickly dashed when Eric strongly recommended that she not be the first into this unknown world. He felt the physical dangers that could be encountered may be beyond what she could handle. The rest had already been through unknown before and not without negative results.

"It is because I love you that I am recommending this."

Immediate disappointment showed on her face though deep inside she felt Eric was correct.

Carlos, at this point seconded Eric's suggestion for safety reasons. Eric then softened her disappointment with,

"Just give us about twenty minutes to check the safety of the damaged structure, then you can join us. I will stay topside with you until all is considered safe."

Violet agreed to this with a big smile, bowing to the experience of these time tested men. Still a bit disappointed she scolded herself for being selfish. After all waiting twenty minutes was not the end of the world.


Finally arriving at their destination Violet was very active in helping to set up her quickly designed air flow system. Dan volunteered to be the first to descend and check out the air supply system. For safety reasons he was harnessed with rope to allow him to be raised up in case of any danger. These safety preparations made Violet aware of how correct and considerate Eric's decision was. She no longer felt disappointed or hurt.

All things set now the group watched Dan descend on the make shift rope ladder. He stopped on what he considered solid footing and called up that everything was okay at the moment. He added that he would wander a bit to check things out.

All was quiet for close to fifteen minutes then Dan yelled up.

"Okay, I'm on my way up."

Just as his head cleared the top of the entrance hole questions were being fired at him. Sporting a big smile he pleaded to let him catch his breath.

"Okay," he finally stated. "You guys are going to like this hole in the ground. It appears to be a giant warehouse with storage of all kinds of things. Most of which I did not or could not identify."

Looking directly at Eric he further added, "You're going to do a lot of picture taking my friend."

The excitement was contagious.  Carlos was his normal calm self and  started to set rules.

"We will take turns staying topside to keep the air flow gadget working.  Violet you will be the second one down following Eric.  Diego you follow Violet and then Mateo.  I will take first shift up here with Dan.  Perhaps we can shift again in about an hour and a half.  Every one will get their chance.  Mario can follow tomorrow."

There were no arguments.  Eric collected his camera gear and started down the rope ladder.

Eric, as Dan had predicted, was stunned at what he saw.  Not wanting to look away but he returned his attention to see to the safety of Violet's descent.  The view was definitely a first for Violet.  She knew she was observing history.  History of long, long ago.  How long was yet to be determined.  They were soon joined by Diego and Mateo who were equally stunned by what presented itself.

Not a word was spoken as the four slowly separated for closer inspection of whatever attracted them.  Eric disciplined himself immediately connecting the equipment necessary and started shooting exposures in situ before anything was disturbed.  The others used to this routine allowed him his time and space.  While waiting Violet proudly commented that the air being taken in was more than satisfactory.  The others commented affirmatively also.

Eric's preliminary work finished they all spread out exploring different areas.  This internal gallery was truly a warehouse.  Mateo guessed the space to be about one hundred and fifty feet square.

Eric cautioned not to disturb things too much until a basic inventory could be made.

Dove of Spring was some how inwardly drawn to a far corner which turned out to be all things Egyptian in nature.  Possibly even pre Egypt.  Mateo was focused on a definite Chinese collection.  Diego found himself viewing art work which appeared to represent the Inuet of Siberia or Alaska or both.  Eric was taken in by all things Maya.

This section appeared to him as a library.  A collection of all things and sorted by subject matter. There was Astronomy, Mathematics, Religion, Architecture, Art and a section of mixed documents he could not read or understand.  His mind was going berserk.

*"If this is not a lost civilization, then he did not know what one was,"* he thought.

Not a word was spoken by the crew until Eric called them together again.

"I hate to spoil your fun, but I think it's best if we all go topside again. This will give Carlos and Dan a chance. Let's just call it a safety precaution but I think more fresh air unlimited will do us some good."

No dissension was given.

Once above ground and breathing deeply they began to share their finds.

"After resting we can take another hour below. This time I suggest we all write about our finds in our notebooks in as much detail as time permits. We can always come back another day. In the meantime Diego, why don't you think about a temporary cover for this treasure of knowledge."

"I have already started on just such a thing." he answered.

Eric noticed Violet was sitting quietly alone. She smiled as he approached.

"Are you alright my love ?"

"Yes, of course. It's just that I got the strangest feeling down there. What I was looking at was all Egyptian, and early Egyptian at that. It seems to be drawing me in. I had the same tingle when I first observed the Golden Lady. I felt that these inanimate things are trying to talk to me, to give me a message, to teach me."

She looked up to Eric's serious face.

"No, I'm not losing my mind. I'm perfectly okay. I find this so fascinating though. Who would have thought about encountering a lost civilization in the muddle of the jungle."

Eric smiled in answer.

"There's a lot more to this wonderful jungle than just trees. Who knows, this may have been the civilization we are all striving to be."

There was light chatter of what they all had observed. Or should I say the overall shocking things they had observed. Things they would have a hard time convincing the Archeological establishment that they even existed. Documentation was going to be extremely important. Photographic, written and witness validity would be necessary. Secrecy and protection of the site would be of utmost importance.

Carlos and Dan had returned as amazed as the others. Eric

reviewed their discussion which Carlos instantly agreed with.

The original four descended again to study in more detail and this time take notes as necessary.

Violet could not wait to return to the Egyptian area.  This time she did not hesitate to touch and actually pick up articles of interest.  One in particular caught her immediate attention.  It was a book of sorts.  She took it to be of papyrus hinged together on the top with gold lacing.  She most carefully opened the cover.  There were drawings or designs in various colors.  She instantly thought of Diego.  Symbols and or hieroglyphs covered the page unreadable to her, yet interesting nonetheless.
The second page froze her eyes.  She was viewing a symbol she was familiar with.  To her it was of Navajo origin yet it appeared as part of a word statement with Egyptian letters.

Did this denote an actual connection from thousands of years past.  She stood memorized and felt that special tingle again.  A sudden noise from another area broke her trance like state and brought her back to reality.  She called to Eric.

"Do you have the polaroid camera with you ?  If so I would like a picture of this for further study."

He complied without question knowing she would explain later.

Mateo drifted back to the Chinese collection again.  He had read and heard about a Chinese connection before but the material he was now viewing appeared to be from very early times.  He studied the collection for a while before he actually touched anything.  A tube like object caught his eye which was carefully wrapped in obvious high quality silk.  He could not resist and reached for the tube.  It was light weight and uncovered easily.  He unrolled the material, which he was not familiar with, and found himself gazing at a navigation chart.  This appeared to be in more detail than the one they found in the king's tomb.  There was a dotted line in red color starting at what would be today's Hong Kong., then going south following the west coast of North and South America.  There were also large red dots at what would be Baja, California and southern Mexico, Guatemala, and then Peru.  He guessed that apparent stops were made at each of these places.  This particular map showed Baja California as a separate island. It also indicated another continent about half way from the US west coast and Australia.  This land mass  also carried a red dot.  Mateo found this map to be extremely detailed as far as harbor, waterways and islands throughout the whole Pacific. Most of the well known islands of the South Pacific were not on this map.  He remembered his history and figured that they had not yet erupted out of the ocean yet.  At least when this map was made.  He stood staring at this striking planned document comparing in his head the maps of his own time.  This had to come from an advanced people yet this was many thousands of years old.  How did it get here ? He wondered.  This is going to topple all thinking regarding the settlement of the entire world.  But would they accept it ?

In the meantime Diego, sought out the Inuit or Siberian section again wondering exactly what was their connection with the Maya, or any part of Central and South America.  The general consensus was a slow migration across the land bridge of the Bering Sea.  But this collection of material appeared to be of an advanced people from thousands of years earlier.  *"We will have much to discuss tonight,"* he thought.

Eric was again drawn to what appeared to be Mayan or perhaps even pre Maya.  He zeroed in on some astronomical charts.  He already knew of the Maya extreme interest in the stars and the accuracy of their plotting.  This may provide more information on the alignments of the sighting areas of the top of the Golden Lady's tomb.  He purposely backed himself away from this area to at least get an overall view of the place which were divided up neatly into sections, each holding a different piece of the world.  Not really surprised but totally ignorant of who, how and why.

"If there ever was a lost civilization, this was definitely it," he mumbled to himself.

*"Do not be surprised, my son.  You have completed my quest as I knew you would.  Your ability to piece together the past will show its strength once again.  Rely on those who surround you as you have in the past.  Heed, also, the counsel of Dove of Spring.  Her deep association and relation with the past grows stronger by the day.  Do not dismiss it as folly.  Share my words with your colleagues and together you will find answers.  I look forward to your success. We will share thoughts again at a later occasion after you piece together your questions and answers.*

Whispering Winds words hung heavy in the air over Eric. At this moment his mind was floating with the clouds.  He was not upset nor was he content.  He drifted to his log home in the forest of Vermont where total peace of mind prevailed.  He listened to the songs of the birds aided by the rippling water of the brooks as the wind whistled gently through the tree tops.  A smile of peace crossed his face.

"Come back to me, my Chosen One," were the words spoken ever so softly by Dove of Spring.

Eric, ever so  slowly emerged from his respite from another world.  He did not know if it was from his sudden contentment or the loving words from his Navajo queen.  He turned to Violet, his mind suddenly of a euphoric respite   and acceptance of his Chosen One status.  Taking Dove of Spring in his arms he kissed her and said "thank you my love.  I am now complete."  She liked the attention but was confused by his words, yet dared not to break his other worldly emotion.  She settled in his arms content with life.

"Okay, you two.  We have work to do," smiled Mateo.  "Lets seal up this place and head for home.

Showing no embarrassment Eric and Violet happily agreed and headed upwards.  The men, under Diego's guidance, sealed the opening to the ancient treasure trove while Violet dismantled her air supply gadget and secreted it away.

It was unusually quiet on the way back to camp.  Physically quiet for the group, but active mentally between Eric and Violet strengthening their mutual bond.  Two people could not be more content.

~ ~ ~ ~ ~

Dinner was every man or woman for themselves.  The thought of food was almost secondary.  Discussion of the days find was foremost on every ones mind.  Each had their time to outline their discovery and impressions.  Each hung on the others words.  Speculation of the whys and wherefores was put off until the next day so that they could reflect and digest the days revealing facts.  Then they would toss around ideas of what they were witness to.

The days excitement was purposely put on hold while they just plain relaxed for the evening.  The night time symphony was suddenly interrupted by heavy rains as they rushed for cover.  The rains only lasted for thirty minutes or so but left the jungle clean with fresh foliage scents.  The serenade continued as they were hammock bound.

# Chapter  27

Yesterdays excitement took its toll on everybody.  There were no early risers this day.  Dan was the first one up and gave himself the chore of preparing coffee.

He too, was slowly being taken in with the jungles quietude and beauty.  He sat there listening to the quiet and staring at the pyramid tomb.  He wondered at the magnificent structure and thought of the lost civilization premise.

*"There had to be."* he thought to himself.  *"There are just too many wonders being discovered world wide that appear too mysterious as to their manufacture and reason for existence. The time span between them and us was also inexplicable.  Why was this topic not in the forefront of today's science and Archeological studies. Our known history only goes back so far in the calendar and that just seems to be ignored.  There appears to be no one to accept the fact that others, of a possible higher intelligence could have existed.  Particularly of our modern existence and thinking.  "WE" are the most intelligent beings on the planet. We are so brilliant and knowledgeable we invented weaponry to destroy ourselves and possibly the planet itself.  Oh yes, we are so brilliant."*

Dan looked again at the pyramid.  *"It's design was mathematically brilliant.  Its construction method was totally unknown .  The materials and stone quarried many miles away.  How were they moved, how were they lifted in place? How and who designed the interiors. The locking mechanisms were mind boggling.  Yet these more than interesting structures are found throughout the entire planet in the most unexpected places. We laugh and criticize these wonders of construction.  Perhaps the reason for that is because we can not duplicate them.  We are much too intelligent for such construction methods.  We will just continue to destroy ourselves and our planet.  After all we are civilized."*

Here Dan stopped himself, even laughing at himself.

"Look at me. I'm turning into another Eric, but then again that's not such a bad thing," He said aloud to no one or at least he thought so.

"Using my name in vain now, are we," questioned Eric.

Slightly startled Dan turned and smiled at his desert friend.

"My thoughts were all good, trust me." Dan answered.

Eric filled his mug and joined his friend in a chair looking at the tomb.

"Magnificent, isn't it. I never get tired of its beauty," Eric said softly. "It makes me wonder sometimes about our intelligence level. We don't appear to be able to answer questions about it, yet here it is in living color."

Dan smiled and laughed explaining how he just went through that whole thinking scenario himself.


One by one they were joined by the others each savoring their morning brew. Dove of Spring was the last to appear and of course was the target for harassment. She took it all in stride and fired back as much as she was given.

Eric sulked at having lost his status of being picked on. Violets kiss soon brought him back to normal.

All in all this joviality made for the start of what looked like a good day. Everyone remedied their own breakfast hungers and at last gathered at the table for their all important insight discussion. Surprisingly the table was suddenly quiet, each sort of looking at the other to start the dialogue. Eric took advantage of this pregnant pause and opened with,

"Well, I guess it's up to me to start this open forum."

All the others smiled and sat back to listen, while Diego refilled the coffee mugs.

"I did a lot of reflecting last night, as I'm sure we all did, and came up with many answers. But one answer really stood out in my mind."

He paused gauging the interest around the table.

"You gentlemen, I'm excluding  myself, Violet and Dan, are here on a specific mission and are being funded for that task. My, or should I say our, progress here is for an entirely different reason. True, they blend well together for the benefit of both our goals, but, and this is a big "BUT,"my goal and ambition should not deter you from your primary interest which , of course, is to further identify this new city and its environs. Besides, it's only fair to Frank Thurber whose dream this was. This I believe should continue to be your primary job.  I consider myself a part of your team and will continue to aid your studies in whatever way I can.  I'm sure Violet and Dan will agree with me.  At the same time I will continue my search for proof and reasons for a lost civilization as I'm sure I will still have your aid in my goal.  Gentlemen, the full disclosure of this wonderful city is our first priority."

Again Eric paused, took a deep breath, then added,

There, I'm finished sounding like a politician."

There were laughs and smiles all around, even a few hand claps.  Eric sat down as Dove of Spring warmly clasped his hand and squeezed.  Carlos spoke up next.

"You took the words right out of my mouth.  My thoughts last night were along those same unbelievable lines."

"As were mine," chimed in the three other Mayans.

A sudden but noticeable relaxation took over the group.


"Now to get down to yesterday," stated Carlos.  "I'll have to agree with all of you.  If this find doesn't hint of a lost civilization, I don't know what does.  What we all saw was absolutely unbelievable.  As we already know the establishment is not going to believe it.  It won't fit into their well planned picture of history as they tell it.  So what do we do ?"

Mario who had not seen the ancient display yet, spoke up with the obvious.

"The first step should be up to our local photographer.  This should be captured for posterity."  Then smiling and looking directly at Eric, "That project should keep him out of our hair for a while.  Then perhaps we can get some real work done without having any more new discoveries."

Eric immediately jumped up.

"I second that motion.  I'm tired of doing all the work for you guys."

"Good" joined in Mateo.  "Now we wont have to think too hard about the Lost Civilization."

They all smiled in agreement now and started on what they considered a normal back to work day.  This left just Eric, Violet and Dan at the table.

Violet still could not get over how great these men were together.  She realized it took some of the hardships of the jungle life away.

"I'm glad I brought along all that extra film."  Eric

mumbled aloud as he headed for his camera and supplys.

Violet, Dan and Eric cheerfully headed back to the buried pyramid with all three posing different scenarios of the how and why of this library in the jungle.  The one good thing they all agreed on was that the conquering Spaniards never found it.

Arriving at the chosen site Violet immediately put together her air supply unit while Dan and Eric set about uncovering the entrance. They all agreed not all three should be down inside at once.  Not only for safetys sake but to monitor the air supply workings.  Dan chose to take the first shift topside.

Once completely settled below Eric set up his camera equipment and began the photo recordings with overall shots first.  Detailed exposures would come later.

As expected Violet drifted to the Egyptian collection still fascinated by its mystical powers.  Powers over her anyway.

After a half hour or so Eric called to Violet that he was going up topside to get more film.

"Okay," she answered with out looking.  "I'll be right here."

Once above at ground level he chatted with Dan for a few minutes and finally gathered the film necessary and descended again into the pyramid depths.

"Sorry it took so long," he spoke to Violet not really looking in her direction.

Not receiving an answer Eric looked in her direction.  She was not there.  He called her name several time a little louder, yet still there was no answer.

*"She must be at the other end and didn't hear me,"* he thought to himself.  He looked around to the many different sections.  She was nowhere to be seen.  "I guess she went back up top and I didn't notice," he mumbled quietly.

Returning to his camera set up he continued his routine work. Time whizzed by and Eric decided to climb up again to some more fresh air.  Once again breathing clean air he looked around for Violet. Again she was nowhere to be seen.

"Dan," he called,  "Where did Violet go ?"

Dan, with a surprised look answered nonchalantly, "I haven't seen her. I thought she was down with you."

Eric felt a sudden panic set in.

"You mean she didn't come up here ?"

"Not that I know of, why, isn't she down in the pyramid ?"

"No, I haven't seen her since I came up to get the film."

The look of panic crossed both faces as Eric headed for the ladder. He was already calling Violet before he reached bottom. Looking about the huge space and using their flashlights in the darker spaces, no Violet was seen.

"Are you sure you didn't see her above ?" Eric questioned.

"I'm positive. I was facing the entrance all the time and she did not come up."

Dan could see Eric was getting upset and spoke calmly to settle his friend.

"I know you are right. I should know better. After all, I have been through rough situations before," Eric responded.

"This just proves how much you truly love her," smiled Dan in return.

Eric, almost embarrassed smiled in return. "Let's finish a detailed search down here and then we'll check topside again. She just can't have disappeared."

They searched thoroughly every nook and cranny of the entire space. They even found a few small alcove tunnels leading away from the main room. They proved to be dead ends and actually were not very deep. All this time they continued to call her name. Frustrated with no results they climbed the ladder and continued a search in the surrounding jungle with the same negative results.

"Why don't you try your mind reading thing," posed Dan

Admittedly feeling stupid Eric voiced, "I should have thought of that earlier.

Back at the underground entrance Eric sat down and concentrated harder than he had ever before. Everything he had in heart and soul went into his concentration effort.

"I was wondering when you were going to answer me," floated the sweet voice of Dove of Spring.

Eric, still in a slight panic mode instantly asked, "Are you alright ?"

"**I** am just fine.  There is no need to worry, but I will need your help to get out of here."

**E**ric now smiling gave a quick nod to Dan  indicating all was okay.

"**W**here are you ?"

"**I**n some sort of secret room, I'm guessing. You should see the history I'm viewing here."

"**N**ever mind that for now, where are you ?"

"**I**'m sorry love.  I forgot that part.  As you know I was at the Egyptian area studying what ever I could.  I moved some sort of sculpture.  That must have triggered something and an opening appeared to the right of where I was standing.  My curiosity got the better of me and I went through a portal to this room.  I was so mesmerized by what I saw I did not realize the portal closed.  I have tried, but not too hard I admit, but cannot find a trigger device on this side."

"**B**e patient my love.  I'll have you out in no time."

**E**ric ended the mental chat and headed for the Egyptian section.  Dan followed while Eric explained.

**N**ow standing where he remembered Violet standing he viewed the space in detail.  He finally saw what could be taken for a sculpture. He picked it up and held it. Nothing happened. Dan reached for a different item in that area yet nothing opened. Leaning in further to reach for different items Dan pushed against the shelf edge. A faint rumble was heard and sure enough the shelf structure slid to the left leaving an opening which showed a few steps down. Eric was quick to start down only to meet Violet coming up. He hugged and kissed her almost knocking them both down the steps.  Quick to catch their balance they both laughed as they continued up.  Dan greeted both with a grin.

"**Y**ou two are going to be the death of me yet," he snickered.  He also gave a big hug to Violet.

**S**till excited as if nothing happened Violet started talking about what she saw.

"**T**o me, this just proves what Whispering Wind referred to as a lost civilization.  I obviously did not have time to study everything but this definitely must be studied in detail."

"Then let's go see what has got you so excited," suggested Eric.

Dan again volunteered to stay where he was for now.

"Let's face it Eric you are the one with the magic fingers like Carlos.  So you will have to find a way to open this hidden door again.  So to be on the safe side I will stay here just in case.  I can join you later."

Eric realized he was correct so he and Violet returned to the hidden room.  Violet immediately returned to searching through the historic articles while Eric waited for the door to close so he could ply his fingertip routine to see if he could open this hideaway.  Soon the entrance disappeared.  He went to work to find the opening mechanism.  He tried every thing he knew around the doorway with no results.  He moved his finger search outwardly in both directions but could still find nothing.  Remembering the tunnel find by Violet, he began to push at different parts of the wall surrounding the opening.  As he was doing the push routine he was thankful that Dan chose what he did.  At least now  they were not locked up for good. Using his pocket flash light Eric examined the entrance way more closely.  Nothing obvious showed.  He checked both floor and ceiling.  Still nothing.

Violet, in the meantime, was oblivious to Eric's struggles.  She was more interested in the history she was seeing.  An obvious shared history.  Shared with the northern Navajo and northern Pacific China along, of course with Egyptian or even pre Egypt.  There were obvious calendar dates she could not read.

*"Perhaps Mario or Mateo would have better luck,"* she thought.

A thoroughly frustrated Eric joined her admitting his failure to open the wall.  They would have to wait for Dan's help from above.

"No matter," responded Violet excitedly.  "That will give us more time to look through this plethora of history.  Look here," she pointed.  "I believe these to be calendar dates, which of course I can not read, but just the way they are presented I believe them to be many thousands of years old."

Her statement drew Eric's immediate interest.

"If what you say is fact this place or library, if you will, absolutely proves  a lost civilization. If this is the case, they were definitely far ahead of us if we compare the approximate same length of time period.  Had they not been destroyed by a cosmic cataclysm, who knows how advanced they would have been in technology."

"In technology yes, but what about in humanism?" Violet answered sarcastically. "We are supposed to be technologically advanced but we are killing ourselves to get there. What is the good in that?"

Eric was stunned by her words but not surprised. He did not disagree with her view.


While Violet continued her detailed study of every and anything she saw Eric decided to look at the overall display. In a far back corner he noticed some scratch marks on the floor. Marks that were just as others that had hidden center pivot or sliding walls.

"Eric, come quick, come look at this. You are not going to believe what I just found."

Eric ,slightly annoyed at being disturbed, walked to the table Violet was at. Without another word she held up an odd but familiar object. An intricate combination of zig zags and curves at a slight off set angle. Eric could not believe his eyes. It was a duplicate of the key to the chest that Whispering Wind held so dear and so valued. The on containing the scroll contracts.

"I wonder if this means there was a duplicate of this treasured chest, or just the duplicate key."

"Just one more thing to prove contact of peoples world wide of many years ago." added Violet.

"To us perhaps, but will the world of today believe it ? Put that aside to show Dan and the others. I know Dan will really enjoy seeing it. Right now let us get back to what we were doing."

Happy he was now at being disturbed and the key still on his mind, Eric returned to the back corner and floor scratch marks. Violet re-buried herself in the historic items.


Allowing his fingers to work again, sure enough after a minute or so he heard the familiar rumble as the wall pivoted open. Compared to the others this one did not allow much room, but he managed to squeeze through finding himself on a small landing before descending stairs. Reaching for his pocket flashlight his arm triggered the all familiar motion sensitive lighting. The stairwell was now well lit yet he still was not able to see bottom. He hesitated and naturally the light went out.

Dove of Spring now filled his mind.

*"I can't just leave her alone, but do I want to risk taking her into*

*the unknown. Then again she will be very upset if I don't allow her."*

These thoughts filled his confused mind. Suddenly he heard his name being called. It was Violet looking for him. Following his answering voice she joined him. Her instant excitement was visible on her face and body movement.

"Let's follow these steps." she suggested quickly.

"Whoa there, love of my life. Is this what you really want to do. Jumping into the unknown without preparation ?"

Violet smiled at Eric. A knowing and loving smile.

"Is that not what you always do, my Chosen One." She emphasized the words Chosen One.

Eric could not help but laugh as he answered.

"Okay, but allow me to go first just in case."

"Of course my love. I'll follow you anywhere." she beamed.

Eric hesitated again. "Wait, perhaps we should notify Dan."

Glancing at her watch Violet answered.

"We have been down here about twenty minutes. We have plenty of time yet."

Not really wanting to but Eric agreed. Moving his arm the lighting beamed again illuminating the obviously deep stair well.

Step by step they descended. Violet was in awe of the steps and walls. How perfectly and smoothly constructed they were. How was this accomplished she wondered.

Eric was slowly taking step by step while counting them. The lighting continued. The steps appeared to go on forever while at the same time were curving round and round, both clock wise and anti clock wise. At last they touched bottom, or at least they hoped so.

Eric did some quick math in his head. There were seventy four steps and he judged a seven to nine inch spacing per step. That roughly added up to approximately a fifty foot descent. And add, if you will the depth that they started from was already about twelve feet below the jungle floor. They were now looking at a subterranean world of sixty or seventy feet underground.

Eric became concerned with air quality yet there did not appear to be any lacking of oxygen. Violet also commented on the same thing.

They stared at each other and then at the long corridor in front of them.  They were silent each questioning in their own minds what to do.  A voice they both recognized interrupted their thoughts.

*"Why do you hesitate.  This is what you both want.  Go and fulfill your destiny."*

As they were accustomed to with Atl's voiced  messages, so too Whispering Wind's voice faded away.

"That could only mean one thing." Eric mumbled.

Violet acknowledged his mumbles with her own answer.

"The lost civilization must be close at hand."

No longer hesitant they started down the long rock corridor as the lighting showed the way.

# Chapter 28

The pair, hand in hand, walked for close to fifteen minutes and Eric realized they were descending all the time yet they had no problem breathing. The lighting was superb. The farther they walked the more it appeared as daylight.

Violet was noticing the walls. Not only were they smooth and highly polished but periodically a painting or wall etching would present itself. The art work was perfection, at least to her untrained eye.

These things did not go unnoticed by Eric either. He also knew they should be considering Dan and the others but this down deep desire to know the truth, the real truth, drove him on. He kind of guessed Violet was under the same pull of discovery.

Checking his watch he realized they were walking and still descending for some twenty minutes now. He had no idea how deep into the earth they were.

Eric hesitated, thinking of turning back, but detected the sparkle in Violet's eyes.

"Why not," he thought. "It's still early yet."

They resumed their trek into the unknown. In a little under a half mile they were at their journeys end. There before them was a wall. Not just any wall. This was floor to ceiling, side to side highly polished, what looked like marble. It was designed and painted to appear as the night sky. If Eric recalled correctly this would be the view from their position in the Yucatan with a few slight changes due to a significant time lapse.

Violet had no trouble recognizing this either. Their silence reigned for countless minutes.

Dove of Spring finally broke the spell.

"Okay, Mr. Magic fingers, what do we do now ?"

Eric smiled and quietly answered.

"We count the stars. I always wanted to know how many there were."

He no sooner stopped talking when she swatted his arm.

"Here we go with the spousal abuse again," he whined.

"Stop your whining or I will really beat you," she smiled.

They both continued to study the sky before them. The first place Eric looked was the floor hoping to see scratch marks but was seriously disappointed. He moved on the corners inspecting each as close as he could. Disappointment showed again. His thoughts were interrupted by Violet's soft voice.

"Eric, come look at this. The constellation Orion. To me it stands out more so than the others. It could just be my imagination because Orion is also very special to my people."

Eric moved to her side.

"Look at the three stars of Orion's belt and then the two on the outside going in the southerly direction."

Eric moved closer zeroing in on Orion's belt as Violet continued.

"Those five stars appear to be indented slightly as opposed to the others."

Eric thought for a moment then mumbled aloud to himself.

"As if made to be touched by the fingers of one hand."

With a smile of recognition Violet quietly voiced,

"Give it a try. Your hand is bigger than mine."

Ever so slowly Eric raised his right hand and placing the first three fingers on Orion's belt he extended his thumb and little finger to the two southern extension stars. He felt the curves indents and gently pushed. He held this position for a few seconds then detected movement. It was the center pivot again but this time there was no noise. Silence still reigned.

Dove of Spring, also aware of the silence, continued her staring as the sparkle in her eyes grew along with her smile.

They were looking at what appeared to be blue sky. A shade of blue neither had ever seen before nor could describe. It seemed to go on forever.

"This is not possible." Eric thought to himself. "This can't be sky. We are almost one hundred feet below the surface."

Violet wanted to think the same yet couldn't.  She was too pre-occupied by the beauty before her.

Simultaneously they each stepped forward, paused then advanced another step.  They were now holding hands allowing the gentle squeezing to do their talking.

Without realizing it the sliding wall ever so quietly closed behind them.  Rather than disturb this newly found serenity with words they communicated with their wonderment by telepathy.

Ahead they could see hills of various shades of green that went on forever.  Their silence was only broken by the sweet song of unrecognizable birds.

"This can't be real," thought Violet to Eric.  "This is impossible.  We will awaken soon."

Eric agreed with her sentiments.  The couple took a few more steps forward towards what appeared to be the sun.  Eric dared to lool behind then only to see more of the same.  It was then he realized the door was no longer there.

"Where are we?" he thought to himself.

"I don't know," was Violet's sudden mental answer.  "But right now I don't care."

She pressed his hand harder to emphasize her feeling.  Each gave into this euphoric state.  In doing so they further advanced towards the distant hills.

*"You have fulfilled my lifelong quest," spoke Whispering Wind ever so quietly.  "I can rest now and join the ancestors in forever sleep as your king has already done.  Learn the lessons well that you are about to uncover.  The world, as it should be, will then be yours.  Teach what you will learn so that others will benefit.  You both are truly Chosen Ones by your own choice.  Do not fight or neglect your destiny.  Peace and long happiness to you both my children.  I am content now."*

There was no fading echo this time, just the sound of silence.

~ ~ ~<br>~ ~ ~ ~ ~ ~ ~<br>~ ~ ~

This silence continued as both stood there contemplating what had just transpired.  Dove of Spring, leaning into Eric's arms and with her head on his chest spoke aloud what they were both thinking.

"What do we do now ?"

"I wish I had a strong answer but I don't," Eric responded. ""I'm just a simple photographer and now suddenly it feels like the weight of the world on my shoulders."

"I share that weight with you," offered Violet.

Eric pulled her closer as they continued to view the blue sky and green hills.

They stood together for the longest time.   Eric finally spoke softly.

"I cannot do this.  At least not yet.  I have responsibilities to others, which in all good conscience, I cannot and will not ignore."

"You really are a man of true honor.  I will be at your side always," Dove of Spring whispered.

As if on signal they both did an about face walking to the pivoting door.

"I just hope I can open it again." Eric smiled.

There was no star pattern on this side of the portal.  Again the sharp eyes of  Violet picked up on a tree pattern design that had appeared to take the shape of the Orion constellation.  On closer inspection by Eric there was a definite similarity.  Gently running his finger tips over the design he did pick up minor recesses he felt would match the same pattern as the other side.  He gently pushed with all five fingers and the silent door opened.

"You have done it again my love.  Keep this up and I'll be out of a job."

They quietly exited the unknown world knowing they would be back.  Heading back to the entry point they remained silent but their minds were working overtime until an unexpected interruption.

*"I would not have expected anything less of you my*

*son.  Tending to the needs of others before your own is what makes you a Chosen One, and not unlike your spouse a better world awaits both of you.  Do what your heart tells you, the rewards will be many. Not monitory gains but an everlasting peace in harmony with those who had gone before.  You are part of the lost civilization."*


Dove of Spring was also privy to the words of Whispering Wind.  Not exactly understanding their full meaning she moved closer to Eric holding his hand even tighter.

They remained silent on their return to the real world which appeared to take longer than expected.  Back at what they called the library level they became themselves again.  They met Dan who had just come down from above.

"I just came down to caution the both of you.  I really feel you should get some fresh air to breath.  I'm not faulting your vent system Violet, but let's face it fresh air never hurt anyone."

Both Violet and Eric looked at each other and smiled, almost to the point of laughing.  Dan, looking confused asked.

"What's so funny ?"

"Nothing special," replied Eric.  "We will explain everything at dinner for all to hear."

"Oh !  So I guess you found something new.  Okay I'll be patient."


~ ~ ~ ~ ~ ~


Dinner was quick and easy with light chatter.  It finally reached the point of silence with five pair of eyes staring at Eric and Violet. Mario was the voice of the five.

"Well !"

There was no immediate answer.  He followed with,

"What's the big secret you're keeping ?"

With smiles from both he and Violet Eric started.

"I don't know where to begin.  This is more than any of us expected.  I don't know if I believe any of this myself."

All eyes were going from Eric to Violet and back again not gaining any insight from either.

Dove of Spring, feeling an unknown heart movement suddenly decided to break the impasse.

"Not knowing how to explain our last encounter with the unknown, I will just use the words as they come out. Please bear with us. It will seem absolutely unbelievable."

Here she took a deep breath looking at everyone.

"As you all know Eric, he could not stand still. I was studying some unknown histories on one of the tables and his curiosity got the better of him as he wandered away from me. The next thing we knew we were following descending steps away from the history room. All told Eric calculated that we were now about sixty or so feet below the surface. As exciting as this was it was no preparation for what was to come next. The usual wall presented itself with the constellation Orion out standing, to us anyway, this , of course was the key. The key to open the wall. Now gentlemen this is where euphoria set in."

Violet purposely paused here searching all five faces. The answer she expected was there. All five grew into the undisputed fact of a lost civilization.

Her head now filled again with the first visions of the new blue sky that went on forever. She stuttered her words realizing she could no longer communicate coherently. Embarrassed, yet not, she outwardly turned to Eric. He lovingly squeezed her hand and continued her story starting with the new blue sky. How they were transfixed by the beauty before them, how they took slow steps forward to what appeared to be the sun. Eric restated his words to Violet regarding his responsibilities to others at this time. They at last retraced their steps returning here to camp.

"That truly is an unbelievable saga," voiced Carlos immediately.

He noticed a reaction to his words by both Eric and Violet and quickly threw up his hands.

"But, I believe every word spoken. I truly feel this is something we all should see together and it should be the first thing tomorrow. Right now I'm sure our minds are going round a mile a minute. I know mine is. We must see this and it must be as soon as possible."

Without hesitation all agreed. Dove of Spring breathed a special relief.

Mario, quietly but authoritatively spoke up.

"Why should we be surprised at something like this. For

years we have been reading of surprise finds of peoples far more advanced then the average population on this planet.  We, ourselves, or at least our ancestors, once held such a distinction.  Our astronomy, mathematics, construction and farming once outdid the rest of the planet.  Yet for unknown reasons fell back to only survival methods.  Why ?  The Egyptians also at one time held sway.  Peoples, even forerunners to Egyptian civilization, once were far more advanced than their neighbors.  So why not find remnants of such advanced people right here.  I personally think the cause of their disappearance is what we should be investigating.  Our welcome friend Whispering Wind obviously had some insight into one of these disappearances, as did our king.  The how and why of this remarkable fact is what we should be looking into."

Here he hesitated putting on a smile.

"I haven't done that much speechifying since college.  I didn't mean to bore you but I believe I made my point."

Diego, to lighten the moment added,

"We didn't even know you could read."

With a broad smile Eric answered all.

"Good, then it's decided.  We all visit this lost world to see what we can determine.  Mainly, I guess, would be why it disappeared, although I think we all agree on the why s already.  Gentlemen, be prepared to look upon beauty as you have never seen before.."

Eric's finishing statement put a glow on Dove of Spring that no one had ever seen.  The air of the camp was light for the balance of the evening in anticipation of the morrow.  Even the annoying monkeys appeared in a happy go lucky mood.

# Chapter   29

The king's pyramid tomb double checked for security and camp cleaned up of all inviting tid bits the seven friends headed out the archway to the buried pyramid.

The trail, by now having been well used, made their travel non confrontational.

The usual levity took place leaving no one free from attack. Violet gave as good as was received. This was truly now a well knit group, each with their own expertise yet all worked for one goal. Today's trek might just be the culmination of that ambition.

Arrival at the almost buried pyramid was most anti climatic. All were ready for the big revelation. The air vent system was triple checked for soundness and at the behest of Carlos various rocks ans small logs were collected to hold open all doors. Not everyone was adept at the finger movements as he and Eric. This of course, was just a precautionary measure.

~ ~ ~ ~ ~ ~

The moment had arrived. One by one they descended the rope ladder, the first step to who knows where. Eric led the way to the corner and the very hidden wall. Once the door was opened they tested it a few times to assure it stayed open. They were all pleased with Carlos's suggestion for this safety escape.

Eric and Violet now took the lead allowing the self lighting to mark their way. Mario and Mateo followed Eric's example and mentally kept track of their descent and with all three coming within a few feet of a final distance below surface.

Here, with inner excitement building, Violet pointed out the Orion constellation they used as the door release. Carlos, of course studied it for a moment before the opening was attempted.

"You may have the honor my friend," Eric voiced as he stepped aside closer to Violet. Without hesitation Carlos put all five fingers to work. After a few hour long seconds there was movement. Silence was maintained, but there was movement. Everyone immediately turned to using the rocks and small logs to block the door from permanently closing. The corridor lighting maintained its motion detection illumination but there was only blackness ahead.

There was no blue sky, there was no sun, there were no distant mountains.

Violet could feel herself start to tremble her mind going wild.

"This can't be," she silently screamed to herself. "Am I going crazy ?"

Eric noticed her reaction and quickly moved to her side pulling her to him.

"Not to worry love, and no you not going crazy." Then with a smile added, "Welcome to the jungle of the unknown."

By now Dan, Diego and Mateo had already taken a few steps past the opening.

Suddenly but slowly there was light. Blue light, blue sky light. It was the blue Violet could not describe. Then there was the same illumination of the distant forever green mountains.

All seven were locked in place by the spectacle before them. One by one they each stepped forward a step at a time. The beauty of nature none had ever witnessed before surrounded them. This was all followed slowly by the sounds of nature, again a nature they had never heard before. The birds, the echo of the wind in the distant treetops, the ripple of the brook water on the various colored stones. The distant call of the larger animals. Not a call of fear but of welcome. Welcome and share. We are all one with the earth.

This sentiment filled and was shared by all seven hearts. This dedication to the planet was solidified in those few seconds by all individually unaware that all were pledging the same.

Dove of Spring appeared to be internally moved more so, her life having been lived with nature more than the others.

She moved forward slowly observing every detail possible. The peace being displayed was unlike anything of her past.

"This truly is a lost Civilization," she whispered to no one.

She stopped her forward motion filling herself with this unbelievable world. Would this ever again be possible to achieve again what with the planets present condition of turmoil.

Violet chose to continue her small steps into the past, or was it the future? She did not know or care. Her whole being was at total peace. She was one with the world, nay with the universe and all its flora and fauna. She was the world, as were all creatures.

Violet dared more steps into euphoria, her mind and heart savoring feelings never known before.

One by one the others were captured by the same elation. Perhaps not to the same degree as Dove of Spring but being taken under its spell nonetheless. No one appeared aware of the other. They had each succumbed to the mysterious, familiar yet unknown environment. The deeper they ventured into this strange beauty the more familiar it became. They were all committed now and they knew it. The more they wandered the more they spread apart, each lost in this ideal world.

Diego, of course, ever the artist, could not get over the perfection of color and the sun being the true light of color. The world he was familiar with and its color now took a back seat to this perfection.

Minutes turned into many hours but as in real life all good things must end. This perfection was at its end when our guests realized that's exactly what they were. Guests. Guests in a controlled environment. A controlled environment beyond their control. Their individual wanderings brought them back to the make believe beginning.

Silence prevailed though each knew they must leave this world of make believe. The logs and rocks were removed from blocking the door and the illuminated hallway greeted them with out fan fare. Questionable glances were passed back and forth without words. Silence seemed to be preferred as they headed back to the main section of the pyramid. One by one they routinely exited till all were again breathing the jungle air freely.

Diego was the first to speak. Not intentionally trying to be funny but because of what they just witnessed his statement broke the silent spell.

"**I**'ll never be able to match those colors in my art work."

**E**veryone started laughing.

"**I** needed that.," followed Mario.

"**W**hat's so funny?" asked a confused Diego.

**C**arlos, still laughing himself tried to explain to the innocent Diego.

"**W**e all just went through an almost religious experience and all you can think of is different colors."

**S**miles were all around of course.  Quick with a comeback, Diego answered

"**T**hat just shows you how pure my intentions are."

**T**his did lighten the mood.  A sense of normalcy appeared tp return to all.

**A** light discussion ensued on the return to camp.  They would all wait until supper for the in depth review of this Disney World they just witnessed, as Eric referred to it.

**V**iolet stayed close to Eric thanking him for bringing her to this remarkable jungle.

# Chapter  30

Dinner was a pick and choose yourself night without much fussing.  Mario appointed himself lead to start the discussion.

"What we all just witnessed was, to me anyway,  a most unbelievable moment.  Here we all work at and are used to discovering things of the past, expected things with the occasional unexpected."

Here he paused looking directly at Eric.  By now both wore a small grin.

"Today's show defies logic.  How?  Why?  And of all places in the world, why here ?"

Eric raised his hand and started speaking instantly.

"After all that has occurred this last month or so I believe in the words of Whispering Wind.  A lost civilization.  A lost civilization that once covered the globe.  And yes was destroyed by an unavoidable cataclysm.  To answer your question of "Why here?" could it be that this advanced culture started here.  We already know of the many advancements of the Maya and perhaps the culture preceding them.  We all know of the reigning paradigm that the start of civilization was in Africa and spread out from there.  We also know that more and more question this everyday.  Could this lost civilization be the start of technology on this planet?"

Mario was about to answer Eric when Carlos chimed in rather forcefully.

"I agree."

All eyes turned to Carlos.  Now smiling Carlos continued more softly.

"It just makes sense.  We are in a jungle setting right now.  People say an inhospitable jungle.  Yet everyday we uncover settlements.  Not just farming communities but structured settlements once ruled by a government framework.  We have discovered Astronomy, Mathematics, Art and construction methods still not duplicated today. We have proof beyond doubt of contact with Egypt, China, the Navajo and North Americans and of course various peoples of Europe. This Disneyland that Eric refers to could be just that. As world contacts are made and representatives visit, what better way to show off this advancement than a type of amusement park."

"Aren't you really stretching your imagination now ?" put in Mateo.

"I don't think so." volunteered Violet's soft voice. "What better way to learn than to have fun doing it. Is that not what we do with our children?"

Her logic sounded simple to everyone.

Carlos picked up again, "What better way is there to demonstrate advanced technology than by keeping it simple."

"So what you really are suggesting is that, here at this site, was the home of the Lost Civilization ?" questioned Mateo.

"Well, if not the home the possible starting place. Look around you. The size of this settlement. And thanks to Eric, look at all the hidden tunnels, the hidden art, the hidden scrolls, the hidden rooms. Hiding things from the Spanish, yes, but not to this degree. This would have been a lot of building and digging just to hide gold over a short period of time."

"If I may quietly interject something," said Dan. Personally I think what Carlos is presenting has merit. We already have beyond a doubt proof of early world contact no matter what the establishment says. We know of early Chinese advances in some things. The same goes for the early Egyptians. We could also throw in the early Sumerians and Minoens."

"They were all early technological peoples. Perhaps each had their own Disneyland so to speak. Because of the world wide Archeology of today we know of such places throughout the globe. Two and two were just never put together before. We are all part of this lost civilization. We now have to catch up to where they were."

Silence ruled now. At least with the humans. The ever present monkeys resumed their chatter at a slightly higher decibel level as if they understood what was being discussed. The other jungle noise joined in. The seven gazed at each other while listening to the monkey dialog.

Each realized in their mind that there was no more to be said tonight. This fact was automatically accepted by all. The subject was dropped like a rock.  Clean up ensued.  The monkey chatter ceased as quickly allowing the symphony of the night to slowly fill the air.  Each in their own unexpressed way of silence made for their rest area. While Eric and Violet, hand in hand, went for a short walk.

-235-

# Chapter  31

All, except for Dove of Spring were up early.  The coffee was being nursed with only two seated and the other four ambling about. Other than the usual "Good mornings" no words were exchanged. Yesterdays surprise was still paramount in their thoughts.  Violet quietly approached.

"Gentlemen",  and I use that term guardedly," she added with a smile. "Please be seated.  I have something to say that I feel is very important to all of you.  And to myself, I guess."

Violets face was non expressive as she made eye contact with each one.

"Humor me on this one please, then I promise you I'll keep my mouth shut."

The six men refilled their coffee mugs and found their favorite seat at the table.  All was quiet.

Violet remained standing and with the air of her tribal elder position addressed the group.

"Yesterdays experience was a bit shocking to us all and understandably so.  This lost civilization thing has literally opened up a whole new world to us.  The word "US" is the key to my whole train of thought this morning.  The "US" or we with perhaps some scattered others through out the globe have found or discovered a lost world. Right here in our own world.  A world, by the way, obviously much more advanced then we are.  The lost world or civilization, what ever you choose to call it, is or could be a boon to our present knowledge."

Here she paused letting he words settle.

"Or it could be a disaster to our present way of living."

She paused again, this time watching her words being absorbed.  She knew at this point that she really had their interest.  Smiling now she resumed control.

"This is all well and good, and I , like the rest of you, want to dive right in and learn as much as I can as fast as I can. Personally, after giving it much thought all night long, that would be the wrong path to take. We can not change the past. Yes, perhaps learn from it, but this past is too far past. It is not just a year or ten years ago or even a century ago. It is so long ago that we know nothing about it. Yes, we recognize certain things but that is all. And just recognizing them does not make them ours. Our world is here and now. Backwards we may be by comparison but this is our only world. For good or bad, we made it this way. Some of it by chance, some of it not by chance. It doesn't matter which way you think, this is our only world."

She lingered again taking a few deep breaths.

"At this point in time we should not let this intriguing new world keep us from our true and real mission. That mission is to develop our own present world into something better,  that better, is gaining knowledge of those who came before us. Those who came before us is exactly why you are in this jungle today. We are studying our direct connection to those who have gone before us, as did they. That is and will be our real connection to this lost civilization. Our job is here and now, not millennia past, as it will be for our progeny. We are being funded to uncover this beautiful city and its people, and to learn from them And that is what we must do. I am also positive it will reveal things long lost which will educate us all whether we realize it or not. Dream we can and dream we must. Preserving dreams is education. That has been handed down by our elders for ever and will continue to be. Our past is our education to the future. We must learn from it or cease existence. We must continue our work here at this settlement so that we can move on and I'm sure this newly discovered lost civilization will aid us to attain that goal.

Gentlemen, our work is here and now. Our future is here and now.

Dove of Spring was silent again. A lingering air of silence she broke herself with a smile.

"Now can I have my mug of coffee ?"

All six men moved immediately to the coffee pot to comply with her wish.

Settled again at the table with all eyes on Violet Mario voiced the obvious.

"Well my friends, it appears we now have a new "Task

Master" so I suppose we should get back to the work we do best." This, of course, was said with a big smile, Mario holding eye contact with Violet.

Diego being his usual self added,

"What work, we don't do any work. All we really do is keep looking at all the things Eric keeps finding.

Eric answered instantly, "Why is it always my turn in the box ?"

Violet, now in a less authoritative mood spoke again.

"Gentlemen, I hope I didn't over step my bounds. Those were just my own thoughts on which I pondered all night."

Carlos assured her she was not out of bounds with her opinion.

"I had similar thoughts my self. I do believe you are right on the mark."

Mateo broke the serious mood with,

"Breakfast anyone ?"

~ ~ ~ ~ ~ ~

While the breakfast table was being set Eric took Violet aside.

"You were wonderful this morning. It was something we were all probably thinking about but hearing it so wonderfully put really brought the message home. I think I'll keep you around. You are good for us all."

Violet answered with a half smile. "I was going to swat you for that but there are too many witnesses."

Hand in hand they returned to the breakfast table.

"I know I'm new here but just a suggestion for today." volunteered Dan. "Let the loving couple spend the day cataloguing and photographing the history room, than we can seal it up again with Diego's magic until needed down the road."

"Good idea," replied Carlos. "Then after that they can finish the same job on the treasure Room of the kings pyramid."

Mario joined in with, "Great, then we will be getting the best of both worlds and I mean the old and new."

They all agreed with the working plan.

Breakfast over they all went  their separate ways to finish the job they came to do.

At the sunken Pyramid Violet and Eric worked non stop almost silently.  Their goal was to finish this in one day if possible.  Eric already estimated the kings treasure room would be at least three days.

The final recording work being done by the others was also going smoothly.  Dan made himself available to all of them besides doing camp duty.  He also was beginning to love the jungle as Eric did.  Teaching the young Navajo was rewarding but there was something extra special about this place.  Perhaps they will let him come back next season.

Almost unnoticeable the afternoon was growing darker.  Dan appeared to be smelling rain in the air.  Having a little time before the others returned he set up a few extra canopy's as protection from the rain just in case.  Dinner preparations would be next.

One by one the groups came back slightly damp from dodging small showers.  Eric and Violet were the last to show.  Both were drenched to the skin with Violet laughing like a child loving every drop of rain.  Eric, just as wet but not quite as jolly explained they spent some time securing and rain proofing the pyramid entrance as best they could.

Dove of Spring was still acting like a child loving every drop of rain.  Of course this made her the brunt of jokes for the rest of the evening

The guys thanked Dan for the extra effort in rain proofing the camp.  Finishing touches were put on from past experience before dinner.

Dinner itself was a big surprise.  Besides all of the other things Dan got involved in he found time for some fishing.  The surprise feast was welcome.

The evening was a lazy one with everyone going to bed early.

An early rise showed us that the rain had stopped, at least for now but we knew this was only the beginning.  It did at least lower the temperature somewhat.  It was now just below one hundred degrees.  Everyone was aware of their assignments with early starts by all.

Violet was fascinated to again be in the kings tomb.  She was now feeling what we all felt on our first detailed visit.  The cre`me de la cre`me was when I opened the door to the treasury as we called it.  As we stepped in the lighting came on showing the treasures of the world.  I secured the door from closing on us as I described what we found upon our first entry.

Violet was frozen in place as she gazed upon aisle after aisle, stack after stack of worldly treasures.  Even at first glance it was easy to see this rare collection was from the global community.  How was this collection ever amassed in the first place.  Eric could see Violet's mind working and looking for answers.

"We all did the same path of thinking, yet we still have no answer.  This could probably be part of that lost civilization thing."

Dove of Spring finally returning to normal jokingly expressed her feelings.

"Well Mr. Photographer, if you expect to finish this job today I thing you should get started."

They laughed with each other as they looked over the repository.  This fifty foot plus or minus diameter room with floor to ceiling shelving held the worlds ransom in unique treasures.

Violet, still in awe of the whole room began to view certain pieces in more detail while taking notes.  I set up my tripod and a small flat working space but hesitation tugged at my thoughts.  Looking around, as I did many times before, I started mumbling out loud.  I was answered by Violets hesitant "What did you say ?"

Speaking more clearly now I joined her at a shelf with gold cups.

"This is just not going to work.  This much inventory is going to take at least two weeks, perhaps more.  And now with the rains starting there just won't be enough time.  The others will still need help with outside work."

"You're the rain expert and I agree with your estimate.  May I make a suggestion ?"

She did not wait for an answer.

"Let's choose one item from each group for detailed work ans an overall picture of the group it belongs to.  I know that will still take some time but I estimate a day or a day and a half."

Eric was smiling now.

"As usual, you are right on the money again my love.  So let's get to work.  We will explain all tonight to the others."

We worked non stop for the better part of the day with our shortened inventory.  The treasured pieces we came across were amazing.  They were definitely from around the globe.  The how of it was still a mystery.  By late afternoon we closed up the treasure room looking forward to supper and relaxation.  As we neared the tomb entrance we realized the rains had been active all day.

"Try and contain yourself today."

I laughed the words to Violet.

"Party pooper," she laughed back.

We ran all the way back to the camp area drenched to the skin.  I explained our decision about the treasure room inventory to the others acceptance.  The rains were endless for the next two days.  Even the usual jungle sounds were absent.  Journal entries and map updates were about all that took place.  Dove of Spring amused herself somewhat with the aerial photos and stereo glasses.  She actually did quite well.

After much boring discussion it was decided we end this seasons work.  We would wait for the rains to subside somewhat and then make the long trek to the river.  The boatmen should be there soon anyway.

It was decided that a lot of our equipment be left here.  Some would be under the water proof tarps while the more valuable things we would lock away in the tomb.  We would pass on the information to Colonel Ramirez..

No one really wanted to quit the season but better sense prevailed with the realization that we all had serious obligations back in the states.  At least our Mayan friends did.  Dove of Spring and I were totally undecided as to where do we go from here.

# Chapter   32

The rains let up enough for us to try for the river and for home.  We said a final farewell to our monkey friends and sadly left our new settlement.

It was rough going because of the new muddy jungle.  We knew the path well enough and our load was light compared to when we arrived.  The closer we got to the river the more difficult the journey.  The rain actually helped redesign the landscape.

Violet took the difficulties in stride.  She had not once complained of any hardship.

After three long and arduous days we reached the river.  Our smiling boatmen greeted us cheerfully.  They even surprised us with fresh fruit and cold beer.  An overnight camp had already been prepared.  The overnight relaxation was more than welcomed along with the fruit and beer.  Violet being the trooper she was took the whole thing in stride.  She also had two beers.

Finally arriving back at Oxtec we had another thoroughly relaxing evening.  It was welcome after a few months in the jungle.  We met with Colonel Ramirez and he reconfirmed his ever vigilance of the king's tomb and surrounding new found city. He wished us well on our return trip and said he looked forward to next season.

From Oxtec, to Mexico City to Arizona to home.  Dove of Spring, Lone Buffalo and Hunter of Stories were welcomed almost as heros.  The only one missing to welcome us was Whispering Wind, though he did leave notes for all three.

~ ~ ~ ~ ~ ~

Dove of Spring had mixed emotions about being home. The excitement and challenge of the unknown jungle stirred her inner person more than she anticipated. She and Eric spent a very quiet two days absolutely alone. Dan instantly went back to his young classes, his real life's true love.

Catching up on things kept both Eric and Violet occupied but happy. Almost a week went by before they remembered the notes left by Whispering Wind. Relaxing after an early dinner they sat together with the large brown envelope well sealed. Carefully cutting the seal Eric emptied its contents. There were five letter sized envelopes inside, marked with the three names. Two marked Teller of Stories, one for Dove of Spring, one for Lone Buffalo. The last was marked for all three. Of the two marked for Eric, they were numbered one and two.

They both just sat there in silence looking at the envelopes and each other, fond memories of Whispering Wind running through their minds. Dan's envelope was returned to the larger one and put aside.

Violet separated herself some what from Eric and broke the seal on her envelope. She hesitated but finally reached for the contents opening it slowly. It was written in English with a few Navajo words mixed in.

To my Navajo Daughter.

I have watched you since you were but a blossom on the wind. You have always been true to yourself and your people. Both peoples. Your heritage, both, is a proud one, which you should never hide. You should always honor that heritage as it honors you. Your chosen life's mate also carries that honor. Be true to him as I know he will be to you. What soon lies ahead of you is for the taking. That is your decision as it is his. Your decisions, what ever it may be is the correct one. It will be correct for the both of you. Do not attempt to out guess your destiny. It is, as for all people, inevitable. Only you can make your forever happiness.

My love is with you my child and always will be. May the Holy Spirit bless both of you always.

His mark *WW* was at the bottom of the page.

**W**ith a single tear in her eye Dove of Spring crushed the letter to her bosom, moved closer to Eric and lightly kissed him on the cheek and whispered, "Whispering Wind will always be with us."

**T**hey remained silent for many minutes with Violet's head resting on Eric's shoulder.

**"W**ell guess I should open the envelope," Eric sort of mumbled not really wanting to. Violet raised her head, kissed him and moved away. Eric hesitated reaching for the envelope numbered one. Breaking the seal he removed the paper inside.

Now that you are reading this I know that you have achieved what I did not. As I have said before, you have fulfilled my lifelong quest.

But you are not finished yet. There is definitely one more quest you must complete to really see the whole picture. This quest is for you and Dove of Spring. Do not hesitate. Your destiny awaits you both. Did I not say your mate would be of great assistance. To further verify both your feelings of the absolute truth you will follow my last request and instructions. They will not lead you astray but to the forever truth. You will find the lost civilization. Not just the one in your mind but the one of reality and truth. Do not run from your destiny. Complete my quest.

As I have already told Dove of Spring, only you can make your forever happiness. The blessings of the Great Spirit I

**F**inished reading he sat staring at the paper and with an unconscious reaction he wrinkled it up in his hand.  Violet was a bit disturbed by this but chose not to say anything at this time.  He returned the wrinkled paper to its own wrapping and put it aside.  Violet was curious about its content but dared not ask.

**N**ow shaking his head as if to wake himself up Eric reached for the second envelope.

**"I** wonder what he has in store for us now," he said in a normal tone.  This was a few pages which contained some drawings also.  The opening was addressed to both and also included Dan.  Eric did a quick scan of all the pages.  Confusion and disturbance again showing on his face.

**"I** think I need a cup of coffee."

**A**s he got up he handed the pages to Violet.  She started reading as Eric headed for the kitchen.

**V**iolet read a few lines then slowly put the papers aside.  She continued to sit alone not even thinking of anything special.  Eric still had not returned.  Ten minutes, fifteen minutes, still no Eric.  Concerned now Violet headed for the kitchen.  No Eric.  Noticing the back door was open she looked outside.  She spotted Eric sitting under the few trees in the back yard sipping at his thick syrupy coffee.  Pouring herself a cup of the black syrup she joined him under the trees.

Once seated she spoke quietly yet in an upbeat voice.

"I'm afraid this is about as close as we get to a jungle around here."

Eric looked at her and laughed.

**"I** was just thinking the same thing," he answered with a smile.

**V**iolet was glad of the smile.  To her it meant they could discuss things openly.  She decided to lay it right on the line and get everything out in the open.

**"T**he "Chosen One" thing has got you down again. Perhaps if we talk about it I could help.  Please let me help.  After all I am your chosen one."

She smiled with her last part.  Eric also smiled and reached out and took her hand.

"And you always will be."

Violet then added,

"Let's not keep secrets from each other."

She said this looking directly at Eric.  Then added with a smile, "Except, of course all my other boyfriends."

Eric picked right up on this and joined with,

"Okay, we'll introduce them to all my other girl friends and then it will be just you and I."

"I can go with that plan," Violet answered laughing.

"Okay, big guy, let's have it.  I'm all ears."


Now feeling totally relaxed Eric agreed that she was correct.  He openly reviewed with her the last few years.  Meeting the king, discussions about being a chosen one, and eventually receiving the same input from Whispering Wind.  How both he and the king kept reviewing with me of their past history and lost civilizations and how I also am a chosen one.

Eric surprised himself at not getting upset while discussing this with Dove of Spring.

*"I guess she really is good for me,"* he thought.

He paused for a few seconds then looking directly at Violet asked quietly, "Why Me ?"

Violet thought for a moment then cautioned, "Now don't take this the wrong way but could it be because you came from the same mold as they ?"

Eric looked at her but did not utter a word.

Violet continued;

"You are sincere, honest, truthful, understanding and mainly you care.  You care about everything and every body.  And you care deeply.  Sometimes to the point of forgetting yourself.  You are intelligent and can think beyond where most people stop.  You accept what most others do not.  You do not let challenges defeat you."

Here she paused gazing at his serious face.

Now with a big smile, almost a laugh, she added, "And

you're all mine."

Eric genuinely smiled at this. "Of that I'm glad." He was feeling better now. "Perhaps you can help me understand how I even got involved in this in the first place."

"From what I understand of this whole thing, from what you have told me so far, it was your relationship with the king. He saw in you what I just outlined. Sometimes I think it's just you who does not want to accept who you really are. It's not like they are expecting you to rule the world. I think they both were wanting you to carry forward on their work of explaining how the world can be. And, if my opinion means anything, I think they chose the right person."

Eric started to speak but Violet shushed him with her finger to his lips.

"I just want to add that just because they chose you that does not mean you have to follow what they said. You have a great mind, my darling, use it how you want to. I will always be at your side. Now , you think about what I have said while I refill our cold coffees."

She took his cup and walked to the house.

Dove of Spring did the best she could in reading Eric's mood returning with full coffee cups. She was pleased with her interpretations.

"Now, Mr. Photographer do we read Whispering Winds letter or do we go and look for more straight lines in the desert sand ?"

"I would not want to disappoint Whispering or Dan for that matter, so we will read the letter and the decide. In the mean time, What's for dinner ?"

"You're taking me out for dinner. I'm too tired to cook after all that talking. But first let's just sit and enjoy our three tree jungle and coffee."

# Chapter 33

Dinner out was the perfect relaxation for Eric. Violet's insightful words finally did register and Eric became Eric again. The change was obvious to Violet which pleased her. She did not like to see her chosen one in his internal turmoil.

Dan phoned shortly after nine A M asking to come over. He has the day free because of outside assignments he had the kids working on. Dove of Spring answered that they would more than welcome his company. The time was set for ten thirty. This would give Eric and Violet both, time to review Whispering Winds papers.

Eric, to Violets pleasure, reviewed the papers with a whole different attitude than yesterday. As he read them he willingly passed them on to Violet.

Basically the message or request was simple. Please follow through what Whispering Wind did not get to finish. It would require further searching back to where they first started. The house they nearly destroyed.

Whispering Wind's second request was more in line with Dove of Springs forte`.

Whispering Wind's hogan was not to be destroyed but turned into an organized museum. It was his wish that the history it contained should be preserved, especially for all Navajo to see. Lone Buffalo was to assist Violet in this endeavor and make it part of the class teachings. Teller of Stories was also to be part of the museum.

Whispering Wind wrote that because of his uncanny knack for finding lost or buried history he should be given free reign in the hogan. (by the way, there is still some lemon drink in the cooler.)

Dove of Spring you will assist him. Your history is part of mine.

This caught Violet's attention instantly. Eric saw her

sudden reaction and was pleased for her.

Dan was right on time with his usual happy attitude. He received Whispering Winds envelope which he read directly. Smiling he said.

"Looks like we are in the search business again."

Eric then passed on the multi page list of Whispering Winds wishes.

"Count me in with a few reservations."

Eric and Violet questioned with their eyes.

"My class will have to come first. Other than that I'm all yours. I wonder what he means by referencing the old house we sort of wrecked ?"

"I guess we will find out soon enough," chided Violet. "This is almost as exciting as the jungle. I hope we are not disappointed."

Eric was not surprised at Violet's enthusiasm.

"Okay," interrupted Eric. "First things first. Dan work out your schedule and let us know of your free time. You my love," he added with a smile, "See to your tribal elders business and calculate your free time."

"And you ?" questioned Violet.

"I have to make a trip to the pet store and,"

Violet continued for him with a broad grin."

"And get some more bribery treats. I'll go with you. I would love to see Mr. Blue again."

"For your information, my kids told me that he is still living at the desert pyramid." Dan added.

This brought quiet a smile to Eric.

The three parted each going their separate ways.


It was almost a week before the three actually got together. They had arranged ahead of time that once they did they would head out to the "Cave In" area. In the meantime Dove of Spring and Teller of Stories spent some time at the hogan of Whispering Wind. Eric brought his camera while Violet brought a note book. They planned to do a detailed inventory along with pictures to learn what they actually had for the museum. To their surprise, it was easier said than done. Whispering Wind had put aside a visible history of uncountable years. And that was just the visible things. There were boxes and make shift shelving not to mention the hidden underground storage rooms.

**W**hispering Wind must have been a very busy man over the years.  Digging and manufacturing all this storage space.  This was going to be one special museum they decided.   This would make the Smithsonian jealous thought Violet while being proud.

**T**he quick, or so they thought, job of inventory, actually took just over three days.  Even then they both knew it was not finished yet.  The many documents they had come across would most likely take close to two days alone, that is if they could read them at all.


**F**inally, hearing from Dan that he had some free time they quickly made plans to visit the old ruins of the lost civilization again.

**O**n the two hour ride to the four corners or north east corner of the reservation they discussed the elder lady "Keeper of the Past"

**"I** do and do not want to see her again.  I guess we should though.  I'm sure she will she will be most helpful.  She knows as much if not more than Whispering Wind about this lost world."

**"I'**m glad to hear you say that," Violet interjected.  "We should not under estimate her.  She doesn't carry that name without reason.  Besides Mr. Blue appears to be familiar with her also."

**F**inally at their destination they were surprised to see some rebuilding had been done on the house Dan and Eric caused to partly collapse.  Upon exiting the car Eric let Mr. Blue loose.

**"Y**ou know what we want old friend.  Help us as I know you will."

**T**he tarantula made a few circles about five feet in diameter and then took off in the direction of the old structure.

**"I**t looks like he knows where he is going," commented Violet almost in a whisper.

**T**he three followed quietly. As they neared the door the old familiar voice could be heard.


"Come in and welcome back.  Whispering Wind said you would be back  My only instructions were to help in any way I can.  I will just repeat what I said on your last visit which was...


Beneath where we are now sitting is the lost technology, an unknown city, nay a massive community dedicated to advanced technology and equality without prejudice.  Unheard of Cosmic forces put an end to that world, an end to that world and all that was good for the planet.

Not far from where we are sitting now is a portal or entranceway to that lost world.  The portal is not a visible thing.  It has been buried, as the city was, for many thousands of years.  When and if you find the entrance Whispering Wind will then share with you further documents to the treasured secrets of civilization we have not reached yet.

You have proven yourself true to your cause my young friend.  The portal you seek may be here.  It is something I have suggested for countless years, but dared not pursue.  Whispering Wind was wise to choose you."

"Now my young friend, you are on your own.  With diligence and your great frame of mind you will be successful.  I will take my leave now.  You need me no longer."

As she left she turned with a smile adding; "Your way with the Great Spirits other creatures will always serve you well."

Then she was gone.  Violet went to the window to follow with her eyes only to find no one.  She shrugged her shoulders and returned to the guys.

~ ~ ~ ~ ~ ~

"Now for the real fun," said Eric out loud.

"And what would that be," asked Dan.

"Follow Mr. Blue," smiled Eric in return.

With that Mr. Blue appeared.

"How does he do that," puzzled Dan.

Violet just smiled quietly.  And that's exactly what the three did, follow Mr. Blue who went to the exact same cavern as he did previously, stopped there and turned to look at the three numerous times.  Dan broke the silence.

"I'll go get the shovels," he mumbled

Returning he sheepishly said, "Seems like we have been here before."

He threw a shovel to Eric and just started digging.  Mr. Blue moved to where Violet was and relaxed and watched.

"Thanks for joining me," she whispered.

He twitched his front legs and further relaxed.


**A** half hour of non stop digging netted many rocks and other debris. Suddenly there was that familiar sound of a wood thud. The pair thumped the same spot a few more times. They next started to widen the area. After almost ten minutes they were staring at a door like structure roughly five feet in diameter.

"LOOK" cried Violet as she pointed to one side. "A pull handle or at least it looks like one."

The two men made room to stand aside while Eric then grabbed the handle. A few pulls netted nothing. From above them came a sweet voice.

"Does it turn and then pull?"

Dan and Eric looked at each other almost laughing. Dan reached down and sure enough it turned. He pulled, it started to lift but was obviously heavy. Eric joined him on the pull. Creaking, the panel started to lift but stopped suddenly as it hit the dirt and rock wall. More edge cleaning would have to be done. Ten more minutes of sweat and they tried the lift again. This time with success. The three froze in place as they viewed highly polished steps to the bowels of the earth

"Do we dare!" posed Eric.

He was answered by Violet with the question,

"Do we not dare ?"

Being more practical Dan suggested,

"Let's rest a bit first. It's not even noon yet."

Rest they did. Violet tried not to show her excitement knowing the men should rest a bit, but was very anxious. After the many wondrous and amazing surprises of the jungle she was like a child at Christmas.

While the two men relaxed Violet inched her way closer to the opening of the hole to get a better view. She picked up a small stone and dropped it to the steps. She listened as it bounced what seemed like forever. It was quite a long time before the sound could no longer be heard. She judged it to be deeper than the steps in the jungle where they discovered the endless blue. She sat back her imagination going wild. She finally turned to Eric only to see him smiling, enjoying the child at Christmas. She felt herself go crimson.

"**N**o need for that love.  I know exactly how you feel.  Well, it seems like I'm holding up the show so let's do it."

**D**ove of Spring was all smiles now saying;

"**I** know I can't go first because of possible dangers.  Let's just go," she added, "Please" long and syrupy.

**E**ric looked at Dan and indicated with his eyes that he go first.  There was no hesitation on his part.  In reality he was as anxious as Violet.  He was only down three steps when a mellow, subdued light came on.  It showed a rather steep descent of the polished steps.  They looked highly polished and very slippery.  That was not really the case.  The highlighted sheen was deceiving.  Foot traction was the best he ever felt.  He relayed that information to Violet and Eric as they were discovering that for themselves.  Each, unknown to the other was counting the steps.

**E**ric was amazed as always at the lighting.  Thousand of years old and they were still working.  This really was advanced technology.  *"We thought we were advanced with solar energy."* he thought to himself.  Even though they did not appear to be treacherous Dan chose not to go too fast.  He wanted to take in every detail there was to see.  He stopped his descent to study a marking on the wall.  A symbol he had not seen before.  Violet saw what he was looking at and instantly recognized it.  That's an old Navajo marking.  It means happiness or joy depending how it is used.  They continued on.  The three started to notice the air quality was starting to decline.  Violet mentioned, what ever system they were using most likely was disrupted during the cataclysm.

"**I**'m surprised we are this deep without problems.

"**P**erhaps we should slow our descent some more," Eric posed.

"**N**o need for that," answered Dan.  "This is the end of the trail.  The land collapse will allow us no further."

"**N**o wait!  Look behind you," exclaimed Violet excitedly.

**T**here were well defined verticle lines in the wall.  She turned to Eric who understood her meaning.  He moved down to Dan level and started his finger search routine.  He barely began when Violet again interrupted.

"**L**ook at the wall design.  They are constellations.  Orion is in the middle."

**S**miling, Eric used his five fingers to cover the pattern as he did in the jungle.  There was a pause for about five or six seconds.  The wall section moved horizontally extremely slow.  It stopped allowing an opening of approximately five feet.  Beyond the wall was pure black.  There was no illumination what so ever.  Dove of Spring with out hesitation said,

"I know what you are thinking, but go ahead."

Still showing a bit of indecision Eric bent down and removed his boots and stood them by the wall opening to keep the door from fully closing.

Dan trying to make of the situation calmly stated,

"You're not as dumb as you look."

With that Violet swatted his upper arm which made him cry out.

"Abuse, spousal abuse.

On that outcry Eric swatted his other arm.

"That's my line."

"If you two clowns are finished can we go forward?"

With all three laughing, Dove of Spring pushed her way between them and stepped into the blackness.  Like a slow curtain rising the darkness dissipated.  It was replaced by the forever blue they witnessed in the jungle.  All three were through the portal now as they watched the forever blue give way to the same forever green mountains.  Then slowly, as if being introduced came the birds and animal sounds.  This was a perfect duplication of their experience in the Yucatan.

The three remained silent.  Violet stepped forward.

"I want to see it all."

Dan put his arm out to stop her but Eric stopped him instead.

"Let her go," he whispered.

The two men gave her space then followed, also marveling at the breath taking spectacle.

The three, with Violet in the lead by over twelve feet continued on.  The pathway curved every which way.  Each curve presented a new showing.  Farm land, tree covered springs, wild flower displays, mountain beauty and waterfalls.  Beaches and oceans.  The true beauty of the world at its best.  Was this not a perfect example of truly advanced cultures ?  There were no disturbances or noises.  Just color and beauty no matter what you viewed.  The three continued on ever so slowly, in awe, each allowing their own interpretation of this magic world.  Not realizing their travel suddenly they were back at the beginning. Eric, enthusiastically put his boots back on.  As they crossed the portal the magic world of color went black yet their tranquil hush remained.  The sliding wall was the only sound and it too faded.

~ ~ ~

~ ~ ~ ~ ~ ~

~ ~ ~

**W**ithout question or comment Dan took the lead retracing their steps back to the world of reality.  Even these steps were hushed.

**O**nce up and out of the world below each took a seat on what ever was available.  Violet went to the car first and returned with three cups and a jug of lemonade which they all shared willingly.

**"I** can't imagine a world of such quietude," Violet said in almost a whisper.

**"W**here is this world, I want to go there," answered Dan seriously.

**"I** can't even imagine it.  Could this actually have been a reality" posed Eric to no one.

**"T**hat is something I guess we will never really know.  At least not in our lifetime" added Violet.

**"B**oth Atl and Whispering Wind were right though.  Whispering Wind spoke of a portal here to the lost civilization.  Atl mentioned it also but said its search would net us nothing," quoted Eric.

**"B**ut we just saw ?" pondered Dan. "Both here and back in the jungle."

**"N**ew world advertising," smiled Violet.

**B**oth men turned to look at her after her crazy statement.

**L**aughing, Violet attempted to clarify what she said.

**"W**e spoke of a similar thing at the lost city, remember.  What better way to show technology than to keep it simple.  Personally I believe there was a lost civilization.  Also that it covered this whole planet.  Why else would we have all these world wide contacts and contracts?  Consider my connection with Egypt.  The trade of China and the world artifacts in the kings treasure room.  We were all different but just as one because of the super advanced technology.  A technology that we will not see in our lifetime but that does not mean it did not exist."  Truly smiling now she added, "I'll bet there are a few more of these Disney Worlds else-

-255-

where.  China maybe or perhaps even Egypt, and I'm sure some where in Europe."


All was quiet for awhile thinking of Violets words.  Eric spoke up,

"You may be correct.  We all know we are talking about many thousands of years ago that this lost civilization existed.  It also took us this long to get this far.  Who knows how much longer it will take us to reach their stage of advancement.

Dan put in with "If we don't blow up the planet and ourselves first."

All agreed and were quiet again pondering the recent spoken words.


Dove of Spring murmured not quite out loud,

"I wonder what we might have to go through to find something like this in Egypt ?"



*"I wonder"*

The Navajo
>by James F. Downs
>Pub. by Holt, Rinehart & Winston

Hopi & Navajo Weddings
>by Emily C. Laskowski
>from Cowboys & Indians Magazine

Lost Cities of North & Central America
>by David Hatcher Childress
>Pub. by Adventures Unlimited Press

Finger Prints of the Gods
>by Graham Hancock
>Pub. by Crown Trade Paperbacks

America Before
>by Graham Hancock
>Pub. by St. Martins Press

Forgotten Civilization
>by Robert M. Schoch
>Pub. by Inner Traditions.

Ancient Maya Civilizations
>by Norman Hammond
>Pub. by Rutgers University Press.

Lost Knowledge of the Ancients
>by Graham Hancock
>Pub. By Bear & Co.

Maya Cosmos
>by D. Freidel, Linda Schele, Joy Parker
>Pub. By Quill, N.Y.

Also by Kenneth J. Goss:

*Simple Short Stories*
(To tingle the imagination)

*Simple Short Stories II*
(To further tingle the imagination)

*The Dead Living Mummy*
(An epic story of a lost city that ended with a lost mind)

*The Innocent Murder*
(The tranquility of an English Manor upset by a sudden death)

*The Ancient Ones*
(Another adventure with Eric Dexter of the Dead Living Mummy)

The Ancient History Rediscovered
(The third book in the Eric Dexter adventure series)

The Librarian Checked Out
(A murder mystery)

*The Jury is Out*
(A sequel murder mystery)

*The Other Planet Earth*
(Travel Between Worlds)

*The True Cost of Ignorance and False Judgement*
( One man's indomitable inner strength against a town that would destroy him)

*The Lost Civilization*
(Another adventure in the Eric Dexter adventure series)

# Squiggy the Squirrel Series also by Kenneth J. Goss:

The Garden Mystery
No. 1 An original story of Squiggy the squirrel
The Christmas Garland Mystery

No. 2 Squiggy's Special Christmas
The Great New Land

No. 3 More Adventures with Squiggy as the
meadow friends move to a new home
New Friends

No. 4 Squiggy's adventures with new friends
Squiggy and the Bear

No. 5 Squiggy's adventure with a Bear
Squiggy and the Storm

No. 6 Squiggy defends the Old Man
The Next Generation

No. 7 Squiggy's last adventure
Squiggy's Maine Vacation and More

No. 8 Another Double Adventure with Squiggy
Squiggy and the Virus

No. 9 Squiggy handles the Bad Virus Bug
Suzette Squirrel

No. 10 Squiggy's other adventures he doesn't
like to talk about

No. 11 Squiggy's New Visitors
Squiggy's adventures with some new friends

No. 12 Squiggy's Adventure in the City
Adventure or Trouble?

No. 13 Squiggy Learns a Lesson